D1364604

Dutch Reckoning

Michael G. West

This book is a work of fiction. Names, characters, places and incidents are the product of the author's imagination or are used fictitiously. Except where actual historical events or characters may resemble those being described for the story line, any resemblance to actual events or persons, living or dead, is purely coincidental.

Dutch Reckoning
Sepiessa Press
64 Madaline Lane
Vineyard Haven, MA 02568

First Edition, First Printing

ISBN-13:978-1492308898

DEDICATION

For Isabella Gardner, friend and mentor
And a fine poet besides

Part One - Thief in Shadow

To tread the razor edge of a sword
To run on smooth-frozen ice
You need follow no footsteps
Walk over the cliff with hands free

Mu-mon, 13th Century

1

Friday, March 12
Capitola, California

It was way too early in the morning when I heard that tap-tap-tapping at my bungalow door. The coffee machine was gurgling, set to an automatic timer, but I hadn't had my first cup of Celebes yet. I pulled on a pair of bike shorts and padded through the shambles, cutting a tight slalom through the ginger ale empties and pizza boxes on the floor.

When I cracked open the front door, there stood a guy in a boxy, double-breasted, navy-blue suit and designer tie combo, cordovan slip-ons polished to a blinding sheen.

I blinked.

"William T. Shakespear?" he said.

His greeting was formal, and it sounded like a summons. I knew at once he was a process server or a lawyer. Either way, trouble.

"Depends. You from Prometheum? Okay," I said. "You can have the Mister Coffee."

"I'm not from Prometheum. It's about another thing."

"My dad sent you." I had a sudden flash that my trust fund had been shut off. For years Dad had been threatening to do it, but as far as I knew he didn't have legal means. Must have found one.

"May I come in? I have a business proposition for you, that is, ah, if you *are*, ah, Mr. Shakespear."

The suit guy smiled in a kind of sneering way. His mustache looked like the yellow bristles on a worn-out toothbrush. What could I do? I waved him into the sitting area. He entered tentatively, as if expecting cobwebs. I thought about picking up a few empties and a pizza box or two. Instead I helped myself to a cup of full-city Celebes, tossed in a thin spoon of sugar and stirred.

I said, "People call me Tommy. Not William T and certainly not Mister. Want some coffee? Just made."

"No, thanks," he said. "I've had mine."

We sat down, and the suit guy flipped open his attaché case. Polished oxblood, matching the shoes. The guy was really premeditated.

"I am Ted Wycliffe. I represent the Butler Museum of Art in Boston. You are, ah, familiar with the Butlers, I believe?"

He handed me his business card. Theodore Wycliffe, Esquire. Heavy gray stock, embossed black letters. I felt the card and looked at it, pausing to consider my reply. The Butlers, one and all, were very very Boston society.

"Yes," I said. "I knew Beatrice pretty well."

Beatrice Butler was a poet, the namesake of her great aunt, Beatrice Longwood Butler, an art collector and consort to one of the world's richest men at the turn of the century. Aunt Beatrice had built herself a Venetian palace in Boston, now the Butler Museum, to house the fabled art collection she'd amassed while traveling through Europe with her beau financier, scattering greenbacks and snatching up masterpieces. Local legend had it that Aunt Beatrice had imported the villa stone by stone from Italy, reassembling it on land she owned across from the Back Bay Fens, where she would walk her pet leopards on sunny days.

Of course, the Beatrice I'd known had little in common with her late, great aunt, except for a love of art and, of course, that *name*, which had become a kind of curse to her. Impossible to live up to. So Beatrice Butler had made that name into a central part of her act, together with the drugs, the neon body paint and the alto saxophone, figuring if you have an albatross around your neck you might as well call it a necklace.

Beatrice had become an over-the-top performance artist to put off her Boston family and get out from under the shadow of the late, great aunt Beatrice Butler. And it had worked. Finally. Too finally.

I looked at Wycliffe and wondered if he'd bring up her suicide. Was that what this was all about? I sipped at my coffee.

"I believe you're also acquainted with Jack Butler," he said.

I nodded. Jack had been Beatrice's favorite brother, the only family member who'd forgiven her the many indiscretions and, especially, the final one, her suicide.

"Mr. Butler has asked me to explore whether you would be available to, ah, consult on a very private matter."

"Which is?"

"The theft from the Butler Museum two years ago of several very nearly priceless art works. Perhaps you read something about it at the time."

Very nearly priceless? The Butler Museum was chock-full of great paintings by Titian, Botticelli, Fra Angelico, Rembrandt, Vermeer and others. But not priceless. Everything has a price.

"I read something," I said, noncommittally. "Jack and I spoke briefly about it when we met. Just a few paintings, wasn't it, and an urn?"

"A Vermeer, three Rembrandts, a Flinck, a Manet, four drawings by Degas, the Chinese Ku or urn, as you term it, and a bronze eagle, French. It was, I believe, the largest art theft in history."

I'd met Jack Butler at Beatrice's memorial service in Boston about six months after the theft. We'd exchanged a few words at the grave site and reminisced about Beatrice later at their family house on Chestnut Hill. When the conversation turned toward me, I'd said something about being in private investigations.

It was not true. Not exactly. For the past year or so, I'd been doing leg work for a lawyer, locating and interviewing witnesses, moonlighting as a security guard at the Coca-Cola plant, because the lawyer, Hank, that is, wasn't paying me much. But I let Jack Butler think I was traveling a lot, doing low-profile investigations—no divorce work, no repo—corporate espionage, art thefts, insurance scams. I knew I was lying, sort of, but Jack, like all the Butlers, had a way of making me feel insecure.

"Why didn't Jack just call?" I asked. And why had he waited two years?

"Mr. Butler is a very busy man. At the moment he's in the Bahamas on business. He asked me to contact you personally. Frankly, we had no idea whether, ah, you were still doing investigations."

"Still doing investigations?" I echoed Wycliffe, mumbling to myself. Hard to believe Jack Butler would still remember that business about me being a PI. Besides, Santa Cruz was a long way from Boston.

Yet, here was his lawyer offering me a job. Too good to be true. I set down my coffee cup and took a deep breath.

He continued. "You were strongly recommended by a mutual friend. Mr. Butler can fill you in on that. I tracked you down myself, and I'll admit you weren't so easy to find. Fortunately, Mr. Butler recalled your, ah, association with the Greenberg law offices. They were able to provide me with your present address and with a reference. Apparently, they think highly of you, too."

"Nevertheless," he droned on, "Present circumstances require, ah, some discretion. We already have a Boston agency working on this case, but we seem to have reached a dead end. We'd like to add another investigator who would try a different approach. You are still licensed?"

"Well, no. I'm *not* currently licensed in Boston."

Or anywhere else for that matter. The work I had done for Hank Greenberg had been as his employee, not as a licensed PI.

"Besides," I said, "What makes you think I'd come to Boston for this?"

"We are prepared to pay you for your consultation," he said. "And first class accommodations. Of course, if you're not interested...."

"But no license...?" I said.

"We can work it out. Mr. Butler is quite set on having you — a trusted family friend— with us. I imagine we can have you temporarily assigned to the museum security staff."

A little whisper started up inside my head, telling me something was wrong here, warning me away. Things that seem too good to be true usually are. But the whisper wasn't loud enough, and it was way too late. Besides, I really needed the money.

"Okay," I found myself saying. "A thousand a day, plus expenses." I'd heard of people getting that much, but I figured we'd bargain some. I was wrong.

Wycliffe handed me a blue envelope he took from the attaché case between us on the table.

"Here's a first class ticket to Boston and a certified check for ten thousand dollars. Your retainer. The next flight to Boston leaves San Jose at two-thirty this afternoon. I think you'd better pack." He snapped his case shut and stood up to leave.

I'd better pack? Pack what? I thought about my extensive wardrobe. Bike shorts, jeans, assorted t-shirts, leather jacket, hiking boots, running shoes.

"You have a reservation at the Four Seasons Hotel. Jack Butler should be back in town in a day or two. In the meantime, drop by the museum and, ah, meet with the director, Dr. Louvenbragh, and the security chief, Fred Peavy. They will be expecting you. Sunday at the latest."

"Sunday?" I said. "People work on *Sunday* in Boston?"

"The museum closes on Mondays, and the staff has a planning session scheduled. Dr. Louvenbragh would like you to be on board as soon as possible. She would prefer Saturday. As I said, Sunday at the latest. Here is her number."

Wycliffe handed me the card with Dr. Amy Louvenbragh's contact data. A cream white card with crimson script. We shook hands, and he was gone.

I looked around my two-room shack. Something of a dump, but it's home. The front room where I met with Wycliffe — lumpy green sofa, matching threadbare armchair, telephone-cable spool for a table, and the black bean-bag chair that Shiva gave me. Shiva's a friend of mine who writes videogames. She thinks the bean-bag chair classes up the joint.

I walked back toward my bedroom at the other end of the bungalow, picking up a couple of ginger ale empties, setting them on the card table. The card table and four folding chairs came from a yard sale only a few months before, along with most of the kitchen stuff.

There's a stove-top refrigerator unit, a microwave, a blender, and a coffee bean grinder and, of course, the Mister Coffee machine I stole from Prometheum the day I got laid off. I poured myself another cup of coffee and toasted my new job.

To the right of the bedroom door is a windowless bathroom with a toilet, sink and an old tub with feet. Outside, through the door off the opposite kitchen corner, I have an outdoor shower stall where I hang my wetsuit and a little backyard plot, eight by ten. Mostly crabgrass, but the neighborhood cats like it.

I peered into the way back where my bed was still unmade, scolding me. Barely enough room to get dressed in there, much less tidy up, just big enough for a double bed and a dresser with my computer stuff and videogames piled on top. But it's cozy in there at night, and magical, when you're lying there in the dark listening to the waves breaking on the beach two hundred yards away.

When I was sure Wycliffe, Esquire was well out of sight, I walked to the front door, stepped outside and tasted the morning air. One of the neighborhood cats, a calico named Slinky, slipped around the corner of my house and rubbed up against my bare leg. A few cars were parked by the beach esplanade, but nobody was out on the street. The air felt cool and sharp, and there was nothing but blue all the way to heaven. I went back inside to get my mountain bike.

It was the perfect morning for a ride.

2
Friday, March 12
Capitola, California

I had dinner that night with Shiva at the Sea Breeze restaurant out on the Santa Cruz pier. My treat. Usually we went dutch, but I figured this time it fell into the category of "expenses" as in "a thousand a day plus expenses." If necessary, we could spend a few minutes talking over the Butler Museum case. Since my rust-eaten Jeep was still in the shop for minor surgery, Shiva drove her Lexus. She was on the car phone the whole time, talking to L.A.

On the way to the restaurant, I thought about priorities. Wycliffe had expected me to take the two-thirty flight to Boston, but so what? I had a date with Shiva, and, besides, Jack was busy in the Bahamas. The Butler art theft was two years ago. So what was the big hurry? I could leave on Saturday and still make the appointment with Dr. Louvenbragh on Sunday morning. Plenty of time. Time to think about things, like where this was leading. My life seemed about to take another unexpected turn. I was hoping it wouldn't be for the worse.

Two winters ago I had moved to Santa Cruz. Why? I was sick of Boston. I liked the location, Northern California, and the climate, Mediterranean, is temperate year-round. Then the atmosphere, and Santa Cruz has plenty of that. Racially diverse, artsy. Political with a capital PC. Attitude to spare. Great surf.

A hot live-music scene, lot of reggae bands, too, with headline groups touring through. And, with a university campus and a junior college, diversions aplenty.

Bottom line, I was trying to forget somebody. And Santa Cruz was three thousand miles away from her.

At first I worked in a Mexican restaurant, washing dishes and sweeping floors. I advanced to short order cook on the breakfast shift. Huevos rancheros were my specialty. After a few months of that I hungered for stardom and apprenticed myself to Chino, the head cook. Under his half-drunken tutelage, I mastered mole, that's pronounced moh-lay, a spicy, chocolatey sauce for chicken. That got me onto the dinner shift. Not big time, but steady.

Unexpectedly, I fell into software. A few days past my thirtieth birthday, I was walking on the beach across the street from where I live, and I met Shiva, who was sitting in the sand working on her laptop computer. Shiva had long blonde hair and bright-green eyes and a body made for lying on the beach. Or anything else she wanted to do with it. She looked almost illegal in her neon two-piece. Peach.

"Uh," I said, "What's that you're doing?" My repartee fizzed and popped like drops of sweat on a hot, short-order grill.

She lifted her amber sun visor to get a better look at me. Our eyes met, and she smiled.

"Writing a fan letter to the Pope?" I tried again. She kept staring, though. Made me nervous the way she looked up at me.

"Nope," she said, finally, "Smash Attack II."

"Smash Attack II. It's a...." Like I was fumbling through my pockets for my car keys.

"A video game," she said. "I did the original Smash Attack last year. You hear of it?"

Had to admit I hadn't. Not being into video games, I didn't know that Shiva was the hottest new games artist around. She had just been featured in Wired magazine as one of the most influential people under thirty. Influential, I didn't know about. What I could see was how inviting and open and friendly she was. I felt like I was digging in a big sandbox with my shovel and pail.

We spent most of that afternoon talking about where we grew up, our families, our memories, our friends. I told her about living in Boston, summers on Martha's Vineyard, how I'd moved out to Santa Cruz to escape my life, and one woman in particular, back on the East Coast. Shiva told me about her parents, the long winters in Wisconsin and how, before her parents divorced, her family used to come out to California on summer vacations.

"We'd visit friends in San Francisco and drive down the coast to Big Sur. We'd bring a tent and sleeping bags and camp out in the redwoods by this little stream that runs all the way to the beach. Once we got a cabin in the mountains near Felton. That's how I got to know Santa Cruz. But I finished school and moved here years ago—and that's before Mom and Dad split up and—he hasn't been out once. Not once."

"Maybe he needs some distance from your mom," I said.

"Yeah, maybe he needs some distance from me, too."

All of a sudden the people sitting around us were talking excitedly, getting up and moving quickly toward the water. What was going on? We turned toward the surf and noticed fins cutting through the shallow waters just off shore. They looked like sharks. I didn't know they were dolphins until Shiva explained. I'd never seen dolphins up close before.

"I see them all the time down here," Shiva said. "Usually in the morning or evening, though. You want to walk down by the water to watch them?"

"Might as well," I said. "Left my spear gun at home." Always sensitive.

We got up and made our way to the edge of the surf. People stood around in groups pointing out the school of dolphins as their slick gray bodies surfaced for a moment and slipped under again, splashing in the water just past the shore break.

"Your parents didn't name you Shiva, did they?" Standing there, I finally asked her the question I'd been wanting to ask her since I'd first sat down.

"No, they named me Rachel." Shiva paused, as though undecided whether she should tell me more. "My junior year at college I got involved with my drama professor. He started calling me 'Shiva the Destroyer' mostly as a joke, because he was married and felt guilty about putting his marriage at risk. After we broke up, I kept the Shiva and added Moondance. Shiva Moondance. Much cooler than Rachel Abrahamson at the time. Of course, I also considered Abrahamsdaughter. Briefly. Very briefly." She laughed.

"So maybe your dad feels you rejected him? I mean, when you changed your name. You haven't changed it back."

"No, well, maybe, but it didn't bother my mom. She changed hers, too, last year."

"Insult added to injury. Poor guy."

"Yeah, but his new wife is an Abrahamson now. So he shouldn't feel too lonely."

We didn't say much after that. We stood there watching the dolphins playing in the shore break.

That afternoon went by in a blur. I became a video game fan on the spot, and by the end of the summer I had a tall pile of videogames, many of them gifts from Shiva. In the fall and winter I took some computer courses and began hanging out with Shiva and some of her friends. I caught on pretty quickly. Soon I found myself working at Prometheum, testing and documenting the latest videogames. Not a lot of excitement in that, maybe, but it was steady money, and I was working my way over to the creative side six months later when the layoffs came. Last in, first out. I left with Mr. Coffee tucked under my arm.

The following week I slept late and went for long bike rides. The Forest of Nisene Marks in nearby Aptos with its giant redwood trees offered a kind of solace. I'd ride my mountain bike to Sand Point at the top of the fire road, around and around in a narrowing spiral, several miles of unrelieved uphill pumping, to burn off the anger and frustration. I'd turn at the top and make the downhill run, spiraling down a rutted dirt track, churning dust and gravel, and squeezing at the brakes until my hands cramped up. Suicidal. Or I'd head over to Twenty-Sixth Avenue beach to body surf the heavy shore break until I was numb and exhausted, floundering in the whitewater backwash. Afterward, I'd return to my cottage, shower and stretch out on my bed, staring at the bare green walls. My fresh new leaf had blown away. Shiva telephoned once or twice, but I felt too discouraged to return her calls. I needed something new to get me going again. Mr. Ted Wycliffe, Esquire, and the Butler Museum had come along at just the right time.

Shiva parked the Lexus on the Santa Cruz pier a short distance from the restaurant, and as we were early, we strolled out to the end to take in the evening air. The pier was busy with weekend tourists drawn by the warm spring weather. A few fishermen baited and cast their lines, but no one seemed to be catching anything. Below us the sea lions barked, their hoarse cries echoed, mingling with the slap of waves against pilings. At the end of the pier, I turned and looked back at the Beach Boardwalk amusement park, its classic wooden roller coaster standing out against the twilight sky. Shiva drifted off to my left to watch the sea birds dip and glide on the evening breeze. The sun was beginning to drop into the ocean, so we turned toward the restaurant and found our way to a table with a view of the sunset splashing crimson on Monterey Bay.

During dinner we talked about movies. Shiva was planning her next video game project, and we argued about Blade Runner and Die Hard and a few other classic thrillers and whether she should base her new videogame on a classic movie thriller or on something new.

As Shiva talked about her plans, my mind's camera framed her against the now-black window pane. Long blond hair twisted up in a braid like a wreath around her face. The little bulge in the ridge of her nose. The fullness of her lower lip. The furrow in her brow. Shiva's beauty shows less in her features taken separately than in the way they all fit together. She smiled, and I could feel my heartbeat quicken. A shiver of heat rushed through me as I looked into her mossy-green eyes—but not for long. I was afraid of getting caught there.

"I'm spending a few days with my mom this week," she said.

Her mother, a psychologist specializing in adolescents, had recently moved to Berkeley.

"How's her place shaping up?" I asked.

"Much better now that the goon has moved out." Her mother's boarder had once come on to Shiva very aggressively. He left shortly afterward.

"She have somebody else lined up for the studio?"

"No, I think Mom plans to get back into doing her art work. Lately it's been seaweed collage. So I think she'll just keep the studio for herself. She doesn't really need the income. I think she just wanted to have someone else around when she first moved in there, but now...."

"She have a boyfriend?"

"Not that she tells me about. I wonder though. She goes out a lot."

I filled Shiva in on the early morning visit from Jack Butler's lawyer.

"You're what?" she said. Somehow Shiva managed to convey skepticism, irony, and astonishment in a single look.

"I'm going to investigate the art theft. Find the thieves and the missing art works. Return the art to the museum. That's what."

"Tommy, what do you know about art?"

"I know what I like," I said. "Let's see, there's Art Nouveau, Art Deco, and Art Carney."

"Very funny," she said. But her tone of voice said, "You know, Tommy, I'm not even going to pretend to take the bait."

"It may interest you to know, Shiva," I said, "That I took art history in college, from the Egyptians all the way to Laurie Anderson, two semesters worth."

"Oh, an authority. I didn't realize," she said. "So tell me what you know about the Butler art theft."

I had to admit I'd been to the Butler Museum only once, four or five years ago, for a Sunday afternoon concert. I'd walked through the place and browsed the collection, but didn't remember anything about the museum, its holdings or the location of the stolen paintings.

So earlier that Friday afternoon I logged onto the Internet and found some newspaper and magazine articles on the theft in a journalism archive and a piece by a college art professor on the museums of New England. That helped to bring it back home. From what I could tell by scanning the pages on the Butler, the thieves had overlooked the most valuable painting in the place, a Titian work called "The Rape of Europa." Somewhat ironic, I thought, given the plundering Aunt Beatrice had carried out in her sweep of the art collections of Europe.

Anyway, as I told Shiva, one of the thieves had gone straight to the Dutch Room on the second floor. He cut two of the Rembrandts from their frames, lifted the Vermeer from a standing easel, frame and all, grabbed the Flinck and a third Rembrandt, a self-portrait etching, while the other thief took four minor Degas pieces, a bronze eagle and an ancient Chinese beaker from the gallery nearby. On the way out of the museum, the second thief had added a Manet portrait to the pot.

"Yeah? How long were they in the museum?" Shiva asked.

"They were able to get in and out fairly quickly," I said. "No more than fifteen minutes in all."

"Fifteen minutes?" she said. "How much did they get?"

"Around two hundred and fifty million dollars, if you want to put a price on it, but one painting, Vermeer's The Concert, accounts for almost half of that. Quite a haul for fifteen minutes, wouldn't you say?"

"I'd say," she said. "They certainly knew what they were after."

"Here's what's wrong, though. Another five minutes would have gotten them the Titian masterpiece, if they were going after the big dollar score. Another two hundred million, minimum. Ponder that one."

"Tommy." It was not a question.

"Yeah?"

"You did say the Butler Museum."

"Yeah. So what?"

"Trade seats with me." Shiva spoke in a firm, but quiet voice.

"What are you talking about?"

"Let's not waste time talking about it. Just do it, please."

Something in Shiva's voice told me I should follow her lead. I stood up, and we switched seats. As I sat down I noticed the hulking presence of Andre Ziff, president and CEO of Prometheum, across the restaurant from us. His party was just being seated. Ziff, his oblong torso draped in an elaborate, blue Hawaiian shirt, probably an antique, stood at right angles to us brushing his brown wiffle haircut with one hand, while directing traffic with the other.

"So, okay," I said. "It's Andre. What's the big deal, Shiva?"

"I don't want him to see me, one. And two, you might be interested to know Andre Ziff is on the board or something at the Butler Museum. He travels back to Boston several times a year for meetings."

"So I should go over and introduce myself? No, thanks. If I had a Supersoaker water gun I could probably hit him from here. I have a pretty clear shot."

"Believe me, I feel the same way. Besides, Tommy...I quit today."

This was big news.

"Quit Prometheum? But Shiva, you're the franchise. What are they going to do without you?"

Okay, maybe I was exaggerating a little, but not much. Shiva's games accounted for a very big chunk of Prometheum's revenues.

Shiva frowned. "Don't know, don't really care. I've got a few things going on in L.A. You know, Tommy, since the layoff it hasn't been the same. The place feels like a battlefield hospital or a morgue. Except you can't see the bodies. They've been swept away, under the carpet, into the closets and storage rooms. But you feel them. I feel them anyway."

"We'd better get out of here," I said. "Let's go for coffee someplace else."

"No. I'm not letting Andre chase me out of here. Let's order."

"No, let's don't, Shiva. I can't stand looking at him and thinking about you and pretending he's not here. You know that cafe near my place?"

"The one upstairs from that bar?"

"Yeah, let's adjourn this meeting and reconvene there."

We went to the cashier to settle our bill. As we passed through the restaurant, Shiva cleaved to my side, partly to avoid Andre seeing her and partly, I hoped, because we were growing closer. After paying, we walked to her Lexus in the heavy mist that had come in with the darkness.

"Guess I'll be back east for about a week or so," I said, apropos of nothing.

"Yeah, if somebody doesn't shoot you." Shiva smiled. "Then, Tommy, you'll be back east permanently."

"Shiva, this isn't dangerous. We're talking art theft here, not murder. It's just a kind of adventure, really, and I'll be helping out a friend. I've told you about Beatrice. I'd like to help out Jack because of her."

Of course, there was also the money. We had reached her Lexus. Shiva unlocked the doors, and we got in. She turned toward me as she fastened her seatbelt.

"Okay, Tommy. It's your corpse," Shiva said. "I can give you a ride to the airport on my way to Berkeley, if you want. What time's your flight?"

"A little before noon."

"Perfect. I'll be just in time for lunch."

"I'll miss you, Shiva," I said, and I realized I meant it. Shiva started her car.

"You won't have time to miss me, Tommy," she said. "You'll be up to your hips in art theft."

3

Saturday, March 13
Capitola, California

In the morning Shiva drove me to the airport. On the way there she handed me a box wrapped in recycled paper and tied with some twine she had dyed red with beet juice. I shook the box. It sounded like a baby rattle.

"It still worries me that you're doing this private eye thing," she said. "What do you know about investigating crime anyway?"

Shiva wouldn't let up, but she was right, of course. Everything I knew about crime came from TV shows, movies or the pulp novels I'd read while working as a night watchman at the Coca-Cola plant in Boston.

I opened the gift box, sliding off the twine, taking care not to tear the wrapping paper more than once or twice. Inside I found a canister of Mace and something called Skunk Spray.

"In case you run into trouble," she said, "you should have some protection. Skunk Spray will handle most of the problems, I expect, but you may want the Mace for the nasty situations."

"That's great, Shiva, but I really don't expect this to turn into anything too serious. I'll probably talk to a few people at the museum, write up a report for their insurance company and be back in Santa Cruz by next weekend.

"I doubt it somehow," she said.

We drove the winding highway through the Santa Cruz mountains in about twenty-five minutes. On a weekday commute, it would take two to three times as long, but on a Saturday morning the traffic was light, and we flew. Shiva liked to drive her new Lexus fast, and she was good behind the wheel, focused, and with enough mind left over for conversation. I was absorbed in the views, jagged mountain peaks, sharp ridges topped by pines and redwood groves, sweeping vistas open only for a moment as we followed the curves of the mountain road. Yet despite its beauty, or perhaps because of it, this road had a dark side. Frequent accidents, for one thing. Last week a tall pine tree had split in two, disturbed by heavy construction equipment widening the highway. The pine's roadside half fell suddenly into the southbound lane, crushing a late model Chevy Citation and killing its elderly driver instantly. It was random and without warning.

Things happen like that. Not always that tragic, but...like the way I lost the five million, for instance.

Used to be I didn't worry about money. My father's side of the family made big bucks in the sporting goods business. That paid my way through college, and graduate school until I dropped out, and there was still a little money that came my way every month from a family trust fund. It just covers the rent on my place in Capitola, but I missed the real jackpot. Five million dollars on my thirtieth birthday if I didn't smoke, drink, or do drugs until then. My grandfather set up the conditions for the five million. He was fanatic about health and physical fitness, and he thought he'd provide the financial incentive for my sisters and me to just say No. His executors, one of them being my father, were going to be pretty reasonable about it, or so I thought. They were even willing to look the other way occasionally on minor transgressions, unless we made the papers or ended up in jail. One summer though on Martha's Vineyard I got caught with a pound of really potent homegrown pot, and Bingo! that was it. Or, I should say, no bingo.

In court the prosecutor dropped all charges for lack of evidence, and so I walked. But I walked without the money, and I walked without much support from my family, except for my sisters. Johanna had already collected her five million and was sympathetic, but she couldn't resist telling me I had to get my life together. She's married to a plastic surgeon in LA, so she's got no worries except for what to do with her life. CC is another matter entirely. She lives in Seattle, and works at a lot of different jobs. We're alike in a lot of ways so I worry about CC. But both of my sisters have been great. True blood. We talk on the phone and see each other once or twice a year, which is easy to do since all three of us live on the West Coast. My mother still writes now and then, but Dad and I haven't had anything between us since the trial. Not that we were ever very close.

The flight to Boston took about five hours. Nothing to write home about, but at least the food was hot. Once we were on the ground at Logan airport I wasted no time getting into a cab. Before you could say, "honest Boston politician," we were through the Sumner tunnel, over Beacon Hill, and I'd checked into a room at the Four Seasons Hotel in Back Bay. I didn't bother to unpack. I left my suitcase in the closet by the door, stripped off my clothes and threw them in a heap on the bed, drew myself a hot bath, climbed into the tub and lay there soaking the shape of an airplane seat out of my bones.

It was after ten by the time I got out of the tub. Out in Lexington, my parents would already be asleep, unless there was a fight on cable. In which case, my dad would be watching guys pound each other silly, and my mom would be waiting up for him in bed reading. I knew I should call my mother, but I didn't want to run into the old man. That could wait. I'd be in town for a while. Later, maybe.

I got out the Boston white pages and found Hank Greenberg's number. He answered on the first ring, sounding a little groggy, as he'd nodded off watching the news on PBS. This was a tough time of year for him. A rabid baseball fan, Hank was only weeks away from opening day, and the wait was killing him, quote unquote. I knew from personal experience that he'd buy every newspaper he could find and throw away everything but the sports pages, just to get his spring training fix. Once the season got underway, he'd settle into a predictable routine. Predictable, that is, for a fanatic. I had worked in his law office and so I'd seen it operate. Hank never missed a home game at Fenway Park or a chance to chow down on those godawful Fenway Franks. He had season tickets for box seats right behind the Red Sox dugout. And when the Sox were on the road he'd watch them on TV or listen to them on the radio, day game or night. He'd even carry a Walkman into court with him. He was famous for that, well, infamous.

Hank's baseball season had a predictable pattern to it, too. Early euphoria, mid-season excitement and then depression in October, as once again the Red Sox went into the tank. As many times as Hank went through it he never seemed to learn.

Hank was hooked on baseball, and he was cursed to live in Boston.

We talked about baseball for a while, but since I'm not a fan, it was a very short while. I told Hank about the investigation and that I planned to be in town for a week, or so. He seemed to have strong feelings.

"You're a fish outa water here, Shakespear. You're in way over your head." He was mixing metaphors beautifully, as always.

"Meaning?" I said. I stretched out on the bed.

"You don't know thing one about art theft. You'll be lucky if they don't prosecute you for misrepresentation, fraud..."

"And impersonating a person? Lighten up, Hank. I can handle it."

"Your funeral," he said.

"Why do people keep saying that?" I asked. "This is just a few paintings, a pot and an eagle. I can handle it." I decided to change lanes. "So what did you tell them about me, Hank?"

"I told them about the jobs you'd done for me. Especially about the Zymanski murder trial. The lawyer, I think his name was Wyman—"

"Wycliffe."

"Whatever. He wanted to know details. So I filled him in on how you'd tracked down Zymanski's girlfriend when the cops couldn't find her."

"What else?" I said. Hank probably told Wycliffe all about her.

"I didn't mention about your getting involved with her, if that's what you're asking."

"Hank, I didn't get involved. She made a play for me, so she could get away. Besides, I was a lot younger then. Less experienced."

"Anyway, I gave them a rundown on some of the cases you'd worked on. It seemed to be what they wanted."

"Yeah, well, thanks."

"Don't thank me. Buy me dinner."

"You got it. How about tomorrow night?"

"I'll have to let you know," he said. "I might be going down to Florida to watch spring training for a few days. That is, if I can clear my calendar. Rain check?"

After I hung up I began to get cold feet about the job. Hank was right. What did I know about investigating art theft? Nothing. In the morning I had a sit down with the Butler Museum director. She was going to know how little I knew. She was going to know I was a fake. Shiva was right, I thought, this would never work.

The minibar was stocked with little bottles of premium liquor. I looked at them one by one, considered having a nightcap or two to settle me in for the night. Instead, I took an Evian water and set it on my bedside table by the digital clock radio. I turned on the TV, snapped off the lights and began to surf the channels. I narrowed it down to three, CNN, MTV and a rerun of Barnaby Jones.

It was the one way I knew to shut off the leaky faucet in my head.

4
Sunday, March 14
Boston, Massachusetts

In the morning I sat across an antique maple desk from Dr. Amy Louvenbragh, director of the Butler Museum, and cleared my throat.

"Nothing in art theft, actually," I said.

"What exactly have you done?" She wondered aloud, skepticism mingling with impatience in her voice. Dr. Louvenbragh was confident and well-tailored in a brown herringbone tweed suit. Her dark chestnut hair hung in waves just short of shoulder length.

"Corporate espionage, executive security. That sort of thing."

"You have references, of course."

"Well, Jack Butler, for one." I knew I was playing my only trump card.

"Jack Butler was under the impression you had experience investigating art theft."

"No telling why, but why don't we get to the case at hand? After all, Jack Butler has already hired me, paid me a retainer and so forth. We might as well cut out this fencing." This was not going well.

"I don't mind telling you, Mr. Shakespear, I have reservations."

"For lunch? Hey, I'm free. And you can call me Tommy. Mr. Shakespear sounds too much like a dead poet."

Dr. Louvenbragh glared at me from within her professional shell. Her brown eyes did not twinkle, and her thin unpainted lips showed no sign of humor. A bit severe, I thought. It goaded me into twitting her with wise-guy remarks. Not that I needed any provocation. She sat with arms crossed and let loose a sigh.

"Don't trivialize this, please. We are talking about a two-hundred-and-fifty million dollar theft, about art that probably won't be recovered and cannot be replaced."

"This museum," she went on, "is a monument in the art world to the ideals of a great American woman."

"Beatrice Cairn-Terrier Butler," I chimed in, still unable to resist playing the picador.

"Mrs. Butler," she continued firmly, "assembled this collection piece by piece. Each work not only has artistic merit, but also personal and historic relevance. Further, according to the terms of her bequest, no new pieces may be added. Nothing may be removed from the collection, nor replaced, even if something is stolen, as in this case. The collection is a whole. Consequently, this theft was a violation, almost a personal assault. As a friend of the Butlers, Mr. Shakespear, you should appreciate this."

"I do, of course, Dr. Louvenbragh, but I am also aware that Aunt Beatrice did a fair amount of thieving and pillaging herself while assembling this fabulous collection."

"Excuse me? Mr. Shakespear, what you are referring to is, by the way, open to dispute. And refuted by most reputable scholars. Certainly that claim is ancient history."

"It may be ancient history, but it is a fact."

We were at an impasse, and I knew I'd have to back off to get anywhere.

"Look," I said. "Time out. Everybody to a neutral corner. We got off to a bad start, but let's move on. Can we get to the particulars of the theft? I am anxious to begin my investigation."

"All right," she said. "On March 18, 1990, at approximately three a.m. two thieves posing as Boston city police officers entered the museum by the security entrance. They sprayed our security guards with mace, tied and gagged them. They then went through the museum taking several irreplaceable art works by Vermeer, Rembrandt, Manet, Degas..."

"And a Chinese bronze vase, Shang dynasty, I believe, an American eagle, carved, wooden...Dr. Louvenbragh, the way I figure it, the Dutch paintings were the real target. The thieves went after the second floor rooms first, got the Vermeer and the Rembrandts, picked up the French pieces and then grabbed the other stuff on the way out." I had to recite it all from memory because I'd forgotten my notebook in the hotel.

"I see you have done some research already."

"Some," I said.

"That's good. You know the collection was not insured."

"Not insured?"

I was stunned. Surely that was impossible. A collection like the Butler's had to be worth several billion dollars. It was inconceivable that they carried no insurance.

"No," she said. "Not insured, not a penny. Nothing."

"Pardon my asking, Dr. Louvenbragh, but isn't it rather cavalier not to have insurance on an art collection with the stature of the Butler Museum's?"

"It's a fair question, I grant you. We do carry damage insurance, but we have no theft coverage. We estimate that to carry theft insurance on our collection, even after these recent losses, would cost nearly $5 million a year, and that exceeds our annual operating budget by quite a bit."

"I see," I said, but I didn't. How could a museum like the Butler not have enough budget to handle insurance?

"You may be surprised to hear we are not alone. Many art museums don't have theft insurance. It's a fact of life. We are limited by the resources of Mrs. Butler's bequest. Besides, even if we had insurance, the terms of Mrs. Butler's bequest prevent us from acquiring any new art to supplement the collection or to replace any stolen works."

"So really all you can hope for is recovery."

"Yes, but after two years the trail gets pretty cold. In Japan, for instance, there is a two-year statute of limitations on art theft, and it runs out in one month. Someone there could legally purchase those pieces and not risk a thing. I am afraid our chances for recovery have grown very slim. Even the FBI was about to call it quits until recently."

"What now?"

"Nothing at all on the valuable Dutch works, the Vermeer and the Rembrandts. However, copies of the French paintings by Manet and Degas have recently surfaced in Barcelona as part of the estate of a recently-deceased professor at the university. He was an art collector, especially of the Impressionists and pre-Impressionist French masters."

"But you said copies. You mean forgeries? Of the stolen paintings?"

"That's right, I mean forgeries. Good quality forgeries, and that's the interesting part."

"Good enough to fool a collector? A serious art collector?"

"More than good enough. The collector in Barcelona was an art historian and an experienced restorer of Medieval art, but also well-acquainted with the French Impressionists. The information is in here."

She handed me a binder of material which had been sitting on her desk. It was labeled "Confidential," and I could see by leafing through its contents that the report had been assembled from a variety of sources.

"You have there a summary of all the relevant information pertaining to the theft. Read it carefully and I will be glad to answer any questions you may have about it. In the meanwhile, we have just a few minutes until my next appointment."

"I appreciate it, Dr. Louvenbragh. I do have one or two questions to ask."

"Go ahead."

"How long have you been director of the Butler Museum?"

"About three years now."

"And before that?"

"I was in Amsterdam at the Rijksmuseum."

"Doing?"

"Doing research on a fellowship for an academic study of Vermeer, actually. I was not employed here until the fall of 1989."

"A few months before the theft."

"Yes. Mr. Shakespear, this is all covered in detail in the material I've given you."

I had the distinct impression that Dr. Amy Louvenbragh regarded me as an underachieving student in her art history class. Maybe I hadn't done all the homework, but I fully intended to ask a few hard questions.

"Where were you at the time?"

"At the time?"

"Of the theft."

"I was asleep in my apartment on the top floor of the museum."

"You live here?"

"Lived. Until her death in 1924, it was Mrs. Butler's private apartment. The apartment went with the position of museum director, but after the theft I moved out."

"I see. And you were asleep. You heard nothing."

"Nothing. I was in a dead sleep."

"Dr. Louvenbragh, I gather you had only been in your position a short while. Who was museum director before you?"

"A man named Titus Moone. He now works for the Commonwealth of Massachusetts in social services, but I can assure you nothing has ever connected him to the theft. I believe he had a long-standing interest in working with disadvantaged persons and chose to make a career change. He left about six months before I arrived. Jack Butler acted as interim director until he hired me."

"So he hired you."

"Yes, he hired me. What is your point?"

"Was this a career change for you, too? I mean, weren't you making a move from academic research to running a museum?"

"I had some previous experience in arts administration from the foundation side of things. When I met Jack Butler, I was at the end of my Fulbright grant, and this position was open..."

"Where did you meet Jack Butler?"

"I was on a short vacation in the Bahamas. We met socially through mutual friends."

I wondered. It was clear to me that Amy Louvenbragh could be connected to the theft. She was a specialist in the Dutch paintings, the Vermeer and the Rembrandts, and she would know their value, possibly even a potential customer or two. Amy Louvenbragh had come to the museum not long before the theft. She lived alone on the premises and could easily observe the comings and goings of the security personnel. In short, she had loads of opportunity. Unfortunately, she had no real motive I could imagine, so I made a mental note to explore her background further. I made another note to explore the relationship between Jack Butler and his prickly museum director, Amy Louvenbragh.

"Mr. Shakespear, I am afraid I have to conclude our meeting. I have another appointment in just a few minutes."

I looked down at a notepad Dr. Louvenbragh had been doodling on. She had sketched several variations on the letter T. For Tommy? Time? Her next appointment? I wondered.

"Thank you for your time, Dr. Louvenbragh. I've got the material, and when I've been through it I may want to follow up."

"Certainly. I understand you will be joining our security staff on a temporary basis."

"I wonder," I paused, "whether it would be possible to meet with your head of security now. I'd like to learn a bit more about how you operate here. And we've got to exchange credentials, naturally." What was I talking about? I had no credentials.

"I'll see."

Amy Louvenbragh pressed a button on her telephone console.

"Yes, Dr. Louvenbragh?" came the voice from the speaker phone.

"Carole? Would you call Fred Peavy and see whether he's free for Mr. Shakespear? Thanks." She rose from her desk. She placed her fingertips on the polished maple surface and smiled for the first time. I had to smile back. It was a complete transformation. Before I had seen Dr. Louvenbragh the serious professional with a tough, no-nonsense demeanor, and now I was looking at this lovely, highly-competent woman with an engaging smile. The Amy underneath Dr. Louvenbragh, probably the Amy who had met Jack Butler.

"Carole will direct you to Fred Peavy if he's free, Mr. Shakespear."

We shook hands across the desk. No rings, firm grip. This was a woman who knew what she wanted. I wondered how far she would go to get it.

"Oh, one last thing," she said. "The FBI thinks that two recent murders in Barcelona may be connected to the theft somehow. That's also in the material I've given you."

"Murders?" I said.

"That's what the pros think, Mr. Shakespear. If I were you I'd be careful. Very careful."

5
Sunday, March 14
Boston, Massachusetts

I stopped to talk with Carole on the way out. She informed me that the museum's security chief, Fred Peavy, would see me right away. I looked at the telephone console on her desk. Ten lines. I could see Dr. Louvenbragh's line was in use, but there was nobody waiting in the ante room to see her. Maybe her appointment was somewhere else, and she was calling about being late. Maybe there was no appointment, and she wanted to get rid of me. I hurried down the hall to the security office in the first floor administrative wing.

Fred Peavy's secretary sat at her desk with shoulders hunched over and hands on her forehead, furrowed in deep concentration. As I came closer I could see it was a crossword puzzle.

"My name is Tommy Shakespear," I said. "I believe Dr. Louvenbragh's secretary called for an appointment."

"Just a moment, I'll see if he's in," she said, erasing a word and blowing the crumbs. The door behind her opened wide.

"Mr. Shakespear, come on in. We've got some time." Fred Peavy was in. He had crewcut hair, a white short-sleeve shirt, soiled blue-and-gold rep tie, permanent press chinos with a black belt and Florsheim shoes, also black. Looked like he was probably an ex-cop. I couldn't see if he wore an ankle holster above his white socks, but I was willing to bet on it. He was not a large man, but he was large for his clothes. And he looked like he could take care of himself in a tough situation.

The night of the heist Fred Peavy was breaking in a couple of college students moonlighting security for tuition money. They'd only been working a week. At 2:42 a.m. two men dressed in Boston City police uniforms arrived at the security entrance and conned the college kids into letting them in.

"Maced 'em."

"What, no guns?" Shiva would love this.

"Just mace and tape. Wrapped them up in heavy gaffer's tape. Gagged them so they couldn't make a sound. Then they went about their business." Fred was playing with a letter opener that had an oooh-la-la French Burle-Q stripper for a handle. He toyed with the blade.

"These guys were professionals?"

"Hard to say," he said with no apparent difficulty. "There are mixed opinions on the subject. Boston cops say no. FBI says yes. An international conspiracy, in fact. I guess that justifies their involvement."

"What do you say?"

"I say they got in like pros, but maybe they weren't experienced art thieves. They hacked two of the Rembrandts from their frames with a razor knife and left some canvas behind." Fred Peavy carved the air with his letter opener. "Of course, they were in a hurry. In and out in fifteen minutes." He stabbed the opener into his desktop.

I looked over and saw there were lots of little pockmarks on his desktop. Still, I was feeling pretty comfortable with this guy Fred. He seemed more thoughtful and articulate than I had expected. And he wasn't rushing me out of the place.

"Just wondering," I said, "why a world-class museum like the Butler would use college kids to guard its crown jewels."

"You ever work security?" He knew I had.

"As a matter of fact, I did," I said. "I used to be a security guard at the old Coca-Cola plant in Allston. Before they tore it down."

"You get what you pay for."

"Are you suggesting that the Butler was under-budgeted for security?"

"You said it, not me. We do have world-class electronics. Motion detectors that can sense a mosquito in any room in the museum. Cameras, too. But someone has to monitor the console, the closed-circuit TV. And someone has to call the cops when there's trouble. Come on. I'll take you for a tour."

Fred did not linger over art work, but walked me through the administrative wing, pointing out offices and commenting on the attractiveness of secretaries. I noticed he was wearing a wedding ring. As we passed by the center court atrium toward the staircase leading to the second floor, I looked across the center court. I saw something out of the corner of my eye that made me turn my head. She was dressed in a slate-gray suit, and she was heading toward the cafe. Her face was a blur at that distance and angle, but I could not mistake the shape, and that walk. It had to be Elaine. Elaine Stockton. I hadn't seen her for more than two years. What was she doing here? I became aware that Fred Peavy was talking to me.

"Of course, your average museum-goer won't notice those little red dots on the floor."

"Little red dots?"

"Yeah, all they can see is the paintings, the furniture. Maybe they notice the frames. Basically, they punch a ticket. Okay, I saw the Titian, the Rembrandts, the Vermeer. Now where's the Tapestry Room?...Shakespear, you with me?"

I had been thinking about Elaine and wondering if it would be good to see her again. She'd let me down pretty hard. I could still feel it.

"Let's head up," he said.

Peavy took me up to the Dutch Room on the second floor and showed me where the missing paintings had been. We walked across the tiled floor under a high wooden ceiling, itself a work of art with dozens of recessed panels, carved, and stained with time-worn pigments. He pointed out the motion detectors and the red dots on the floor. He explained that the red dots defined the placement of furniture to comply with the Butler will's proviso against changing or moving any element of the collection.

I asked about the Vermeer. The stolen Vermeer had hung from two picture hooks on the top of a simple easel covered with brown felt, standing four feet off the ground. It was easily removed.

"And nobody saw this? No cameras? I thought you mentioned cameras."

"We had no cameras in these rooms, unfortunately. We are planning to add cameras. It's in the budget for next year, but the thieves would have shut them off anyway. When the police arrived later that morning, they found the guards bound and gagged and the hallway cameras shut off."

"Who called the cops?" I asked.

"Anonymous."

"Just in time for the morning news?"

43

Fred chewed on his lower lip as if he might say more. I waited to hear.

As we stood there, I watched a young couple with a five- or six-year-old daughter and a pre-teenage son move from painting to painting in the room. The little girl approached one of the row of chairs lining the walls, wanting to touch its salmon-pink upholstery. When her mother caught her hands, she pulled away and turned her attention to the green-silk wall covering. Her brother, dressed in a hooded warm-up suit and Nike Airs, looked as if he'd rather be playing baseball or street hockey. His father tried to interest him in a Rubens portrait of an armor-suited nobleman, hanging alongside a sixteenth-century carved oak throne, but the boy's mind was not in the room. Both were apparently oblivious to the bare wall on the other side of the throne where the stolen Rembrandt portrait once hung.

My attention wandered, too. Had that really been Elaine a few moments ago downstairs? Was she still in the museum?

Three years ago I was standing at a car rental counter at the Martha's Vineyard airport talking to a friend of mine when Elaine walked into view. Tall, her dark hair pulled back and set in place with a tortoise-shell barrette, she wore a rose-pink sundress with a scoop back and a button-up front. The hand-tooled, brown leather bag she carried looked like a knapsack, but Italian and expensive. Down for the weekend, maybe longer, and she wanted to rent a car. As she spoke I watched her hands move, her fingers long and graceful, her nails manicured and painted pink. And her face, piercing, cold blue eyes, long dark lashes and frosty-pink lips. Her weekend turned into a week, and then a month, and then Elaine was down for the summer, and I was down for the count.

Elaine and I did everything together. Rode bikes, went to the beach or swam in the Great Pond. Wind surfing, sailing, fishing off nearby Cuttyhunk Island. I had set up a tent on a three-acre parcel a friend of mine owned up-island in Chilmark, and, in case of heavy weather, I had a studio with a bed and a shower in Lambert's Cove. I painted houses and tutored "academically challenged" preppies in English and math, while Elaine worked in a boutique in Edgartown. She had her own rented room in a big white whaling-captain's house in town, but usually we stayed in my tent in Chilmark, unless it was raining or something.

During the week, that is.

There was this one problem with our relationship. Elaine was engaged to a guy named Winslow, a securities analyst just out of Harvard Business School. According to Elaine, it was some kind of family thing, a marriage arrangement I thought had gone out of style back in the nineteenth century. This guy Winslow was working in Boston and came down to see her on weekends. Friday afternoons she would move into her room in Edgartown. Needless to say, she did not tell him about me.

Our Monday-through-Friday relationship continued throughout the summer. By August, however, I got down to thinking about how much fun we had together, how close I felt to her, and I really wanted to change things. Elaine really didn't belong with Winslow. But when I tried to bring it up, Elaine would laugh like she was embarrassed at being found out. Why spoil it, she'd say. Before I knew it we'd be horizontal in our sandy bed, making the mattress move.

"A hundred and twenty-one maintenance workers in all, seven gardeners, nine or ten sales clerks, cafeteria and kitchen workers and my security staff."

While I was lost in reverie thinking about Elaine, it seemed Fred had taken the conversation down a new corridor. I tried to follow and catch up as he continued.

"I have a staff of twenty-nine guards, nine patrolling at night in shifts. On the night of the theft there were only two on duty when the thieves hit."

"What about inside information?" I asked. "It seems like the theft occurred at the low point in security coverage. Who would know the schedule?"

"There were supposed to be three on duty, but one guy got sick and went home. In fact, the other two were complaining of stomach pains. This is not general knowledge, by the way. One of the guards bought a bag of donuts from a donut shop in Kenmore Square earlier that night. It had been spiked with detergent. FBI chased it down, but couldn't connect it to anyone. The counter man knew nothing, the guys in the back knew nothing. FBI suspects that a dishwasher was paid to do it, but the guy they were after left town, disappeared."

"How was it possible to poison just one bag of doughnuts?"

"It wasn't," he said. "A lot of people got sick that night." Somebody went to a lot of trouble to knock out those kids.

"What about inside information? Who would know the schedule?"

"I make up the schedule a week ahead. Carole types it and posts it in the security office. Remember, these guys were college kids, at least the two remaining on duty were. That's probably why they stuck around."

"FBI check them out?" I asked.

"All three. Clean as a whistle. Good families, doing well in school, good kids all around really. Just green, no experience, no judgment. I am sure you can appreciate that."

Fred looked at me and smiled. It was a perfectly innocent smile as far as you could tell, but my instincts told me he was making a point about me.

"Yeah," I said, "I can appreciate that." I smiled back.

"You've got their names and addresses in the case folder I put together."

"Right here," I said, looking down at the folder in my right hand. I'd forgotten I had it.

"Let's head down this way," Fred said. We cut through the Tapestry Room, where I'd heard the concert a few years back, and entered the Short Gallery. "Here's where they picked up the Degas sketches. Small stuff mostly. And the bronze eagle. Up there." He indicated the place on the wall where the eagle had been hanging.

"Anyone on the museum staff quit or hired around the time of the theft?" I asked.

"Only one," said Fred. "Our director, Amy Louvenbragh. Of course, she's in solid with Jack Butler. Probably more than that, if truth be told."

"I wondered about her," I said, hoping for more.

"Jack's a good guy, the finest kind, but—pardon me— he's a sucker for her bushwa." Inwardly I winced because Jack had fallen for my bushwa, too.

Peavy continued.

"The director she replaced ran into trouble with the board of trustees. Snotty Boston blue bloods. Jack Butler is the only one of them who really cares about the staff. You know, he keeps track of everyone's birthday and sends them a card every year with a little check in it."

Like my grandmother used to do, I thought. Could he be that corny?

"And Dr. Louvenbragh?" I asked.

"Dr. Louvenbragh should have stuck to researching art forgery," he said. "She knows nothing about running a museum and doesn't really seem to like the job. She'll probably move on in another year or so." Apparently Fred was not a fan of Amy Louvenbragh's.

"How about you?" I asked.

"Me? I've been here eight years next month. Came here when I retired from the force on disability. I expect to stay here until I am old and gray. Unless I die first."

Fred Peavy had an accent I was trying to place. Philadelphia? No, Baltimore, somewhere near Chesapeake Bay. I wondered what his background was.

As we walked downstairs, I went through a list of action items in my head. Check into Amy Louvenbragh, her references and her connection with Jack Butler. The security guards. The former museum director, Dr. Titus Moone. And last, but not least, Fred Peavy. One thing was very clear to me. This had been no amateur operation. Someone had taken the time to prepare and plan carefully for this job, and that included covering up the trail that led to him. Or her. Amy Louvenbragh had mentioned the recent events in Barcelona. Some art forgeries had turned up there, the Degas and Manet paintings, and a couple of murders, possibly tied to the theft. So the trail wasn't completely cold yet. I'd have to pursue those new leads before it was.

"Fred, I was wondering about Amy Louvenbragh and her relationship with Jack Butler." I said.

"What do you want to know?"

"Are they personally as well as professionally involved?"

"Sorry," he said. "I've already said more than I should. Does that about wrap it up?"

"Okay, but what did you mean when you said that Amy was in solid and 'more than that if truth be told'?"

"No comment," he said, firmly. "Look, Shakespear, I'm not going to get into that any further. You want to talk about the theft, fine. Or museum business. But I have to draw the line."

He seemed to be talking more to himself than to me.

Fred Peavy and I shook hands in the corridor outside his office. He said he had other business to attend to, but invited me to check back with him if I had any questions after reading through the case folder. I looked down at the thick sheaf of papers in my hand. I didn't look forward to going through it all, but it would probably answer a lot of my questions. That and raise a few dozen more. I remembered Elaine. It was early for lunch, so she might be meeting someone in the cafe for coffee.

As I walked in, I felt a little nervous wondering what we'd say to each other after almost four years. I scanned the clusters of tables and chairs and caught sight of Elaine sitting by herself, browsing some papers, sipping from a cup. Looking at her like that, I tried to imagine how I'd see her if we didn't have so much past between us. And then something strange happened. A smile bubbled up from inside, and I felt completely relaxed, as if we had been together last night for dinner and were meeting again, as planned, for coffee in the morning. I walked up to her table feeling rather giddy.

"Ready to order, Madam? I can recommend the edible etchings. Or the tiramisu with ginger tea, if it's something sweet you have in mind."

I mimed waiter, slipping a napkin over my left arm, bent as though age had curved my spine.

"Tommy?" she said.

"Elaine," I said. "Is that you? Elaine?" Now I was the ancient, nearly-blind, Homeric waiter.

"Tommy Shakespear!" she said. "How are you?"

"Elaine, let's see. What is it? Stockton, Winslow? I can't keep track." I knew I was over the top.

"Tom-my!!" she said, exasperated. She was glad to see me.

Elaine stood up, and I dropped my charade. We moved toward each other and embraced warmly. Her body felt soft and familiar, and she smelled like a narcotic flower. I felt something starting up inside of me that I couldn't quite control, and I held her a little too close for a little too long. Elaine broke away, gently.

"Hey, fella," she said. "Is that any way to treat a married lady?"

6
Sunday, March 14
Boston, Massachusetts

As I stood there, I'd forgotten the past three or four years of my life.

"Tommy! What are you doing here? Please sit down and tell me what you are doing."

What was I doing? I had forgotten what I was doing. My God, she was great to look at! I sat down at the table and took her in. The cool blue eyes that sometimes made me shiver. Rosy lips, light coat of gloss. Her hair, several shades of brown, pulled back, pinned up. As always a few strands had worked loose, careless curls with unmade minds of their own. As though she could hear me think, Elaine brushed those curls away from her face. I glanced down the graceful curve of her neck and could see she had no blouse on under her gray suit jacket. Knowing Elaine, I had to wonder what else she wasn't wearing. She was wearing two rings, though, one with a large glittering rock set into it.

"Hey, amazing, Elaine." I said. "You feel almost like yesterday." I must have been more than a little dizzy.

"Yeah, almost like," she said, taking the tea cup in her hands as though for warmth, and smiling. "It's great to see you, too, Tommy. What are you doing in Boston? I heard you were living in California."

"Well, I am. I came here on business."

"Business? You?" She laughed, incredulous. Ironically.

"Butler Museum business, in fact." I patted the thick case folder I'd set down on the table in front of me.

"Really." Elaine looked as though she didn't quite believe me. She sipped her tea and set the cup down in its saucer. "Museum business."

"And you, Elaine, what brings you to the museum?"

"Well, I do some volunteering here. One day a week in the museum shop. And I am also on a fund-raising committee that has been meeting a lot lately." She played with her teaspoon on the table top. I picked up another.

"Have plans for lunch?" I hoped she didn't.

"Unfortunately, I do, and I have a doctor's appointment at two. But I don't have to leave for a while yet. Tell me more about your business with the museum."

"Tell me more about those rings on your finger." I said it as lightly as I could, but it made my gut tighten up to think about it. I tapped the spoon.

Elaine pulled back from the table and looked at her left hand. She glanced across at me and smiled. It was not a newlywed smile. It was a smile that said, Sorry, Tommy, this is what I had to do.

"Well, you remember Whit, I am sure. It all went off as planned. The big church wedding, the Ritz reception, honeymoon in Venice." I dropped my spoon on the faded pink and green tablecloth.

She reached across to touch my arm. I let her.

"Tommy, I am sure you didn't expect me to change my mind at the last moment, like in some kind of movie."

That felt like a cut, but Elaine was more complicated than that. I knew she'd had some second thoughts. I looked down.

"Elaine, I'd love to have changed your mind." I said, almost choking on the words. "But what's the point of talking about that now?"

Neither one of us said anything for a while. Finally, Elaine spoke.

"You know, it's not so bad for me, Tommy," she said, brightly. "I have a pretty good life. Of course, Whit's busy with work. He travels a lot, so I have to cultivate my own interests. I've got the museum, the tennis club, lots of friends, and, of course, the house to look after. A pretty big house, in fact."

"I am sure it is." Without thinking, I took a shot. "Any chance Winlow's away on business tonight? We could have dinner, and catch up."

But, as soon as I'd said it, I regretted it.

"No chance, I'm afraid. But thank you for asking, Tommy," she said. "We're having a little dinner party tonight. Some museum people, our friends from the local art scene. I'd invite you to come, but I am not sure Whit would appreciate it."

"Probably not," I said.

There was an awkward pause. Fortunately, Elaine changed the subject.

"So what are you doing with the Butler museum? I can't imagine."

"Jack Butler hired me to look into the theft," I said.

"The unsolved major mystery? I'd have thought it was old news by now." Elaine looked away, avoided my eyes.

"Some new developments apparently. Bodies. Two of them. At La Sagrada Familia." I'd stolen a peek at the dossier earlier while Fred had been rambling on about the absurd prices people pay for art.

"I'm on my way to Barcelona tomorrow to learn what I can."

Barcelona? It was out of my mouth before I could stop it. I was trying to make myself sound important to Elaine. And surely Barcelona sounded important. Besides, two fresh bodies had to mean something.

"Spain should be beautiful in the spring, Tommy. You know, I had forgotten you knew Jack Butler," she said. "He's coming tonight with Amy."

"Amy?" I said.

"Dr. Amy Louvenbragh, our ambitious museum director? I'm sure you must have met her by now."

"I have had the pleasure, Elaine. It's true." Actually, pleasure wasn't quite the right word.

"Not the warmest person, maybe, but she can be fun sometimes. She certainly has her hooks into Jack."

"Hooks? Are they..."

"You know, since you're working on this investigation—but, Tommy, I just can't picture you as a private investigator."

"That's because you've seen me with my clothes off."

Elaine smiled, indulgently.

Why was I saying these things?

"Sorry," I said. "Go on. Since I'm working on this investigation...." I tried to recover.

"Well, I was going to say maybe you should come to the party tonight."

"Why? Who is going to be there?"

"Art people mostly. Jack and Amy. The Globe art critic and his girlfriend. A Newbury Street gallery owner and his boyfriend. And there's me."

"And your husband."

"Well, I am sure we can find some time to talk. If that's what you want."

I had to make eye contact. Her blue eyes gleamed at me, and her lids narrowed. Elaine was always hard to figure, and now she had me going.

"I thought you said that Whit would mind."

"I did, but never mind Whit. I want you to come."

As I looked at Elaine, I realized we weren't the people we'd been two years ago. A lot had changed, and now I was feeling a little wary of her.

"Where are you staying?" she asked.

"Four Seasons."

"Jack, or rather the museum, must be paying your expenses."

"Yeah. He's..."

Elaine stood up to leave.

"Six-thirty for cocktails. Don't dress. We're a pretty casual crowd."

I got up and kissed her on the cheek. We stood there holding hands, looking into each other. Our eyes had locked on, and, for a moment, I felt that we were going to make love standing right there. But it passed like a flight of birds overhead, and I was relieved.

As I watched Elaine walk away, I was beginning to think that maybe I was lucky she'd turned me down.

7

Sunday, March 14
Boston, Massachusetts

I walked all the way back to the hotel. It took me well over an hour, but the sun felt good on my back, and I had a lot to think about. My own life had been on track such a short while now that this reminder of my unsettled past was a little threatening. I could easily be persuaded to take a detour, it seemed, and I was afraid of what it could mean. I tried to focus on the case, but Elaine had become a distraction and a hard one to ignore.

Two years had not been enough time to forget her. After we'd split up that summer, I'd tried throwing myself back into the job with Hank's firm in Boston, but it was no use. Her face would be everywhere I went. Every woman I saw on the street had her hair, her hips. Or her pink lips. It got so bad I finally quit my job and left town.

California still hadn't done the trick.

The first thing I noticed when I entered my hotel room was the blinking red light on the telephone. The room was spotless. My notebook was on the desk where I'd forgotten it, and the hotel maid had placed my ticket and taxi receipts alongside. I emptied my pockets, tossed the case folder onto the bed, called the operator and picked up my messages. The assistant hotel manager had called. Call Jack Butler at his home number. Hank Greenberg called, he'd decided to fly down to Florida to watch spring training. He'd be gone a week. And Shiva called to say hi.

I returned Jack Butler's call first. It was time to check in with my client. The phone rang and rang and rang. I kept expecting the answering machine to click in, but it never did. After about ten or eleven rings he picked up the phone.

"Jack Butler."

"Jack, hi. This is Tommy Shakespear."

"Oh, hello. Just one moment, would you?" He was gone for a while, and I heard the sounds you get when someone switches over to another extension.

"You there, Shakespear?"

"Here," I said.

"Good. How was your flight?"

"Fine, Jack. I just got in last night, but I've had meetings with Dr. Louvenbragh and Fred Peavy this morning.

"Wasting no time. That's the idea."

"I gather there've been some recent developments in Barcelona."

"The Manet and Degas."

"Yes," I said. "And a couple of men found dead there. I had the idea of going over to get a bead on the situation."

"You're comfortable with the assignment? Ted Wycliffe said he had briefed you, and so I take it you're interested."

"Curious, anyway," I said. "I can be on a flight to Barcelona tomorrow, but when can we get together, Jack? There are some questions I'd like to ask you."

"Not sure. I've just got back from the Bahamas, and I am going to be engaged this evening."

"Congratulations, Jack. Who's the lucky—"

"Not engaged to be married, Shakespear. No, I meant I have a social commitment this evening."

Oh.

"Would that be Elaine Winslow's party?"

"Yes," he said. "I gather you've been in touch with her."

"We met by chance this morning at the museum."

"You know, Shakespear, Elaine Winslow was quite keen on you."

Uh oh. How much had she told him?

"That was before her marriage, though," I said.

"Sorry?"

"Well, I meant, Jack, that our relationship was before. Maybe they were engaged, but, you know, well, really, it was..."

He interrupted. "I think you misunderstood, Shakespear. Elaine Winslow had recommended you for this assignment. She and her husband are important museum patrons. He's on the board, in fact, and she's involved in the committees. Elaine Winslow put me in touch with the Greenberg law firm, and they provided a reference."

"Oh. I wasn't aware of that."

"Apparently," he said. There was a pause. "You will be coming tonight?"

I was noncommittal, unsure now whether Jack really wanted me there. "Elaine thought I might find her guests interesting. I understand there will be a few art scene movers and shakers."

"Well, I don't know, Shakespear. Amy, that is, Dr. Louvenbragh, will be there. Clark Bouton, Kara Penny-Wise. One or two of the Newbury Street contingent."

"Maybe we can get a moment aside to discuss the case and your requirements, Jack. Like I said, I've already interviewed Dr. Louvenbragh and Fred Peavy, and I'm on my way to Barcelona. Things are moving quickly. Still, there are a few questions I'd like to ask." More than a few, I thought to myself.

"We can certainly get started," he said. "See you then."

I set down the phone, somewhat puzzled by what Jack had said. At the museum Elaine had acted surprised to see me, astonished to learn I was working for Jack Butler. Why had she been playing dumb? What was she up to? I looked forward to confronting her.

Hank Greenberg was out of town. There'd be no point in calling Hank until he got back from Florida. He'd be totally obsessed with Red Sox baseball even then. The man was seriously ill, but he was my friend. I hoped we'd find some time when he got back. I could use his advice.

Shiva was out when I called, but her answering machine was in. It was Hawaii Five-O this time. The musical theme was in the background.

"Hi, it's me. Well, not exactly me, I'm out right now, but I would like to know who called. So do what you have to do. And...Book 'em, Danno!" I could almost see the big waves crashing on the beach as the Hawaii Five-O theme faded to the beep. Shiva's answering machine had a new tape every week or so. Once in a while she'd have a trivia contest with prizes like a can of Spam, a Slinky or an old-time paperback like *Franny and Zooey*. I left word that I'd called and would get back in a day or so.

After lunch, I called the concierge and made plane reservations for the following day. I had a few hours before the party, but I sure didn't feel like working. Jet lag had got me in its magic spell. And I didn't feel like talking to the assistant hotel manager. He probably wanted to make sure everything was fine. Fine as fine could be. I knew I should read the case folder Amy Louvenbragh had given me, but I was just too tired. There would be plenty of time on the plane to Barcelona, I reasoned, to delve into details. For now I would be better off if I got some rest. I placed the case folder on the bedside table in case I should later change my mind. I stripped off my clothes, stashed my wallet under the mattress and slid between the cool, clean sheets. My head burrowed into a soft pillow. Down-filled, I thought. I closed my eyes.

When I woke up it was dark. I looked at the clock on my bedside table. Glowing red numerals—7:02. I was going to be late for Elaine's party, but I was too groggy to care. I turned over and adjusted the covers.

Now what? I thought I could hear someone in the walk-in closet. Going through my suitcase? How could anyone get in?

Even though the Four Seasons was a top-drawer hotel, I doubted it would be a valet unpacking my clothes. I lay still, scanning the room, adjusting my eyes. Pitch dark. Nothing. You couldn't see the closet from the bed anyway. It was around a corner and across from the bathroom. Maybe the burglar didn't know I was there. Why would anyone...?

The phone rang. I hesitated, uncertain whether to answer. It rang again. If I answered the phone, the burglar would know right away I was there. The phone kept ringing. Whoever was calling wasn't giving up. I decided to pick up the phone, as if I had just awakened, and give the burglar a chance to leave unseen. Finally, I grabbed it on the sixth ring.

"Hello?" I said loudly, but, I hoped, sleepily.

"Tommy, it's Elaine. Aren't you coming to my party?"

"Oh, hi, Elaine." I forced a yawn. "Yeah, of course. Why? Am I late?" Another, more prolonged yawn. For the benefit of Mr. Kite, the burglar.

"I woke you. You were sleeping." Good old Elaine was accusing me.

"No, I was just sitting here in the dark — loading my gun," I said loudly. I listened for noise from the walk-in closet but could hear nothing.

"Well, hurry up, Tommy." Was she pouting?

"Okay, Elaine," I said, rustling around in bed. "I'm going to get up now, shower, and dress in record time. See you for cocktails."

"Dinner's at eight-thirty, so hurry."

"What kind of gun? It's a nine-millimeter Browning."

"What?"

"Never mind," I said. "See you in forty-five minutes. In fact, time me."

I hung up the phone, and a moment later I heard the hotel room door click softly shut. I jumped out of bed naked, ran around the corner to the door and opened it. Down the corridor I could see the door to the back stairs closing. Across the hall, only four doors down. I considered chasing after the intruder, but my birthday suit would be a bit too casual for the Four Seasons lobby, so I closed my door. In the walk-in closet I checked my suitcase and found it still full of my natty threads. The little canisters Shiva had given me were in the side pockets. Had I imagined the intruder? No. I turned on some lights.

The spiral notebook I'd bought to take notes in was missing from the desk, but the ticket and receipts, spare change and pocket lint were there. I looked around the room and turned on a few more lights. The thief had taken my notebook. That was odd, but no great loss. I'd made a few notes at the library in Santa Cruz, but had forgotten to bring it with me to the Butler. Otherwise it was a blank notebook I could replace easily.

Wait a minute! An extra card key...but this one had no hotel logo on it. I thought about calling hotel security before the thief left the hotel. I thought about calling the Boston Police and reporting the break-in. But I decided against it. I didn't want to face anyone who might ask me why I lay in bed talking on the phone while the burglar rummaged through my belongings. It might get back to my employer.

At least I knew one thing. Somebody knew I was on this case, and I'd have to find out who that somebody was. Somebody who knew how to counterfeit a hotel master key.

I walked into the bathroom, showered and shaved. I put on my blue denim shirt and buttoned it, some clean blue jeans, hiking boots, leather jacket, retrieved my wallet from under the mattress and left the hotel.

The sky was already dark with night. Through the open window of the cab, the air felt wet and heavy like a big thunderstorm was coming around the next corner. It was warm for March, and, rain or no rain, intruder or no intruder, I felt glad to be back in Boston. I had money in the bank, a place to stay and a new job. What could be better? A plane ticket to Barcelona? Hey, I had that, too.

It took only fifteen minutes by cab to Elaine's place on Beacon Street in Newton. Stone lions stood atop of a pair of white-washed pillars at the entrance to her driveway. We paused to check the number, continued up the drive and around the side of a hill to a three-story, red brick Victorian mansion at the top. Behind and to the right of the main house stood a three-car garage with a second-story apartment, probably a maid's or butler's quarters. The front entrance had white-washed brick columns like the driveway, but the lions this time crouched beside the columns, as if they had leaped down to greet the guests. I paid the cab driver and lifted the heavy bronze door knocker, rapping twice. I looked at my watch. It was seven-forty-eight.

After a moment the door opened, and Elaine slid out. She held her finger to her lips, warning me to be quiet. She closed the front door, grabbed my hand and began running across the front lawn toward the garage, pulling me with her. When we reached the garage, she unlocked a side door and led me up a flight of stairs to the apartment above. Elaine snapped on a light and pulled the white wooden shutters closed.

"My studio, Tommy. What do you think of it?" she asked, turning toward me, sweeping her arm across the room's expanse.

The air smelled stale and musty, but with faint ribbons of paint and thinner threading the air. I looked around at bold splashes of color, abstract paintings piled in corners, leaning up against easels. Alongside them were stacks of stretched canvas, spattered drop cloths piled like dirty laundry, clusters of brushes soaking in thinner, sketch pads and boxes of charcoal and chalk. It was haphazard-looking, almost random, yet a certain personal order seemed to be at work, although it would be hard to describe the organizing principle.

"It's like you, Elaine," I said. "Beautiful, well equipped, but disorderly."

"Is that what you think, Tommy? That I'm a pretty mess?"

Elaine came toward me, brushing the hair from her face with the back of her hand. She moved in close without saying a word, her cold-blue eyes peering into mine and through me to someplace beyond. She pushed my leather jacket back and off my shoulders. I shrugged it to the floor. I wanted to run, but my feet seemed miles away. Elaine pressed up against me, and I could feel the heat from her body. I could feel her breasts, nipples hard, through the thin silk blouse. We kissed with our eyes and mouths open, and I could taste lipstick and the Scotch whisky in her breath. We bit into each other again with our lips and tongues, and my breathing slowed. She unbuttoned my shirt and grazed my nipples with her lips. I knew I was about to go over the edge. We moved toward the couch and fell into it. Clouds of paint dust rose up, drifting through angled shafts from the track lighting overhead.

Suddenly I came to. What was going on here? I pulled away from Elaine and sat up and looked around the room.

"Jesus, Elaine." My heart was still pounding.

"What?" she said.

"What do you mean what? You know what." I said, still looking away. "Is that any way to treat an old boyfriend?"

"Shut up, Tommy. You know you liked it, so don't be a hypocrite." She was pouting.

"Okay, Elaine, let's talk about hypocrites and about telling the truth."

"Yeah? What, Tommy?"

"Earlier today at the museum you acted surprised to see me. Like, 'Tommy, where did you come from?' And talking to

Jack this afternoon I find out you recommended me for this job. Is something missing here, Elaine?"

She didn't answer me right away. I figured she was caught off guard. Of course, I wasn't sure what to say next either. How come I was being so assertive with Elaine? That wasn't the old me. Maybe something had changed.

"It's a long story," Elaine said.

Of course it was, and we didn't have time for all of it now. We both knew that.

"Just the headline, okay?"

"Oh, I think you can guess," she said. "It's not working out between Whit and me. It was supposed to be, you know, the perfect situation, but it's never really been that. I think Whit doesn't even notice because he's so intent on being Whit Winslow and all that stands for. I thought if we got together again, you and I, I could get some distance. Maybe. Maybe I *could* decide what to do about Whit. Or whether to do anything. I thought maybe...Well, I don't know what I thought really, Tommy. I wish I knew what to say."

Wait a minute, here. She had her dumb act on.

"Elaine, you mean I'm here in Boston so you could *maybe* get up the courage to think about *maybe* leaving Winslow?"

Elaine reached over and touched my cheek. "We were close once, Tommy, weren't we?"

She said it in a way that showed her pain and put me in touch with mine again. Yeah, we were close. More than close, the way it felt to me. And now I was feeling manipulated again, yanked around like a puppy dog on a three-thousand-mile leash.

"So you conned Jack Butler into bringing me to Boston? Like, 'So, Jack, I know this great investigator who can solve the mystery of Thelonius Monk. He'll find the missing paintings and help me get my husband's attention.'"

Who was she trying to kid?

"Jack was looking for someone. I knew you'd done this kind of work before. You know, Tommy, when you worked for Hank Greenberg. You found Zymanski's girlfriend when nobody else could. Not even the police. And Jack remembered you from the memorial service for Beatrice. So why not, Tommy? Can't you handle it? Or is it me you're afraid of?"

"I can handle it. That's not the point."

"So what is the point, Tommy?"

Here we go again, I thought.

"Once again, I feel like you're using me, Elaine. Like on the Vineyard that summer. And when you're through with me, you're on to somebody else."

"It's just not that simple, Tommy. You can't judge me like that."

"Oh, I can't? Why can't I? And, meanwhile, Elaine, what about your party?" I said. "Won't Winslow and your other guests be wondering where we are?"

Elaine grabbed my wrist and she looked at my watch.

"It's a little after eight. Dinner's not for thirty minutes yet. But you're right, Tommy, let's get back. Tommy —" She paused and tried to fix my eyes. "We do need to talk about this. Maybe another time."

Yeah, sure. Another time. Sure. Sweet Pandora. I was relieved we'd put off what almost started up again. It could only lead to, well, who knew what it would lead to? One thing I knew. This was not why I'd come to Boston.

I dressed quickly. Elaine disappeared into the bathroom for a moment and reappeared with every hair in place, her makeup fresh and beautifully composed. She walked up to me and stood there smiling, so close I could almost taste her perfume. It reminded me of how I used to feel about her.

As though she had read my mind, Elaine smiled and said, "Another time, soon, Tommy." She brushed her hand against my thigh and walked past me down the stairs.

8
Monday, March 15
Boston, Massachusetts

This thing with Elaine had gotten out of hand. I knew that. And I knew I'd have to try to put it back in the box I'd been keeping it in. Not easy, given the way I still felt about Elaine, but there didn't seem to be any other way. I couldn't risk getting involved with her again.

After our little adventure in her studio, we entered the main house through the kitchen. We killed some time there talking with the caterers and catching up on the hot hors d'oeuvres. Elaine poured herself another Scotch, and I took a glass of Poland Springs, no bubbles, for myself. Then we pushed through the louvered saloon doors that led into the informal dining room and then to the sitting room beyond.

Maybe it was because the furniture was as uncomfortable as it looked, but everyone in the sitting room was standing around, drinks in hand, pretending not to notice us walk in. I recognized Jack Butler right away. He was a fairly tall man and slim, but not athletic. He carried himself in a way I could only describe as formal, as though he might have to present an award at any moment. His slightly receding hairline, aquiline nose, and deep tan accentuated the effect. At the same time he was relaxed, even nonchalant in his conversation. He turned as I approached.

"Mr. Shakespear, I presume?" he said. We shook hands. "Hello again, Elaine. We wondered if you had gone out for the evening."

"Very droll, Jack," said Elaine, taking a sip of her scotch. "I was just showing Tommy my etchings." Jack smiled and turned toward the young woman he'd been speaking to.

"Kara, let me introduce Tommy Shakespear. Tommy, Kara Penny-Worth. I'm going to have a word with Elaine. Excuse us a moment."

Jack took Elaine aside just out of earshot. While I couldn't hear what Jack was saying, I assumed it had to do with Elaine and me. I was feeling slightly paranoid, thinking everyone knew what we had been up to.

"Are you and Elaine old friends?"

Kara Penny-Worth was trim and blonde, in her mid-twenties, and her question seemed innocent. I told her how Elaine and I had met on the Vineyard a few years ago, and it turned out that Kara had spent some time on the island, too. Kara was an aerobics instructor and avid wind surfer, and had taught windsurfing there one summer. We'd been to some of the same places, knew some of the same people. Gradually, I began to relax. As I looked around at the others, it seemed that the party had gotten livelier. Probably people were getting hungry. Well-oiled, too. Jack was now talking to Winslow. Elaine was talking to two men I hadn't met. I wondered where Amy Louvenbragh was.

Kara's boyfriend, Clark Bouton, joined us, and the conversation turned to art and eventually the Butler Museum. Clark, tall and very thin, covered art for a Boston newspaper. He had opinions.

"The thing is," Clark was saying, "though it was sloppy, nobody believes that it could have been an amateur operation. It looks too much like a professional hit, like the Marmottan theft in Paris in 1985. By all appearances that was a contract job. They got Monet's "Impression: Sunrise," a Renoir, and several other major works. All of them have been traced to collectors in Japan. And there have been others. Two separate thefts in the Netherlands in 1988, involving works by Van Gogh and Cézanne. The one in Amsterdam was worth over $50 million, the one in Otterlo about $90 million. Fortunately all of it was recovered, but that's the exception."

"Art-to-go for the very rich. Hey, it's a free market, I guess." I was feeling a little giddy with hunger, and Clark was the kind of guy I liked to needle. He furrowed his brow to let me know I'd succeeded.

"It happens more than you'd want to believe. Interpol tracks over 200 art thefts a year, most of them amateur, but an increasing number of contract hits in recent years. There was even one at the Boston Museum of Fine Arts a few years ago."

He was ignoring my wisecrack, saying something about art theft being second only to drug smuggling on the international hit parade, and I felt Kara touching my arm. I looked over at her as Clark was talking. She seemed to be asking me to let Clark be Clark. Then our little group opened up, and Jack and Elaine's husband Winslow joined us. Still no sign of Amy Louvenbragh. Still no sign of dinner.

"You know Whit Winslow, don't you, Tommy?" said Jack.

"Indirectly," I replied, shaking the damp hand in front of me. "My pleasure."

I felt uncomfortable, though. This was the guy whose wife I'd nearly just made love to. This was the guy who I'd hated for so long. He stood about my height, but leaner and finer-boned, with dark hair cut shorter than mine, brown eyes and a gleaming smile. Looking into his face I felt sorry for him.

"Good to meet you, Shakespear. Tommy."

"Whit."

Winslow and I had never actually met before because Elaine had preferred it that way. Now that I'd met him, I could see what Elaine saw in him. Old money, good looks, and very little to say. He embodied nearly every stereotype I despised — this rich, good-looking, preppy, jock, investment banker — all the things my father thought I should be.

Jack took control again.

"I've asked Tommy to help out with this museum theft," he said to Winslow. "Lord knows we can use the help."

"I thought you had Charley Howell on the theft."

"Now don't get me started on Howell. I know Fred's high on Howell, but two years of steep fees and very little to report...We need a new approach, Whit, and I'm hoping Tommy, here, will bring a fresh perspective, stir things up a bit."

"I'd like to do more than stir things up," I said. "The Butler, I believe, by the terms of its bequest, can't replace the stolen works with others, even by the same artists. I don't know what the chances are, Jack, but I'd like to get your art back. It seems unfair that these works may never be seen again."

He beamed. I seemed to have pressed the right button.

"Grossly unfair. Unfair to us at the museum, to the art world and to the general public. What concerns me most is that most stolen art, probably ninety per cent of it, is never found again," said Jack, looking directly at me. "It's two or three times as big as the legitimate art business, you know. And almost all of it is going out of circulation, either into private collections, or it's being destroyed or damaged beyond repair by bungling. Most of these so-called professional thieves know nothing about handling art. They're bunglers, idiots, ham-fisted fools."

"You'd think they'd get some training," I said, unable to resist.

Jack gave me a questioning look. I scrambled to recover.

"What I mean is, if I were going to rip off a masterpiece, I'd want to know how to get the best price for it. Damaged goods don't usually bring the best price." I knew something about damaged goods. So far my life was damaged goods.

"I wouldn't think so," Jack replied. "But my deepest concern is the irreparable loss to the world of art. For instance, 'The Letter' by Vermeer, possibly his greatest work, was stolen in 1971 in Brussels. Cut from its frame and rolled up by the thief, who then sat on it in the back of a taxi, ruining it beyond repair. And that makes just fifteen known surviving works by Vermeer, assuming 'The Concert' can be recovered." He paused.

Amy Louvenbragh had made her arrival and joined the conversation group. Jack kissed her on the cheek and took her hand. She had changed into dark-blue worsted slacks and a white blouse with a ruffled front, which gave her a more expressive look than I had seen that morning. Her eyes shone brighter and larger, and her lips were blood red.

"You know Amy, of course," he said to me.

"Yes. Hello, Dr. Louvenbragh. We met this morning." I thought I'd better assume we were not on good terms. Keep it friendly, but formal, I thought.

Fortunately, Elaine announced that it was time for dinner, and we moved into the dining room. I took a chair between Amy Louvenbragh and Randall Stine, a Newbury Street gallery owner. He was about fifty-five going on thirty. Dyed hair and a beard to match. I made an attempt to converse with Amy, inquiring about the research she had been doing on her fellowship. I didn't really want to know about it. I didn't think it would be very interesting, but it was. She had been studying variations of signatures on works by Vermeer. Apparently Vermeer almost never signed a painting the same way twice. Sometimes he used a monogram, and there were several variations of those. Sometimes he used his full name, or part of it, in a signature, and again several variations. Apart from the psychology of it, I wondered at the exceedingly difficult task of authenticating Vermeer paintings.

Randall Stine found his way into the conversation at that point, speculating that the paintings had been taken by a forgery ring who could sell copies of them several times over to unscrupulous but unsuspecting collectors. Then somewhere between the lemon sole and tiramisu, Randall mentioned something that piqued my interest. The Sotheby and Christie auction houses had offered a reward for information leading to the return of the paintings. $1 million. Jack hadn't mentioned that.

After dinner, Elaine, Winslow and their guests moved back into the sitting room for coffee. I decided to return early to get a good night's sleep before my flight, I should say 'flights,' to Barcelona. So I skipped the old ports and liqueurs.

Elaine called a cab, and we said our goodnights, postponing our talk until sometime in the indefinite future. Leaving Elaine with Randall and his friend, I walked to the front door with Jack.

"Jack, if I could ask you something..."

"Yes."

"Why me?" I said.

He didn't answer at first. So I asked again, or started to.

"What I mean is, you already have someone working on the case, and..."

"Shakespear, I saw something in you when we met at the funeral, a kind of resourcefulness most people and even most investigators do not possess."

Jack was standing with one hand on my shoulder in a fatherly sort of way. He was gripping it a little too firmly, I thought.

"Added to that, you were a personal friend not only of my late sister, but also of Elaine Winslow, a good friend, and you had excellent references locally. In short, you were someone I could trust. When I learned you were possibly available, I had Fred Peavy run a search to locate you. We discovered you worked at Prometheum for Andre Ziff, who by the way is one of our trustees. Were you running security for Andre?"

"Actually, no. I'd taken a brief career detour into computers. You never know when that stuff will come in handy." I was improvising, something I do fairly well and far too often.

"True. Remind me, Shakespear, we need to discuss something about Andre."

Oh, oh, I thought. This could be a problem. What had Jack found out?

"Okay, Jack," I said. "When I get back from Barcelona." It was time to change the subject. I brought up the Sotheby-Christie reward.

"Well, Shakespear, you get paid whether you find the paintings or not," said Jack. "If you do find them, and I am very hopeful of that, I'll give you a bonus of $50,000. After all, we are bankrolling this little adventure."

"What about the one million dollars?" I asked.

"We feel that any reward money should be donated to the Butler Museum Foundation. It would be applied toward restoring the paintings, purchasing insurance, improving museum security and defraying the costs of these investigations. I am sure you agree that this theft has been a great loss, not only to the museum, but also to people all over the world who love art. No one wishes to profit from that, I am sure."

"Well, okay," I said, not feeling entirely okay. "A deal is a deal, and we've already agreed to terms." I could see my cab was winding its way up the driveway. "I'm on my way to Barcelona tomorrow. I'll see you in a few days."

"By the way, Shakespear," Jack said. "I'd advise you to steer clear of Elaine. I realize you two are old friends, but she and Whit have a marriage to work out. You don't want to get caught in the middle of that."

He was right. I certainly didn't want to get caught. But there was still something about Elaine that drew me to her. We had old business to work out, and until I had a handle on that, it wasn't going to be all that easy. As I got into the cab, I looked back at the red brick Victorian mansion.

Behind a filmy curtain in an upstairs window Elaine was looking out at me.

9
Monday, March 15
Herndon, Virginia

I called Elaine from Dulles airport. I had a two-hour layover until the Madrid flight departed and needed to talk to her.

"Elaine," I said. "There's no way we're going to start this up again."

"Why not, Tommy?" she said. "Don't you even like me?"

"Quit playing around, Elaine." Elaine loved to play games.

"I'm not playing." She emphasized the word not.

"No games, then?"

"No. No games."

There was a pause as we listened to each other's silences.

"Who is she, Tommy?" Elaine changed the subject.

"Who's who?" I replied.

"What's her name?"

"Who? Who are you talking about, Elaine?"

"The woman you're in love with."

"Nobody."

"Nobody. Tommy?" Elaine was not going to give up.

"Nobody you'd know anyway."

"Now we're getting somewhere."

"Her name's Shiva," I said. No pause. It came right out.

"That's her real name?"

I told her I had to board right away. That it just wasn't smart for us to get involved again. I told her I wasn't sure about being in love with Shiva. Or anyone for that matter. I told her I had to go.

"Okay," she said. "Call me when you get back." Elaine never gave up.

"Bye, Elaine."

"Wait, Tommy. There's one more thing. You remember that R&B band on the Vineyard at the Hot Tin Roof?"

"Yeah, vaguely. Your friend was the bass player?"

"Right. His name is Yards."

"Sure. The guy with the Mona Lisa tattoo. Got busted for coke, I believe." Where was this going?

"That's him," Elaine said. "Okay, well, he's out of jail now. A friend of mine saw him last night, playing in a band on the south shore. And, supposedly, he's not doing coke anymore."

"So?"

"Well, it turns out he had a prior conviction. According to my friend...."

"For?" Drum roll. Elaine had me playing the straight man again.

"For art theft." Rim shot.

"Interesting," I said. "What kind of art?"

"I really don't know. I thought you might want to meet him and talk to him. He's pretty well connected, and he's not a bad guy."

"Just a convicted felon."

"I seem to recall you had a little trouble with drugs, too."

"But not art," I reminded her.

I had to board the plane, but we agreed to get together when I returned. Elaine was right. Maybe the guy knew somebody who knew somebody. Never can tell.

Once I got on the plane and settled into my seat, I took out the case folder Dr. Amy L had given me. I opened it up and skimmed the materials. There was plenty of detail. Photos and descriptions of the missing works, a catalog of the museum's holdings, copies of news clippings, police reports, reports by a series of hired investigators, descriptions and sketches of the thieves, background on the security guards, a list of uniform rental companies, a scenario reconstructing the events of that Saturday night in 1991, photos of the security entrance, a description and inventory of the security system, names and addresses of museum employees. And more, much more. One curious thing. I came across the name Prometheum written in the margin of the report. It looked like Amy Louvenbragh's handwriting. I wondered if she'd made the note during our interview. Otherwise, it was an interesting coincidence. During the seven-hour flight I read through every inch of paper in the case folder. Twice I fell asleep. But by the time we had landed in Madrid, I was intimately familiar with the formal record. It confirmed the speculation I had heard from Randall Stine. A European art theft and forgery ring, possibly operating out of Barcelona, dealing forgeries to rich, but unsuspecting collectors. But where were the stolen masterworks?

I was looking forward to seeing Ferran Olzet in Barcelona. We'd been friends since college. When Amy Louvenbragh had mentioned the art professor in Barcelona with the forgeries, I thought of Ferran. When I'd called him from Boston, he was already familiar with the case. I asked him to look further into it, but he was reluctant.

"Tommy, I don't think you know what you are getting into."

Why was everyone saying that?

Ferran reminded me of the two men found murdered at La Sagrada Familia. He urged me to forget about it and enjoy Barcelona on holiday. In the end, however, Ferran agreed to ask some friends of his what they knew, and we made a date for dinner.

In Madrid, I cleared customs and then took a short hop to Barcelona. At the Barcelona airport I rented a car and drove the short distance into town. It took a while to get used to all the traffic, even more chaotic than Boston's, and never mind looking at the signs in Catalan.

On the way into town I saw large apartment buildings, laundry hanging out windows to dry. They could have been anywhere, I suppose. Hong Kong, Sao Paolo or the Bronx. A few moments later, I saw a Gothic-looking building with gargoyles leaning out to frighten passersby. No one seemed to notice them except me. Here and there were medieval stone remnants of the era when Barcelona ruled the Mediterranean, side by side with modern office buildings and hotels with imposing black glass facades. And churches; every corner seemed to have a church. Barcelona was a jumble of styles. Old, new, exotic and just plain functional.

I turned right at the Avinguda de la Diagonal and a minute later pulled up onto the tiled apron outside my hotel. It was Tuesday, Jueves, el 16 de Marzo, and I was exhausted from traveling. The sun was shining as I left the car for the doorman to park. It was going to be a beautiful spring day, but as I entered the hotel lobby, I had other plans. Sleep. Lots of it.

But I couldn't sleep. As I lay in my bed with the curtains drawn, eyes closed, pillows fluffed up around my head, pages of the case folder turned before my mind's eye. Again I saw the police reports, photos and descriptions, the scenarios, detectives' reports, sketches, lists of names and addresses. I got up and opened the minibar, taking out two bottles of cold spring water, agua mineral sin gaz. I drank one and set the other on my bedside table. Then I tried to sleep again, but still I couldn't. This time I thought of Shiva and my conversation with Elaine.

"What's her name?" she asked.

"Who?"

"The woman you're in love with."

"Her name's Shiva," I said.

"That's her real name?"

Why had I said that to Elaine? Shiva and I were friends. Maybe there was potential for something more, but our relationship hadn't yet developed into anything. So why had I said that? And then, before I could answer myself, I was asleep.

When I woke it was getting dark outside, but until I opened the curtains it could have been anytime. I looked at my watch, saw it was almost noon and realized my watch was still set to Eastern Standard Time. Lunch time in Boston, breakfast in Santa Cruz. I reset my watch to local time, a little before seven p.m. That gave me an hour or two before I was expected at Ferran's house for dinner. Drinks at nine, dinner at ten, Spanish-style. I uncapped and drank the second bottle of spring water and then unpacked my toiletries. I took a nice, long, hot shower and soaked. With all of that sitting in an airplane and lying on a too-soft hotel mattress, I needed a chiropractor.

After getting dressed I had some time to call Shiva, but I hadn't worked out in my mind what I would say. I punched in the international access number and then her area code and number and then my phone card number. Out of curiosity, I counted up the digits. Thirty-four in all.

"Hi, it's Shiva." She answered on the first ring.

"Shiva, it's Tommy."

"Tommy, I got your message. How's Boston?"

"Great, but I'm in Barcelona."

"You're in Spain?"

"Yeah, Barcelona. How's life in Santa Cruz?"

"Cruzin' as always. I'm just having breakfast. What time is it there?"

"It's about seven-thirty. I'm going to dinner in a little while."

"How's the case going?"

"Complicated."

"You'll figure it out."

"I don't know, Shiva. A lot of people have already worked on it. A lot of professionals. Cops, private detectives and the FBI. And if they haven't been able to get anywhere, I don't know about my chances."

"You're as smart as they are, Tommy. Maybe smarter. Besides, you know what they have already tried and found out. You don't have to start from scratch."

"Thanks for the pep talk, Shiva. I wish you were here to help me with this."

"The Thin Man. William Powell and Myrna Loy. All we need now is a dog, preferably an Airedale. We can call him Asta."

"So how was your mom?"

"Not bad. She still tries to climb inside everything I do, but otherwise fine. What about you? Any excitement?"

"Not really," I said. "Well, there was one thing." I hesitated.

"What was it? Tell me." Her interest was piqued.

"There was this intruder, a burglar, I guess, in my hotel room in Boston."

"Are you sure, Tommy? How do you know? Something missing?"

"I was there."

"You were there? Where?"

"In my hotel room. I already told you."

"And the burglar was there, too? At the same time?"

"Yeah. He woke me up."

"Let me get this straight. A burglar came into your hotel room in Boston while you were sleeping and woke you up."

"Well, he didn't come over to my bed and shake me awake or anything. I woke up while he was going through my suitcase."

"How do you know it was a he?"

"I guess I don't. I didn't actually see the burglar, but I could hear him in a closet around the corner."

"What did you do?"

"Nothing. I pretended to be asleep."

"And then?"

"That's pretty much it. The phone rang. I answered it like I was just waking up and the burglar left."

"Wow! Good thing I gave you those sprays."

"Yeah. Good thing," I said. "Except they were in my suitcase at the time."

"So who was on the phone?"

"Phone?"

"Yeah, the phone."

"What do you mean?"

"I mean, who called? You know, Tommy, whoever it was might have saved your life."

"Elaine," I said. "It was Elaine Stockton. I told you about her."

"Elaine from Martha's Vineyard?"

10
Tuesday, March 16
Barcelona, Spain

I drove to Ferran Olzet's house for dinner. I had gotten directions from Cali on the phone, and everything was pretty easy until I got off paved surfaces onto the dirt-and-cobble back streets of Barcelona. The houses in this district were built of stone blocks and thick wood planks. Thick vines curled down their outer walls. Among these ancient houses the streets wandered according to the twists and turns of family histories, not the dictates of city planners or developers. Eventually I spotted a familiar name on a street sign partially obscured by a tree. I pulled off the narrow drive and parked under a thick canopy of leaves.

The Olzet house stood close to the roadway behind a stone wall. The evening air had cooled off fast, and I felt a chill. I grabbed my cotton sweater from the passenger seat and put it on. I pushed open a doorway in the arched stone gate and entered the courtyard lit by a single lamp near the front door. The scent of a wood fire hung lightly in the air. Through an open window I could hear piano music which stopped when I rapped the door knocker.

Cali greeted me at the door and escorted me to Ferran's study. She was a tall woman with graceful, elongated features. Her wispy reddish-blond hair was cut short as though to emphasize the high cheekbones that shaped her face. Ferran and Cali had met in Paris at the Sorbonne, where he was doing graduate work in Romance languages. At the time Cali was studying piano and dance.

"Old friend," he said. We weren't that old, and it had been more than ten years since we'd roomed together as freshmen in college. Ferran had always been like that, though. It was as if we'd fought together as revolutionaries somewhere. I assumed it had to do with his being from Barcelona.

"Ferran," I said, clasping his hand. He'd gained a little weight, but carried it well. Or concealed it well beneath his expensive clothes. His beard was trimmed but still unruly, his hair short and showing early signs of gray.

Ferran introduced me to Cali and then to his study.

"I'll leave you two to catch up while I get dinner ready." Cali went off to the kitchen. Ferran closed the door. He sat at his desk, and I took an armchair across from him.

"I tell you, Tommy, it is good to see you, but I wish you were here on holiday." He seemed worried.

"Ferran, I couldn't afford it. Look, do you mind if we talk business first? I've got some questions I'd like to get out of the way before dinner."

"Of course not. When you called, Tommy, I thought...this must be a joke."

"No joke, Ferran. Did you know Barneto?"

"He was a senior professor in the art history department. Not friends, but we spoke. I did attend his funeral service last month. I knew he collected art. French paintings and drawings, especially."

"Some French paintings stolen from the Butler Museum turned up among his estate. Not the originals though. Forgeries. Good forgeries."

"He wasn't that discriminating. I am not surprised."

"As I said on the phone, the originals of these paintings were part of a major theft involving a Vermeer and some Rembrandts."

"He wouldn't have been interested in those." Ferran toyed with a carved Meerschaum pipe.

"One theory is the theft was run from Barcelona. There is a syndicate of sorts. Masterworks by request. You place an order, pay a price and it's delivered to you like pizza. But you don't necessarily get what you pay for. These guys employ professional forgers who make copies of the stolen paintings. You get the copy. They keep the original. Of course, even if you suspect, you can't complain. Who do you complain to? The syndicate can sell the same stolen painting over and over again. Everybody thinks he has the original."

"Diabolical." He was very dramatic, like I said, but he was also concerned.

"Ferran, you know Barcelona."

"I've lived here almost all my life."

"Ever hear anything like I just told you? Were you able to find out anything from your friends? Do you know anybody who..."

"Tommy. Slow down. I will answer your questions." He filled the pipe with some shreds of dark tobacco and lit it. He went on.

"I do not know these people. I have heard about them, yes. But I have no direct knowledge of them or their dirty business. I asked around after you called me. I didn't learn much, but I can tell you you are right about this syndicate. It is said the leader of the group is a Dutchman. He is unscrupulous, yes, also vindictive and cruel. The two men found recently murdered? They had been tortured. Horribly mutilated. They died of their torture wounds, from shock."

"Why were they tortured? Does anyone know?"

"Again, there is no way of knowing, except by what you hear. I hear perhaps these men had sold the French paintings to Barneto. Without authorization from this Dutchman. To line their own pockets, perhaps. Or to strike out on their own. And when he found out their betrayal, the Dutchman left their bodies as a warning to others."

"Who is the Dutchman?"

"The police here in Barcelona may know who he is. That is what I believe. But he is much too clever and too powerful for them. Of course, they have no evidence. Probably he can pay to have evidence disappear. Probably he has some arrangement with a senior official."

"Not good," I said.

"Not only not good, but very dangerous to you."

"Maybe I should talk to the police anyway. Tomorrow."

"Or maybe you should not. Tonight, Tommy, let's move away from these things. Let's go see what Cali is doing in the kitchen."

But it was hard to put aside what Ferran had told me. Two of the Dutchman's thieves tortured to death as a warning to others. The police powerless, perhaps even compromised. The Dutchman and his syndicate seemed to have everything going their way. Ferran was right. This would be dangerous. What was I doing here?

I probably should have been scared, but I wasn't. I have very little fear of physical violence. When you grow up getting hit, and you grow up hitting back, you can actually get to where you like it. In fact, the only thing I fear anymore about violence is what I might do to somebody else.

My dad was a Golden Gloves boxer when he was a kid. I guess his dad pushed him into it. So when I was about nine, I started getting lessons from two generations of Shakespear pugilists. We had a fairly complete gym set up at my grandfather's estate, less than a mile from our house in Lexington, Mass. Being in the sporting goods business, my grandfather had easy access to all kinds of equipment, and we had one of everything. By the time I was seventeen I was skilled enough to hold my own with my Dad in the ring. He was bigger and stronger, but I had speed on him, and he'd knocked me down so many times by then I knew all his best moves. Meanwhile, I was picking up a lot from the guys I got to know through the AAU boxing in Boston.

One guy especially. His name was Harold Ory, but he went by Kid, as in Kid Ory the blues man. Kid was a year younger than me, but he knew a lot more about life. His parents were both dead or else had moved away or were in prison or something. I don't exactly know which because there were all kinds of stories, and Kid was evasive on that subject. Anyway, he lived with his aunt and uncle just off Huntington Avenue, and they worked in one of those huge slabs of concrete office building in Government Center, so Kid had a lot of freedom to come and go as he pleased. Probably too much. Anyway, while we were in high school we got to know each other in the ring. And we got to be friends outside the ring besides.

Kid was pretty light-skinned, but he was still black and he wore his hair in an Afro. That made a big difference during the time we were growing up together in Boston. In fact, race was a front-page problem then. Resistance to school desegregation and forced bussing, especially in South Boston, had created a very negative climate. Some of the hostility was racial, and some was anti-government, but the targets of hostility were usually innocent black men and women. Sometimes children, too.

One night after we had been sparring around at a gym in Allston, Kid and I were walking back to my car, a baby-blue VW bug. It was a cool September night. You could almost feel the autumn weather coming in. I was going to give Kid a ride home so he wouldn't have to take the train. About two blocks from where I had parked we passed by a gang of kids about our age, maybe younger, sitting on a stoop, shooting the shit.

"Hey faggot!" One of them said as we passed. Out of the corner of my eye I caught a look at him. Irish kid in a varsity letter jacket.

"Keep walking," I said. Kid looked over at me, like, to say, "Let's wail on these guys."

"Hey, you faggot niggers. I'm talkin to you." We stopped then and turned around. There were two of them, both big. I figured they were on the football team at this local Catholic high school from the jackets they wore. Kid and I were both seniors at other high schools in the area, so we knew their reputation. A few weeks before some guys from their high school had beaten up two friends of Kid's pretty badly after a concert in the Boston Garden. The girl had her face cut. Her boyfriend lost an eye.

We were looking at two on two, a fair fight. Kid was telling me which one he wanted. "You take the first guy on the left." I was leaning toward running myself, but I wasn't about to leave Kid standing there. Besides they were beginning to piss me off.

"Nigger, why don't you go back to Africa? We don't want you here. Or your nigger-loving, faggot friend." He was mine, the guy on the left, a big Irish pimple-faced teenaged thug with the world-class vocabulary. Only five feet away. I thought about how he moved and where I was going to hit him.

"Look, you guys," I said. "We're not looking for a fight. Why not let it alone?"

The one on the right, a lanky guy with thick, dark hair and a dark complexion, began making noises like a psycho-chicken, mocking me. So much for diplomacy, I thought.

No knives I could see. I exchanged a look with Kid, and we rushed them.

Those two guys might have been good at football and yeah, they were tough, but they sure didn't know how to use their fists. Kid did, and I did, too. My fight was over in the first round. I snapped the big Irish guy's head back half a dozen times with short jabs. It was like working on a speed bag. He was game though, didn't want to give it up. He was also a bleeder. It came pouring out of his nose like a stream of rats from a sinking ship. Blood everywhere, on my fists, his face, my face and all over our clothes. I remember thinking, how am I going to get the blood out of my clothes. Then I slammed the door for him with a big right hand he never saw. He crumpled and fell to the sidewalk.

Meanwhile, Kid was taking his guy apart with body shots. I caught the end of it, saw Kid land an uppercut that came from somewhere underground. His lanky, long-haired sparring partner went over backwards and nearly left his feet with the force of it.

The two of them just lay there on the sidewalk, not moving. Not making any noise. Either they were unconscious or they weren't in the mood for more. Kid and I slapped high fives, picked up our gym bags and resumed walking toward my car. We hadn't gone five steps when I heard shots. Kid dropped to the sidewalk. At first I thought he was getting out of the line of fire, but when I looked over I could see the look of pain on his face. And disbelief, too.

"You okay, Kid?" I asked.

"Those suckers shot me, man! It stings. Shit."

I scrambled down to check out Kid's injury, but I couldn't see where the bullet had entered. As I looked up the two football jocks were running away down the street. I left Kid there and went after them. A block away I caught up with the big Irish guy. He had to be a lineman he was so slow. His partner, the one who did the shooting, left him far behind.

I grabbed the guy by his letter jacket and spun him around. He made a windmill of his arms and fists trying to keep me away from him, but I was not about to be denied. This time I was going to use the Marquis of Queensberry, Bruce Lee, Chuck Norris and anybody else who came to mind.

I knocked the air out of him with punches and kicks to the stomach and groin. He was big and tough but there wasn't much he could do against my fury. Soon I had him down on the ground, gasping for breath, squeezing his knees together and holding his hands over his head.

His nose was already bloody, broken probably. I knew the fight was over, but I wasn't done yet. I kept hitting him, trying to smash his head to a pulpy mass with my fists. I wanted to drive his bloody face into the ground. Finally his eyes rolled back in his head, and I got up and began to kick at his ribs. A small crowd had gathered to watch, but I was nearly oblivious. My whole body was caught up in a frenzy of retribution.

I kicked him for insulting Kid and me, for calling Kid a nigger and me a nigger-loving faggot. I kicked him for his friend shooting Kid, for what his schoolmates had done to Kid's friends, for the young black girl with a cut-up face, for her boyfriend who lost an eye. I kicked him for the racism and the injustice and the cruelty and the poverty. And finally, I kicked him for no particular reason at all. And then I was tired, very tired, and I began to walk away.

But I would never be able to walk away from what I had done to that boy, hateful as he was. The boy I fought was in the hospital for months after that. He'd lost one kidney and needed to have his ribcage rebuilt. Reconstructive plastic surgery put his face back together almost like new, but he'd have false teeth and blurred vision for the rest of his life. His buddy disappeared. The cops never found him or the gun. Kid recovered well enough from his gunshot wound in a month or so, and later that year went on to win the Boston Golden Gloves. I quit fighting for good. There was something inside of me I just couldn't trust anymore.

Cali brought me back into the present with her magic in the kitchen. Dinner was a spectacular concoction of seafood served over pasta with fresh bread and salad greens and wine. During dinner we talked of Cali's dance career and of the local arts and culture in Barcelona. We talked of the rich history of Cataluña and of Mediterranean trade. We talked of contemporary Spain, the troubled economy, and where the future would lead. It reminded me of late night bull sessions in college. I felt at home.

A little after midnight I said good night to Ferran and Cali and walked to my car. The air was still. The night was cool and clear. I put on my jacket and slipped behind the wheel. In this part of Barcelona there were no street lights, and the sky was black with countless gleaming stars. I could smell currents of scent in the air that I didn't know by name. As I drove away from their house toward the center of town, I felt a sweet contentment that comes after a wonderful meal and conversation with old friends.

Gradually I became aware that a pair of headlights had been following behind me for a short while. Coincidence, I thought. But I began to reflect on my earlier conversation with Ferran. I wondered if someone could be watching me. Luckily I had brought the canister of SkunkSpray. I felt for it in the pocket of my jacket. When I turned into the hotel and the car behind me continued down the avenue, I breathed a little easier.

The lights were off in my hotel room, and I couldn't remember where the light switch was. I felt along the wall to the left of the door, while I kept the door open for some light from the hallway. When I found it and turned on the lights, there were two guys sitting on my bed. Dressed in blue denim trousers, boots and tank tops, they would have looked at home in New York City.

"Hey, I didn't ask for room service," I said. They looked at each other and exchanged a few words in something that didn't quite sound like Spanish. I guessed it was the Catalan dialect. I took out the SkunkSpray and began to threaten them with it.

"I warn you," I said. "I will use this if I have to. It won't be pleasant."

They looked at each other again. This time they burst out laughing and pointed at me as they exchanged glances. I had no choice. I sprayed the can directly in their faces, full on. I felt an exhilarating rush. I felt powerful.

I felt something hard colliding with the back of my head, and I went down and out, unconscious.

11
Tuesday, March 16
Barcelona, Spain

Apparently there had been a third guy, waiting in the bathroom. When I came to, I was lying on my side in the dark, my face against the cold metal in the trunk of a car. Exhaust fumes leaked in and mingled with the cool night air through a rusted out place in the floor of the trunk. My head throbbed. I could feel each and every bump in the road. I reached up to touch the back of my head. The skin was tender, torn, and my fingers felt sticky as I brought them away. The car bumped on through the night.

After a while the car turned down a rough, dirt road and came to a stop. Doors opened and closed, everyone got out and their voices receded as they walked away from the car. Again I could hear them talking in the Catalan dialect. For a long time, it seemed, everything was quiet. I looked at my watch. I had begun to feel more cramped than tired. And cold. No wonder. I'd been in the trunk for at least an hour. I wondered who these guys were, although I was beginning to have some idea. I considered where they might have brought me. Somewhere outside Barcelona, less than an hour away. Had they driven me around for a while before arriving at a nearby destination? I figured they had probably brought me to their boss. Obviously they were not running things. But who was? The Dutchman?

It added up to this much: someone knew I was coming to Barcelona, knew when I arrived, must have been following me. But only a few people could have known. Unless I'd been followed in Boston. Or my phone tapped. I thought back to the intruder in my hotel room in Boston. Coincidence?

I heard someone walking toward the car down a gravel path. The trunk opened, and someone shoved a gun in my face. Possibly he was the third man in my hotel room. I didn't recognize him, but I would know that smell anywhere. He reeked of onions. I mean, he was a walking cloud of onion breath. Staring down the short barrel of a gun, however, I decided I was in a cooperative mood. I pulled the black hood he gave me over my head and scrambled out of the trunk. I followed the guy down the gravel path, walking with one hand on his shoulder a step behind. He led me up some steps and into a house through a corridor to a room off to the left where he pushed me into a soft, comfortable armchair. In a moment I became aware of another person in the room, as he spoke.

"Mr. Shakespear. I have had you brought here to explain a few things. I want you to listen carefully to what I have to say. Do you understand?"

"Who are you?" I said.

Someone struck me hard across the face and neck with an open hand. The hood took some of the sting out of it, but did nothing to blunt the force of the blow. It was a moment before the stars had settled back into the darkness. The man spoke again.

"I do not intend to answer your questions, so you may as well not ask them. I want only that you listen closely to what I have to say. Do you understand?"

He spoke with an accent that might have been German or Danish or Dutch for all I knew. I was willing to bet it was the Dutchman Ferran had told me about. I heard two others enter the room.

I said, "Okay, I understand you. But what am I doing here? Did I ask to be struck on the head and brought here in the trunk of a car? I am sure that Spanish law prohibits kidnapping as well as —"

Someone threw a punch that emptied me of breath. I gasped for air. Then several more fists struck my midsection and chest. They emptied me out completely, even of the thought of breath. It was several minutes before I could breathe normally again. My ribs ached. I smelled skunk. It must've been one of the guys I sprayed.

"Mr. Shakespear," the man said. "I want to make my intentions perfectly clear to you. I am going to try once more, and if you fail to cooperate I will have you killed. You see, I can do that quite easily. And no one would be the wiser. Now, do you understand?"

"Yes, I believe I do," I said. He had my attention.

"I hope so," he said. "You have been intruding into matters you have no business in. Your friend Olzet has been asking questions for you. Very dangerous to you both. This is my business. My business, not yours. I will not have you intruding into these affairs."

"Okay. I get it," I said. "Your business, not mine, Dutchman."

"Who I am is also my business. Do you understand that, Mr. Shakespear?"

I said nothing. I was in deep petunias. I was busy thinking about how I had gotten myself into a mess so deep I might never get out when someone struck me in the face, just below my left eye. This time with a fist. My upper lip was cut and the inside of my mouth, too. I didn't like the taste of my own blood.

"Hey!" I protested. "I didn't say anything."

"I was waiting for an answer," the Dutchman said.

"Look, Dutchman. This isn't getting us anywhere. There's no doubt you can kill me. No doubt you and your thugs can continue beating me all night long, if that's what you want to do. But I think you have something else in mind. I think you want to tell me something. I think there's something you want me to do. What is it?"

"I want you to leave Barcelona immediately. Return to your home in California. You are in way over your head, Mr. Shakespear. I speak as one concerned from a business point of view. Purely business, nothing personal at all. But those who do not heed my wishes..."

"Like those two guys you left murdered by La Sagrada Familia."

"La Sagrada Familia," he said. He was silent for a while.

I was expecting someone, the Dutchman or one of his thugs, to slug me again but nothing happened. Maybe it was because I was feeling hapless, but I thought about Groucho Marx and Matilda, the duck that used to drop out of the sky on You Bet Your Life when you said the magic word. Shiva collected old Groucho tapes.

Before replying to me again, the Dutchman dismissed his men.

"Leave us," he said.

When they had left the room, he spoke again.

"La Sagrada Familia. An unfinished cathedral facade. It is a beautiful monstrosity, the ecstatic vision of a disturbed mind. You know, the architect, Gaudi, is revered in Barcelona. He is said to be the expression of Catalan genius, in the same way Picasso and Miro were. But his work is a tortured beauty, Mr. Shakespear."

"What about those two dead men?"

"They were disloyal. They had stolen from me. Nothing personal, I assure you. It was purely business to them. And it was purely business to me."

I took a shot at prying loose some information.

"And the Vermeer and the Rembrandt paintings?"

"True Dutch masterworks, expressions of sublime beauty. The Vermeer, especially. Take 'The Concert,' for instance. Not merely color and form, but life, intimate life. People who share music together. Looking into that canvas, into that room, at those people, you can almost hear the music."

Whoa! This was getting weird. It seemed the Dutchman was some sort of demented art connoisseur. Interesting, but he still wasn't telling me what I wanted to know.

"Was stealing that piece pure business, too?" I said.

"You disappoint me, Mr. Shakespear. I took you for an educated man. Stupid, yes, but educated. Now I see you are merely stupid." I had little to lose, though, the way I figured it. He had probably already decided to have me killed.

"Your knowledge of art is impressive, Dutchman. I just wondered how the Vermeer and the Rembrandt fit in, from a business point of view."

"Men who rise to wealth and power, Mr. Shakespear, often collect art. As they are not ordinary men, they do not have ordinary art collections. Some of these extraordinary men are very private people, and they have very private collections. Do you understand? As you say, I am an art connoisseur. Sometimes I advise these men on acquisitions."

"Meaning, you make acquisitions?"

"I am not a thief. I am a businessman who advises other businessmen."

"And has people killed." I said.

"Mr. Shakespear, I am tiring of this discussion." We both were. "And I am tiring of you." I was beginning to wish I had kept my mouth shut, but that's always been a problem for me. I hadn't learned very much from the Dutchman, and he wasn't about to tell me what I wanted to know.

He called in his men and spoke in the Catalan dialect again. I listened for words that sounded like "hotel" and "take him back unharmed." Instead I heard something that sounded like "dispose of him" and "forest." I got the feeling I was not going back to my hotel room. My friend, Señor Onion Breath, was assigned to escort me outside. I knew that because he kicked my feet, grumbled something, and when I stood up he spun me toward the door. The onion cloud enveloped me. I felt both his hands shoving me through the house to the front door and realized he must have holstered his handgun.

I nearly fell on the stairs going out. When I regained my balance I realized that I didn't have much time to plan what I would do. I was pretty sure the Dutchman had ordered me taken somewhere to be killed. My heart was beating fast now, but for some reason my head felt clear and in control. Everything seemed to be moving in slow motion.

Señor Onion Breath walked me down the gravel path toward the car alone. I could hear no one else coming, only the sound of our feet crunching on gravel. This would be my only chance to avoid burial in Barcelona. If he put me in the trunk again it would be over.

We stopped at the car, and he paused, reaching into his pocket to get the key to the trunk. The moment. I knew I would have only this one shot at escape. And it was now. While I couldn't see out through the hood, I could see down, and by the position of his feet and source of the onion breath, I guessed where his head would be. I lunged out with my hands and grabbed his head behind the ears. I slammed my forehead into his face while pulling his head toward me with all the force I could summon. I imagined heading a soccer ball into the net. His nose crushed against my forehead at the hairline. I saw a few stars, but he went limp and fell unconscious. I tore off the hood and looked at him. Though it was still dark outside, I could see his face was bloody. Blood covered his mouth and chin and continued to flow from his broken nose. I reached for the gun in his belt and looked around. No one had heard. No one was coming. I remembered the car keys and found them nearby on the gravel path. I opened the trunk, lifted his body into it and closed the trunk. I felt like I was on automatic pilot. I felt like I was following some script. I got into the car, started it, turned on the headlights and drove away down the dirt road.

12
Wednesday, March 17
Barcelona, Spain

I managed to find the highway after a few wrong turns and made my way back into Barcelona. I almost took the road toward Badalona by mistake when Señor Onion Breath began pounding against the walls of the trunk. My heart was pounding, too, and I was distracted by fear. Even though I had escaped and was now in control, I was struggling against the fear of getting caught again. I had the bad guy in the trunk, and I also had his gun. I thought about using it to silence him. Maybe that would silence my fear, I thought. The traffic light turned red. I joined the line of cars wondering whether they would hear him.

Somehow I had to get rid of the car someplace where Señor Onion Breath wouldn't be discovered for several hours. The light changed, and I drove on toward my hotel. As I drew closer to the hotel I noticed some heavy equipment a few blocks away at an apartment complex under construction. Perfect. Heavy machines, construction trailers, cars and trucks crowded the parking lot nearby. I left the Dutchman's car between a back hoe and a flatbed truck at the far end of the lot and walked back to the hotel in the softening darkness of early morning.

When I reached my hotel I was mentally composing a phone call to Shiva.

"Hi," I'd say. "How've you been?"

"Great!" she'd say. "You? How's life on the trail of the outlaws?"

"Well, now that you mention it," I'd say. "Things got pretty rough last night."

"Are you okay?" she'd say. "Tommy?"

"Well, now that you mention it," I'd say. "I almost bought the farm last night."

"You mean?" she'd say. "What do you mean, Tommy?"

And so on.

In the elevator I became conscious of the gun I was carrying and began to think about doing something with it. I had lost faith in the SkunkSpray, but I still had the Mace. Now what would I do with a gun? I couldn't get it past airport security. So it would have to remain here in Barcelona. But should I ditch it now or later? Later. Though I was still opposed to violence in principle, at least, I had to be practical. People out there were trying to kill me.

I went into my room sure of only one thing. I needed a shower. I smelled of skunk and day-old sweat, and that sour smell had begun to get on my nerves. Whether to stay any longer in Barcelona was still up in the air. In fact, it was circling overhead like a hungry vulture.

Ferran had said the Dutchman was connected inside, but I knew I should go to the police and file a report on last night anyway. Of course Señor Onion Breath would attract somebody's attention in a few hours, get out and come looking for me with reinforcements. So I had very little time unless I decided to stay and fight back. I did have a gun. I also had enough good sense to realize I didn't have much of a chance playing their game. I wasn't good at it, and I might get killed. I was going around in circles trying to figure out what to do when I opened my hotel room door. The curtains were drawn. It was dark. I turned on the light and saw another guy sitting on my bed. He was wearing gray wool trousers and a navy blue windbreaker over a white shirt.

"What is this?" I said, "A homeless shelter?" He was too well dressed to be homeless, but then I knew that. "Don't tell me you're from room service, too."

I pulled the gun out of my belt and leveled it at the guy. As I did so, I realized that my room smelled faintly of skunk. I decided to ignore it.

"Mr. Shakespear, I would be so grateful," he said, sounding a little like James Mason, "if you would please put that thing away." He held his hands out and away from his body. He wore a black diver's watch on his left wrist, but no rings.

"Pardon me," I said. "I don't normally carry a gun. But then people don't normally break into my hotel rooms. So until I know who you are and why you're here, I'll keep it pointed right at you. And keep the hands up."

"I'm with Interpol. Agent Bassett. Sam Bassett. Sorry to break in, but I needed to see you right away. And in private."

I approached the bed.

"Mr. Bassett, I am going to need ID, but first I'd like you to unbuckle your pants and slide them down to your knees."

"I beg your pardon?"

"Take your pants down." I said.

"Kinky, aren't we. I must warn you, Shakespear, my legs aren't as good as you might expect."

"Just do it, please. I've had a rough night, and the morning isn't going so well either."

Bassett stood up and dropped his trousers. I had him do it because I was afraid if he wasn't who he said he was, he might outwit or overpower me and get away or worse. With his pants down, I figured, he wasn't likely to try anything.

"Now walk to the wall," I said. It was about three feet away.

Bassett shuffled along toward the wall, his belt buckle wobbling in the air. He was a tall man, well over six feet, and rather thin. He looked more like a college professor than a police agent. But right now, with his pants down around his knees, he looked very silly indeed. When he reached the wall, I had him place his palms flat against it and spread his legs wide. I had seen that part in a movie. Then I reached inside his coat and felt for a gun. I found it in a shoulder holster and took it away, tossing it on the bed. I continued searching for his wallet, but could not find one.

"No wallet?" I said. "Where's the ID?"

"It's in my trousers," he said. Bassett turned to look at me and shrugged.

"OK, kick them off."

He kicked off his trousers and I went through them, finding a book of matches, English coins, some pesetas and, in the back pocket, his wallet and ID. He was who he said he was. Agent Sam Bassett, Interpol. Of course, it could be a forgery.

"I guess that's you," I said, "but not a great likeness." I handed him the wallet.

"I had it taken with my trousers on."

"Sorry," I said, "I had to be sure."

I put the gun on the dresser top.

106

"I'm Tommy Shakespear," I said, offering to shake hands.

"Call me Sam." We shook.

He dressed himself quickly and retrieved the handgun from my bed, holstering it inside his jacket.

"What did you need to see me about?" I asked.

"I am on assignment as interagency liaison to the U.S. Department of Justice, representing Interpol in a large-scale international operation called..."

"Operation Bogart," I said. I read about it in the case folder.

"I see. Yes. Well, what do you know about it?"

"'Bogart' equals bogus art. The goal is to crack down on counterfeit art works. From what I've read, it's international, involving a dozen or more police agencies like the FBI, the Surete, Scotland Yard, Interpol. I can't name them all. "

"Very good."

"Let me see. The Butler Museum theft, the two bodies at La Sagrada Familia, the Dutchman..."

"Right. Well, we got word you'd be coming this way and to keep an eye out. The Dutchman, as you call him, and his merry men also seem to have been watching for you, too."

"Wait a sec, here," I said. "You knew I was coming and the Dutchman knew I was coming. Why so much interest in me?

"Good question. I haven't any idea. I just follow orders."

"Let's start with how you knew," I said.

"We have people in Boston. They alerted us."

"And the Dutchman?"

"Another good question," he said. "I was surprised he picked you up so quickly. Unfortunately, that means there must still be one or more of them in Boston. Who knew you were coming to Barcelona?"

"Jack Butler. Dr. Louvenbragh, the museum director, and Fred Peavy, head of museum security. Elaine Winslow and her husband, friends of Jack Butler's. One or two other people at their dinner party Monday night. Shiva, a friend of mine from Santa Cruz. Fewer than ten people in all."

"What about your friend Olzet and his wife?"

"Ferran and Cali."

"One of them seems to have let your friend the Dutchman in on your plans. Possibly Ferran Olzet asked one too many questions in your behalf. Oh, and by the way, Shakespear, your room in Boston wasn't bugged. We swept it when you arrived, and we've had our people watching it twenty-four hours a day."

"So you must have seen my burglar," I said. "Unless he was one of yours."

"That wasn't ours, unfortunately. And the burglar was a she."

"Nearly scared me to death."

"Sorry about that. Not our fault though."

"How did she get in?" I had been wondering.

"She had a card key. Possibly she convinced the desk clerk that she was with you."

"Was that you last night, Sam, following me back from Ferran Olzet's?"

"Yes. As I said, we didn't expect the Dutchman to grab you then. Or I'd have been a little closer by."

"I nearly didn't make it back from the farm house," I said.

"We had people watching the house, Tommy. We followed you there. You weren't in serious danger unless..."

"Unless the Dutchman surprised you again. I thought I was headed for the mulch pile."

"You handled yourself better than we—better than I—had expected, given your relative lack of experience. By the way, we took your man out of the trunk and into custody. He's a local thug, like most of the Dutchman's people, a short-term hire."

"Terrible onion breath," I said. I stifled a yawn.

"It's the annual onion festival. They eat them by the pound. Speaking of scent," he said, "your room smells a bit like a civet cat's ass."

"SkunkSpray repellent. I tried to use it on my muggers, but one got me from behind."

"Certainly leaves an impression."

It was time to put some cards on the table. We had done all the preliminaries, and if we didn't get to something concrete soon, I was going to have to get some sleep.

"How can I help you, Sam?" I said. "It seems to me there are ways you can help me find the missing paintings. Maybe we can work out a trade of some sort."

Bassett walked to the window and stood a moment looking out at the traffic. I could see him in silhouette against the orange-pink glow of the morning sky.

"Probably," he said, "you should get on the first plane back to Boston. This Dutchman is no fool. By now he knows something has gone wrong. Either you have escaped or his man has gone off to get drunk. He'll send someone looking. They will be here to search your room. They may already have checked the airport."

"Who is this guy, this Dutchman?"

"Dieter Kockhorn. Half German, half Dutch. He has two passports legally and half a dozen under other names. At one time he was a gallery owner in Amsterdam. Years ago he became involved in dealing stolen art and forgeries, and eventually he learned to combine the two. He never steals anything unless it's already sold. For example, we think the Butler theft was at least partly designed to fill a request from a wealthy Silicon Valley collector of Dutch art. And, of course, this fellow never delivers the original, always a forgery. Those collectors who do discover it have nowhere to go to complain. We estimate his personal collection is worth nearly a billion dollars."

"Where is it all stashed?"

"Hopefully in a climate-controlled vault somewhere. We have no idea where it is located."

"Wouldn't it be fairly easy to follow him to it?"

"You'd think so. The problem is that Kockhorn, your Dutchman, is very good at evading surveillance. Sometimes he disappears for several weeks. Then he reappears a little too obviously somewhere else—Paris, New York, London—which, we assume, must be far from his vault's location. Although, who knows? He may have art stored in all the capital cities. We've tried getting people inside his organization, but he trusts no one. No close associates. No lovers. No friends. Lots of little people who don't make headlines when they end up dead."

"What about the buyers? Wouldn't a collector who discovered a fake be willing to work with you?"

"To this point, no. Possibly they are afraid of being identified to authorities. Or perhaps they fear the Dutchman will get back at them somehow. We tried a sting operation, but our buyer didn't pass the Dutchman's credibility tests. He deals almost exclusively with collectors known to him, so our present hope is to catch one of his regular collectors and convince him to testify in exchange for immunity on the art-theft conspiracy charges."

"Listen, Sam. I'm willing to help out in any way I can. But I'd like to get some sleep first."

Sunlight was streaming through my hotel window, and I had not yet been to bed. My body had no idea what time it was, but it knew tired.

"Not a good idea to sleep here. The Dutchman will try again, and this time he will take steps to ensure he takes care of you."

"Where then?"

"I'll help you get safely on a plane back to Boston. You can sleep on the plane."

"I'm not running away from this," I said.

"That's right. You're not running, but you're of more use to us in Boston than here in Barcelona where we'd have to watch out for you. The Dutchman has associates in Boston. We'd like to know who they are. In exchange, we'll help you find the missing Butler paintings."

"How will we stay in touch?"

"Here's a card with a number where you can contact me."

I put the card in my pocket and knew my stay in Barcelona had come to an end. I hated to admit there was little I could do. If the Dutchman was too well-organized for Operation Bogart, he was probably beyond me. At least using a direct approach. If I was going to get him or his Boston accomplices or the stolen paintings, I would have to retreat, regroup and try something different. Trouble was, I didn't know what that would be.

I threw my things together quickly, leaving behind the SkunkSpray, but taking the Mace. It didn't take long to pack. I gave the handgun I took from Señor Onion Breath to Sam Bassett, who could dispose of it properly. I didn't feel comfortable with it, and I didn't want to be tempted to use it.

Sam followed me in his car out to the airport and stayed with me until I boarded my plane. We sat in the restaurant, had breakfast and drank coffee until the time came. The coffee was good, and Sam proved to be an entertaining storyteller. If half what he told me was true, we owe the peaceful resolution of the Cold War not to the CIA or MI6, but to Interpol.

Interpol? Sam would have made a great salesman.

At about three-quarters of an hour before departure I said good-bye to Sam Bassett. I promised to stay in touch and to let him in on any major developments in Boston bearing on the Dutchman or on the Butler theft. We shook hands, and I walked toward the passport control with my suitcase. But I wasn't quite ready to leave yet. I lost myself in a crowd of German tourists and slipped behind a pillar. After a short wait I made my way back to the car rental, picked up another car and drove into town.

This time I checked in to a different hotel in a different part of Barcelona. I even used a pseudonym just in case the Dutchman, Onion Breath or one of the Skunk brothers came around to look for me. A bed. I desperately needed some time in a bed. Tired as I was, I felt as though I had entered the twilight zone. It would not be long before paranoia began to set in. I decided to get some sleep and return to the farmhouse, if I could find it, for a look around. If the Dutchman was still there, I might be able to observe him and his men. If not, I could see what he left behind.

Around two in the afternoon, I woke up to the phone ringing on my bedside table. I considered ignoring it. Who would know I was there? Perhaps, I thought, it was the management inviting me for a drink at the bar. Or asking how my room was.

No, it was Sam Bassett calling from a lobby phone.

"Hello, mate."

"Sam," I said. "You're late. I expected you hours ago." I was still groggy from sleep and thought I was being witty. I couldn't imagine how he'd managed to find me so quickly.

"Thought I'd let you catch up on your sleep. Look, as long as you're here, we might as well work together. Get dressed and meet me in the lobby. We'll go for a ride out to the Dutchman's farmhouse."

13
Wednesday, March 17
Barcelona, Spain

I was running out of clean clothes since I hadn't done laundry in nearly a week. Unless I bought new clothes in Barcelona I'd have to find a laundromat soon. So I began the process of sorting and recycling according to scent. There was no time to have the hotel laundry get them clean.

Purple bruises had sprouted on my neck and face and a painful lump on the back of my head. I was also hungry. It had been quite a while since breakfast, and it would be a while longer until dinner. My hotel room had a minibar and I stuffed my pockets with Spanish peanuts and American candy bars before going out the door.

Sam Bassett was in a surprisingly good mood. I had expected he would take my return as some sort of betrayal, but if he was angry with me he gave no sign of it.

"Another lovely day in Barcelona," he said, as we walked together toward his car. And it was. Blue sky overhead seasoned lightly with high wispy clouds. No rain had fallen since I'd arrived. It had been cool and unusually dry for a March in Barcelona, and that was fine with me. In fact, the weather reminded me of Santa Cruz.

"What do you expect to find at the farmhouse?" I asked.

"Nothing, but who knows?"

"Then why are we bothering?" I was a little grouchy and sleep-deprived.

"Tommy, Tommy, Tommy. How do you expect to find the Dutchman if we don't look for clues?" Clearly, Sam was disappointed with what he felt was a lack of initiative. Or maybe resolve.

We drove out to the farmhouse in about twenty minutes. It was north of the city in a slice of countryside wedged between suburbs on the west and an industrial area to the east. We drove past a factory that made, according to Sam, little chocolate fizzies you put on ice cream.

Before long we found the dirt road leading to the Dutchman's farm house The farm had seen better days. There was no sign of anyone's having lived there for a long time. A large barn to our right had partially collapsed, the fields beyond the house were overgrown with weeds and sprouted rusting parts of cars and farm equipment. We stopped near the gravel path where I had struggled with the Dutchman's thug, Señor Onion Breath. The gravel still showed signs of that struggle. The car they brought me in had leaked oil apparently. I observed a pattern of oil spots where it had been parked.

The Dutchman and his crew had cleared out. That much was obvious.

"No one at home. What a shame," said Sam. Was he kidding? He seemed a little disappointed, but I was relieved.

Sam wasted no time getting to the front door of the farmhouse. It was open. He went in. I continued to examine the grounds. It looked as though the owners had been gone for a year or two, but the farm had been in decline longer than that. I turned over a hub cap. I opened a cellar door. I walked to the edge of the field. I found nothing and turned back toward the house.

"Why don't you tell me about the other night?" said Sam. We were standing in the room where the Dutchman had interrogated me. Like the rest of the house, it had been sparsely and shabbily furnished.

"Didn't we go over that already?"

"Just refresh my memory."

"Well, I was blindfolded. Hooded actually. I couldn't see anything except shoes. And the floor. I saw a lot of the floor."

"Go on."

"They brought me into the room and pushed me into this chair." I sat down in the armchair heavily as though to recreate the events of that night. "And then the Dutchman began talking to me. He was insisting that business was business, and I should not get into his."

My left hand slipped between the seat cushion and the frame of the chair, and I felt something. But I went on talking.

"He didn't like some of my answers and had his guys punch me around a little. But I've had worse plenty of times."

In my hand I had something that felt like crumpled up cardboard. It was a matchbook. I could feel the abrasive strip.

"Why did you smart-talk him? I am curious. He is a dangerous man."

"I couldn't really help it. He sounded so pompous, so self-important and the wise remarks just popped out. I was nervous and afraid, yes, but more afraid of seeming afraid, if you know what I mean. And, to tell the truth, I wanted to see what would happen."

As I spoke, I wondered if Sam would ask me what my hand was doing under the seat cushion.

"You are lucky nothing did happen," he said. "Of course we were outside."

"He was standing over there, just behind you."

I pointed with my right hand, and Sam turned his head just long enough for me to slip the matchbook cover into my pocket. I realized I was holding out on him. I didn't know why. I don't know why I do a lot of things.

"Probably leaning against the desk," he said. "When did he send the men out of the room?"

"When I mentioned the bodies at the Sagrada Familia. He began talking about Gaudi and the art of Barcelona. It's odd, though, you know?"

"What's odd?"

"He makes a big deal about how it's strictly business, but you only have to mention some art object and he goes off on a tangent. Like, it's more than just business to him. Some kind of obsession maybe."

"Interesting." Sam leaned against the desk.

"You go through it yet?" I asked.

"The desk? Not yet. How about you checking the upstairs, and I'll do the kitchen and the rooms at the back of the house."

"Okay," I said. I was eager to see what I'd found in the chair.

I went upstairs and into the bathroom off the front bedroom. I looked at the matchbook. Black with a cowboy boot logo in neon blue. It was from the Boot Hill Steakhouse outside Boston. I knew the place. But what was it doing in the seat cushion of an armchair here in the outskirts of Barcelona? I laughed in utter amazement at the absurdity. Boot Hill.

There it is on Route 1 just north of the city, a shrine to the American carnivore, featuring giant cactuses, cowboy boots and other icons of the Old West. This one restaurant, Boot Hill, is said to account for the weekly disappearance of entire herds of cattle and, over the past few years, a sizable chunk of the rain forest. You'd expect to see a serious feeding trough like Boot Hill in Dallas, Chicago or maybe Kansas City, but not Boston. On a busy night, a thousand diners kneel down at the trough, consuming bloody slabs of beefsteak and prime rib. And, apparently, one or two of them work for the Dutchman. Someone from Boston had recently visited the Dutchman's farmhouse or else one of his men had returned from a trip there.

I was standing in the upstairs bathroom thinking this over when Sam tapped me on the shoulder. I was so startled that I let out a whoop and dropped the matchbook.

"Heard you laughing," he said. "What's so funny?"

Caught with the goods. No way out. I bent down and picked up the matchbook and handed it to Sam.

"This matchbook I found. It's from a restaurant in Boston."

"Boot Hill." He turned the matchbook over and examined it.

"A Boston area steakhouse. Looks like someone from Boston has been here." I said.

"Fresh goods, too. Probably left here very recently." He turned it over and examined it. "Nothing written inside. Where did you find it?"

"Under the bed in the bedroom." I lied, not exactly sure why.

"Not to flog a dead horse..." he said.

"Dead cow, you mean." I corrected him, jokingly. I had cows and parts of cows on the brain.

"Horse, cow, pig, whatever you please. You know, Tommy, it really does make sense for you to follow up that matchbook in Boston and leave this end of things to me."

I had a feeling Sam was hiding something. He had a look on his face I couldn't quite interpret.

"What did you find, Sam?" I asked.

"Don't change the subject."

"You found something downstairs. What was it?"

"I smelled something foul coming from the bathroom at the back of the house. I went in there, Tommy, and I found two hands, two feet and a head, sealed up in clear plastic sacks, in the bathtub. Just beginning to decompose."

Where was the rest of it, I wondered? I felt sick. I wanted to ask Sam if he knew who it was, but I couldn't make my mouth work.

"I'll say it again, Tommy. I think you ought to go back to Boston and work on those leads." This time I needed no convincing. I'd made up my mind to return.

"Agreed," I said.

"You agree?"

"Yes. I'll take a plane tomorrow."

"That's what I thought you were doing today." He reminded me.

"I wasn't ready to leave yet." The body parts in the bathroom had convinced me. We both knew I had narrowly escaped similar treatment.

"Now I've got a few leads I can take back with me. The matchbook especially. Sam, how about you get someone to check airline passenger lists for the past week or so?"

"Possible, yes, but very tedious. Could take days to pull it all together, even a week or more."

"What? You don't have computers? I thought Interpol was computers, mostly."

"Yes, of course. No, but you're right. I suppose we should put someone on it. I'll make a request right away. Frankly, I don't know what it will take."

I took out the bag of Spanish peanuts from my hotel minibar.

"Want some? I'm starving."

"No thanks," he said. "Those little red skins get stuck in my teeth. How about we go find a paella somewhere?" Sam took a handkerchief from his coat pocket.

"I'll just take care of our fingerprints before we go."

Part Two - The Fine Art of Murder

There is no lostness like that which comes to a man
when a perfect and certain pattern has dissolved about him.

John Steinbeck

MICHAEL G. WEST

14
Thursday, March 18
Barcelona, Spain

The next morning I was on my way to Boston, all but empty-handed. It would not be a triumphant return. There were only a few leads to follow. At least I had the Dutchman. Well, I didn't have him, but I had his name. Dieter Kockhorn. And I knew something about how he operated. I also had the matchbook. The Boot Hill matchbook was a link, but to what? Unless Sam Bassett could pull a familiar name or two from the airlines' computers, I would have nothing new to go on. For now, the Dutchman had given us both the slip, and I doubted the police would get anything much out of Señor Onion Breath. I began to dread the appointment I'd made with Amy Louvenbragh for Friday morning. What would I tell her?

The flight to Madrid was brief, fortunately. Unfortunately, European airlines feature an abundance of cigarette smoke, and this one on Avionica had been no exception. I was seated in a non-smoking row in business class between three smoking rows in front of me and three behind. For some reason it was the only non-smoking row in the entire plane, and, of course, I was the only one in it. The flight attendant informed me it had been set aside just for me.

I had a short wait in Madrid airport. Madrid airport was like a shopping mall, but with fewer stores and a few more people hurrying by. In an international airport like Madrid's you can hear the languages of every nation, and occasionally you can spot people dressed not in international chic, but wearing their native clothing, serapes or turbans or djellabas. I was tempted, as I surveyed the throng of strangers coming and going, to take a flight at random to Khartoum or Delhi, Helsinki or Copenhagen, to enter another unplanned avenue of my life.

On the flight to Washington I sat next to a young woman with eucalyptus pods on a string around her neck. I didn't notice them at first. The book in her lap got my attention initially. It was a fat and serious-looking book about society and people. When I made the mistake of asking her about it, she went off on a long tangent about the world of commerce and wealth and the world of politics and power.

As she talked on, I began thinking about my meeting in the morning with Amy Louvenbragh. I was dreading that meeting. My trip to Barcelona had been less than successful, and she would not be a sympathetic listener. Silently I began to rehearse how I would present my findings. I decided I'd be better off citing only known facts and suppositions, like the Dutchman, his Boston accomplices, the Boot Hill matchbook found in a Spanish farmhouse, art theft on request, forgery, murder. And stall for time. That would be my best ploy.

It was then I came out of my trance and noticed the eucalyptus pods on a string around my seatmate's neck. She was still talking about that book and how it had changed her life forever. I interrupted. Where had she found that necklace? She had found it in a little shop in London off Portobello

Road. Imported from Australia, crafted by aborigines. And on she went about aboriginal art and the dreamtime consciousness discussed so brilliantly by Bruce Chatwin in his book....Omigod, another long tangent underway!

Soon the food parade began, seven courses in all, if you count the three desserts, and the movie started up after that. It was a thriller about crooked lawyers which I had so far avoided, but it was better than another in-depth discussion with my seatmate. Again my mind drifted off.

Sam Bassett had been very quiet during the drive to Barcelona, and that had been okay with me. We hadn't quite established a bond of trust between us. I wasn't about to trust him. For one thing, his agenda wasn't clear to me. I knew he'd wanted me out of town, but I was unable to guess where he would go then, what he would do next. Stay in Barcelona? Pursue the Dutchman elsewhere?

We'd meandered through the Mediterranean streets of Barcelona in the little Fiat, dodging pedestrians strolling in groups. At one point Sam pulled the car to the curb for a moment and indicated a building just ahead. I stared at it stunned, unbelieving. Another Gaudi, like La Sagrada Familia, only domestic, if you could describe anything by Gaudi as domestic. Its fantastic surreal facade sprouted balconies like blue Zorro masks in front of every window with ornate technicolor blue, red, and yellow discs several feet in diameter dotting the exterior walls. Overall, it gave me the feeling of melted icing, stalagmites and mushroom-eating troggs. It was a private house, apparently. I compared it to the Butler Museum, its ordinary exterior concealing the ornate Venetian palace within. I could imagine the Dutchman living in a Gaudi palace, plotting his latest heist while drinking absinthe.

Before I left Barcelona, I called Ferran to say good-bye. Sam had warned me there could be a tap on the line. I took no chances. I told him only that nothing had turned up, and that I was going back to Boston to file my final report. He was glad to hear I was leaving.

We landed in Washington around three-thirty in the afternoon. The people-mover took its time getting out to the plane. At Dulles you don't dock at the terminal. You park at a gate out on the tarmac, and a huge bus about the size of an office building comes out to get you. That's the people-mover. If you have to change flights, as I did, you take one people-mover into the terminal and another one out to the next plane. I'd read somewhere that the Dulles terminal is a thing of beauty, composed of graceful, sweeping curves and a vast, ribbed space. As you approach it, you're supposed to think of flight. But to me it looks like a gigantic potato peeler. Eero Saarinen designed it. I wondered if he thought of the people-movers, too, or if he had a committee of bureaucrats to help him.

The weight of travel sank into my shoulders and arms as I walked through the Logan airport terminal in Boston. It was just after five o'clock in the afternoon, but it felt like five a.m. I could feel a twinge in my low back. I needed to take it easy for a while. Hadn't slept much in Barcelona, and with the jet lag and day of air travel compounding things, low-back pain had full command of my attention. I paid a dollar for a luggage cart and collected my bags.

In winter and early spring the city of Boston is gray, cold, and colorless. The lack of color is so imposing that you are grateful for the hard black of a wrought-iron railing or the dull brass of a Beacon Street door knocker. In another few days or weeks, crocuses would be up in the nearby Boston Common. Little specks of color breaking up the gray and gloom. That was the hope you clung to during a winter that stretched late into early spring.

I took a cab into Boston. I was lucky to get one. It was raining, a cold, thin, silent rain that cuts into your skin like the sharp point of a wire. I saw a few homeless people huddled in doorways, as the mid-week rush hour clogged the sidewalks and city streets. In another few hours they would have the rain all to themselves.

15
Friday, March 19
Boston, Massachusetts

I could have slept until the crocuses came up.

That is, if I hadn't had my body clock set to Barcelona time. At two a.m. I sat up, wide awake and exhausted. Part of me wanted sleep, but another part wanted to get up and chase the Dutchman around Barcelona. I aimed the black remote control at my television set and fired once. I fired again and again as faces and animated strips of color whirled past in a carousel of reruns, late night news, infomercials, and old movies. It came to rest on a familiar face, Steve McQueen in the Thomas Crown Affair. I lay back watching the scene I came in on, the eating scene with Fay Dunaway. I thought about Shiva for a moment, but Elaine Winslow kept coming to mind. What would life be like with Elaine? I guessed I already knew the answer to that one, based on our time together on the Vineyard. Until we grew bored with each other, the lovemaking would be great, but Elaine was really more than I could handle on a day-to-day basis. Maybe she was even a little crazier than me. For a moment I thought of calling her, but I closed my eyes to rest them, and before I knew it I'd dropped off to sleep with the TV still on and the channel changer in my hand.

At exactly six o'clock the phone rang. It was a woman's voice, my wake up call. The next thing I knew it was a little before eight o'clock. I threw off the covers. I had an appointment with Amy Louvenbragh in her office at eight, and I knew I wasn't going to make it on time.

Hair still wet from a two-minute shower, I finished dressing in the cab on my way to the museum on Huntington Avenue near the Fenway. Once I finished dressing I noticed that the cab reeked of stale cigar smoke and gas fumes. That plus the jet lag had me feeling slightly nauseous. I was in a hurry to get there, but the going was slow through morning traffic, even with the short cuts and back-alley routes the cab driver took. It was also very cold outside and clouding up, like it might try to snow once more before winter let go. I shivered in the back of the old Checker cab and asked the driver to turn up the heat. She responded by punching the accelerator.

I arrived at the employee entrance, where I'd been instructed to go, at about 8:30 or 8:35. I was in such a hurry I'd left my watch at the hotel, but I knew it couldn't have taken more than twenty-five minutes to get there. I explained to the security guard who I was. I wasn't on his list, so I asked him to call the museum director to verify my appointment. Her phone was busy, he said. A few minutes later he tried again. When the phone had been busy for ten minutes or more, I suggested he try Fred Peavy, the head of museum security.

My appointment had been for eight, and it was getting close to nine. Fred answered his phone, apparently, and gave the guard his okay, because the guard handed me a clip-on ID. I passed through the security door into the administrative wing of the museum.

It was early on a Friday morning and there were very few people at work yet. The museum itself would not be open until ten. I passed Fred Peavy in the corridor, and we greeted each other. He stopped briefly, but the look on his face said very busy, no time to talk. I thanked him for getting me past the guard. He waved it off and continued on toward the security station. I arrived at the director's office and opened the outer door. Her waiting room was unattended. Apparently her assistant was not in yet or maybe getting coffee elsewhere in the museum. It seemed odd though. I began to feel a bit apprehensive, but didn't know why exactly. The inner door to Amy Louvenbragh's office was open, and as I peeked around the corner that feeling of apprehension invaded my heartbeat and turned my stomach sour.

And then I saw it. What I saw took a full minute to understand, but my feelings had it pegged from the start.

The room was a shambles. Papers scattered, lamp on the floor, chair overturned. Blood splatters on the papers and on the green ink blotter on the desk. I had a really sick feeling come over me when I saw the blood. My stomach retched, turned inside out and dumped its sour contents into my mouth.

Amy Louvenbragh, the woman I had come to see, was lying on the floor, tied to the overturned swivel chair with telephone cord, a silk scarf stuffed in her mouth. Her throat had been sliced from ear to ear, laying bare layers of flesh, tendons, her severed esophagus. I held my breath, hoping it would keep my stomach from heaving again, but the spasms continued anyway.

Oh Jesus, Jesus, Jesus. I felt like a little lost boy. Please don't die, please don't…

I knelt down to feel for her pulse, but I couldn't find one. Please?

I touched her face, tear-streaked, flushed from a vicious beating. She was bruised red, battered and cut. She'd resisted her attacker. You could see that. One arm had worked free of the phone cord tying her to the chair. Despite being tied to her chair and gagged, she'd fought back. She was still warm though. She was dead, but only recently, it seemed.

The room started to pulse with shadows in a slow-motion strobe. My vision blurred at the edges and a dizzy sensation came over me.

Behind me I could hear someone, a woman, enter the room through the door. I turned and looked up toward her, past the blood drying on my hands. The woman at the door, Amy's assistant, began to scream. Her face was clenched in a pure terror. As I turned back toward Amy's body, the index finger on her perfectly manicured hand brushed my white shirt leaving a bloody streak.

The next thing I knew her assistant was there behind me pounding on my back. She was still screaming. Her screams drew others. A small crowd gathered. Fred Peavy arrived and pushed through the crowd. Fred was all business, showing no reaction at all to the horror of Amy Louvenbragh's cruel death. He cleared the room efficiently and moved me out into another office nearby. Eventually, the police arrived, a lot of blue uniforms and gray suits, and the questions began. The police sealed off the museum and the crime scene with yellow tape and searched everyone there. It was still before opening hours, and only museum staff and volunteers were present. It was plain to me that everyone was upset over her death, even hard-boiled Fred Peavy, who didn't especially like the museum director. Once his authority had transferred to the Boston police on the scene, Fred began to let his feelings show a little on his face and in the way he carried himself. He sat in a chair next to me for a while, and we exchanged glances, but we said nothing. I was caught up in my own thoughts and speculation. Who could have killed Amy Louvenbragh? It sickened me to think about it. I couldn't imagine anyone there having done it. What was the point? What motive could there possibly have been? Maybe the art theft was somehow connected? I went around in circles like that for quite a while. I felt responsible.

A few hours later, I sat alone in a lime-green room on a black metal folding chair, breathing stale air mixed with Lysol and dead cigarettes. Groggy from jet lag and from the exhaustion of my feelings, I sagged in my chair. I had dried blood on my right sleeve, flecks of blood on my fingernails. I could see it clotted in the hairs on the back of my right hand.

Amy Louvenbragh was dead.

I was waiting for a detective to question me again. I'd been waiting for at least an hour since the first session. The Boston police had brought me to the substation for informational purposes, they said. Did I mind answering a few questions, they asked. I said no, why not? I wanted to help somehow.

The police had offered to let me use the phone, and I had tried to reach Hank Greenberg, but I'd forgotten he was out of town. He was in Florida, to be exact, watching the Red Sox spring training and pre-season exhibition games. He'd be back on Monday.

The door to the interrogation room swung open. A Boston police detective entered and sat in the chair across from me. Detective Sergeant Dave Raymond was average height and a little bit heavy for his frame. He had a rugged Irish face and a bit of a barroom tan. He was going bald on top with a droopy mustache to compensate. Big hands, hard calluses on them like a carpenter. I figured he did fix-up carpentry in his spare time.

Sergeant Raymond seemed interested in the bruises on my face. Of course, they were two days old and had turned purple already, but it established me as a combatant of some sort. Raymond wanted to know the details. Barcelona. Museum business. Art theft. The more he learned, the more curious he became. He kept pulling on his earlobe when I said something that piqued his interest. I was involved, somehow, even if he couldn't quite establish how. His tone of voice said that, and it also said he would get me eventually, so why not give up now? His questioning continued.

"You're from Capitola, California, according to your driver's license. Where's that?" He had the kind of accent you get in South Boston or Dorchester. Real working class Irish.

"It's near Santa Cruz, south of San Francisco, north of Monterey. It's a beach town."

"I understand you're working for the museum." The look on his face was mocking me, baiting me.

"For the Butler Museum Foundation. I was hired by Jack Butler to look into the art theft. That's why I was in Barcelona and why I was at the museum this morning."

"Where's your license?"

"You're looking at it."

"Your P.I. license, Mr. Shakespear."

"I don't have one."

"You are not licensed as an investigator?" He said it with such relish and sarcasm that I knew he'd been working up to it in his own mind.

"No. I'm more like a consultant." I answered him as plainly as possible, but he rolled his eyes when I said it and looked away.

"Tell me again about how you found the body."

We'd already been over a lot of territory. I'd answered a lot of those questions about who I was and why I was at the crime scene and what my relationship was to the deceased. Still, the questioning continued. He must have asked the same questions two or three times.

"Why didn't you call police?"

"I didn't have time," I said. "I was too upset to think straight. Her assistant found me with her and began screaming. There was a crowd of people there. The head of security, Fred Peavy, came in and he called..."

"How did you come to know her ?"

"I was working for the museum investigating an art theft. I interviewed her last week."

"Who is your employer?"

"Jack Butler. Or rather the museum, but Jack hired me."

"What was the purpose of your meeting this morning?"

"To review the status of my investigation. I'd been in Spain checking into some developments there."

"Where do you reside?"

"I told you already. Santa Cruz, California."

"When did you arrive in town?"

"First last Sunday and then again last night."

"Explain that." I did. I explained for the third time how I'd come to Boston, gone to Barcelona, and returned.

"What did you do last night?"

"Went straight to bed."

"Who saw you?"

"Nobody."

"Can anyone vouch for your whereabouts since last night?"

"Nope." I thought about the cab driver, but decided it probably wouldn't be worth tracking her down.

"How did you get the bruises again?"

"In Barcelona. A few days ago. Nothing to do with this."

It went on like that for several hours until Sergeant Raymond was satisfied he wasn't going to hear anything new. But, hours later, he was still no clearer about who did what, though he still seemed to believe I had a hand in Amy's murder. I probably could have ended it sooner. Technically, I wasn't under arrest. Nobody had read me Miranda or cautioned me in any way. I wasn't advised to contact a lawyer. Nothing like that. It was just a friendly chat at the substation. Except it had gone on too long, and I wanted to leave.

A little while later we were standing in a little room with vending machines on the ground floor. Sergeant Raymond didn't look quite so large and imposing standing there. He looked tired, not just tired from that day, but tired from head to toe like he needed a long vacation. The hard questions were over, it seemed.

"Want some coffee?" Raymond gestured with a paper cup in his thick right hand toward a square metal coffee dispensing machine on the wall opposite. "It's on me."

"No thanks." I said. I could have used a cup of coffee, but I don't like instant coffee from vending machines. The way I felt I doubted I could keep it down.

Raymond slipped a few coins into the slot, and a fresh paper cup dropped in place. Seconds later, brown and white liquids streamed into the cup. He added sugar, sipped.

"You're free to go, Mr. Shakespear. We may want to ask you more questions later, but for now, that's it. Just don't leave town without checking in with me." Raymond reached in the pocket of his gray suit coat and fumbled around in there. "Here's my card."

He handed me a thin paper business card with his name and contact data printed on it. I made a mental note to have cards of my own printed. And maybe I'd get a license. That is, if I stayed with this detective business. I had my doubts. It was getting a lot rougher than I liked. The crowd I met up with in Barcelona hadn't been any too friendly either. They'd treated me like a shipping crate, bounced me around, but at least they didn't break anything. A few bruises weren't much to worry about, though. Not when you compare that to what Amy Louvenbragh went through.

As I left the police station on that Friday afternoon, I was puzzled by several things. Who had been able to get in and out of the museum without being seen? What had the murderer done with clothes that must have been stained with blood? What had happened to the knife? Who could have wanted to kill Amy Louvenbragh?

I thought about the dead woman. I'd been in her office a few days before. She and I didn't get along that well. Nothing personal, she just resented my involvement in the case. I couldn't blame her for feeling that way. I might've felt the same in her place. I wondered how her killing was connected to the art theft I was trying to solve. There had to be some connection. But where to look?

I left the station and walked out to the curb. It was sunny at the moment and cold, but the sky was full of clouds, and high, high up in the sky I could see the stratocumulus clouds beginning to collect, as though Boston needed just one more snow storm to finish off its winter.

Snow would be nice. It would make everything clean and white again.

16
Friday, March 19
Boston, Massachusetts

Jack Butler was waiting for me at the curb. His face was set in a grave expression I could see from thirty feet away. He waved to me from the front seat of a green Range Rover. How would Jack be feeling now? I climbed aboard feeling more than a little uncertain.

He wore a camel cashmere topcoat and crimson scarf, gray Harris Tweed jacket, white shirt and a black knit tie. His gray wool trousers were pleated and recently pressed, but his cordovan wingtips were in need of a shine. Without a word Jack slid the gear lever into first and we lurched into traffic, peeling rubber like teenagers on hormone patrol. I looked over at him. He was absorbed in his grief, it seemed. I caught scent of a familiar sour smell. Whisky?

"Jack, I am deeply sorry about Amy. Are you all right?"

He tensed up at the mention of her name, then glanced toward me.

"I'm well enough, Tommy. Thank you. Look, we're nearly at my club. If you don't mind, I'd like to wait until we get there to talk. All right?"

We parked on Commonwealth Avenue. I zipped up my leather jacket, as it had grown noticeably colder in the past few hours. The sky was clouding over. A storm couldn't be too far off, I thought. Jack turned up the collar of his topcoat and pulled his scarf tight. We walked a few blocks past the stately rows of townhouses on Comm Ave, then up the staircase of a rather large brick townhouse with a U.S. flag and a Commonwealth of Massachusetts flag hanging down in the chilly air.

We entered and left our coats with a woman at a cloakroom near the entrance. To our left was a large, sweeping staircase leading up to the ballroom and other function rooms on the second and third floors. To the right was a smoking and reading room, an informal bar and grill, and further toward the back a billiard room. There was nobody checking memberships, nobody to sign you in. We headed toward the back.

Jack indicated the bar and grill, and I entered with him. It was a wood paneled den with a brass rail at the bar and hunting prints framed against the dark wood paneling. The parquet floor was worn but recently polished.

"Care for something to eat or drink?"

"Maybe a sandwich and a cup of coffee."

"Hot or cold?" he said.

"Coffee?" I wondered.

"Sandwich."

"I'll have a medium-well hamburger, if they've got it." I said. "Coffee black."

Jack went over to the bar to order. I sought out a private place to sit, eat and talk. We did have things to talk about. A less public table would reduce our chances of being interrupted. I chose a table set in the corner to the right of the door.

By the time Jack arrived at the table, I had readied my opening lines. Earlier at the police station I had composed and rehearsed them almost without thinking. As upset as I was about Amy's death, condolences were not easy for me. I thought of Beatrice and how awkwardly I'd expressed my friendship and admiration for her. Jack had been warm and receptive then. I hoped to be able to strike the right chord with him again. Before I could speak, however, Jack delivered some bad news.

"I am afraid, Tommy," he began, "We are going to have to conclude our investigation. I've given it quite a lot of thought. I don't want to risk anyone else's life."

Jack's face looked years older, wrinkles lined his forehead, and his voice was slow and unsteady. I felt bad about losing the job, but even more concerned about how Jack was doing.

"Jack, I'm sorry about Amy. It was horrible finding her. I can just imagine what you must be going through." I fumbled for the right words. Inwardly I thought, "Are you okay, man? Is there something I can do?"

"Really, I appreciate your concern, Tommy, but it's all taken care of. I've been in touch with her family, her mother, her brothers. Once the police have finished with her body, it will be shipped to Pennsylvania. I'll go there for the funeral early next week." Jack sighed heavily. I was beginning to feel a little depressed myself.

"Jack, I turned up one or two interesting details in Barcelona."

Jack sipped at his whisky on the rocks. I hadn't noticed his drink before, perhaps because his hands enfolded the glass almost completely. He shook his head.

"No, really, I've decided, Tommy. You can take a day or two to wrap things up. Just let me have your bill and final report."

"Have you dismissed Charley Howell, too? Or just me?" I said it a bit anxiously. But I had the feeling Jack wanted me out of the picture for some reason.

"Actually, not yet." Jack looked at me as though caught off-guard, but he recovered his composure quickly. "Howell is pursuing another aspect of the case." He rattled the ice in his glass.

"What aspect?" I looked closely at Jack for anything his face might reveal. He finished his drink and turned toward the bartender. When he looked back at me, I could see him weighing whether to tell me what was on his mind.

"Some letters began arriving at the Museum this week. Addressed to the museum, to Amy. Crazy, threatening letters. The one arriving today...." He stopped.

"What about it?"

"The letter mentioned a killing as the proof of their sincerity."

"Sincerity? Who were they from?"

"The letters were signed 'La Sardana'."

"La Sardana. What kind of crackpot group is that? What do they want?"

"Look, Tommy," he said, "I don't know much about them. Howell tells me they are a resurgent faction of the Provos."

I knew something about the Provos, but not much. "Weren't the Provos an anarchist group in the late sixties? I think they were based in Germany or the Netherlands."

"Whatever." Jack flicked his wrist as though brushing away a fly. "Apparently this group springs from the same political roots. They claim they want the return of all art to its country of origin. They've demanded we dissolve the Butler Museum and the Foundation and transfer all of our art works to museums in their originating countries."

"Jack, those letters could be some sort of crackpot or college prank, unconnected to Amy's death. Just a horrible coincidence."

I couldn't believe what I was hearing. Not that the Museum hadn't received some threatening letters. That was perfectly possible. There were all kinds of radical groups around making threats.

"It's no joke, I assure you. I've checked with some friends. Similar letters have been received at other museums and private collections. Hearst Castle for one. The Met. The Getty."

"Well, it's absurd."

"Not after what has happened. We believe this group, La Sardana, means business. Bad business. And who knows what they'll do next."

"What else do you know about them?"

"Nothing really. Just what Howell has told me, and I've told you."

"The name La Sardana sounds Spanish."

"I believe it's a peasant dance of some sort," he said.

"From Spain?" I could sense that Jack was withholding something.

"Yes, Spain. From around Barcelona, as a matter of fact. Catalonia."

"And the letters? Where were they postmarked from?"

"The first from Boston, Back Bay Station. The second from Herndon, near Washington D.C. The one arriving today came from Barcelona."

Herndon was the town nearest Dulles Airport. It only took a moment for me to realize that the postmarks coincided with my recent itinerary.

"Jack," I said, "Those letters came from places I've been. I was in Boston, Herndon, and Barcelona. What were those dates?"

This was too much of a coincidence. The La Sardana letters, Amy's murder. It seemed that someone had been setting me up, posting threatening letters to the Butler Museum and to the late Amy Louvenbragh.

"I don't recall exactly, but all within the past week, more or less."

"And the letters, Jack," I asked, "Could I see them? Where are they now?"

"Unfortunately, I've had to turn them over to the police. They consider them evidence in Amy's murder." He paused. "Tommy, I'm sure you weren't involved, and I've told the police that. I believe we've got a pack of crazies on our hands. That's why I think it's best we end our investigation and leave it to the police and the FBI from here on."

"But how do you account for the postmarks, on the very days I was in those places? Better yet, how do the police account for them?"

"I don't think they have made a connection yet. I've only just delivered them," he said. "Besides, I'm sure there will be some other acceptable explanation. A deliberate attempt by this La Sardana group to derail the investigation, for instance."

"Which has succeeded," I said.

He winced. "Yes. I'm afraid it has."

I was silent, dead in the water with no hint of a breeze. I sat unable to focus my thoughts on anything but the beating of my heart.

"Excuse me a moment, Tommy. I've got to go wash my hands. I expect our food will be arriving soon."

I watched Jack leave the bar and realized how much trouble I could be in. Someone was painting me into a corner, and if I wasn't careful he or she might dump the rest of the bucket on my head. I began to run through what I knew that could help me. First, I wondered, was there any known connection between the art theft and La Sardana? Jack hadn't mentioned one, and I only knew the content of the letters in very general terms. Second, I may have had the opportunity, and just barely, to kill Amy Louvenbragh, but I had no motive. At least I could think of none. That seemed to be on my side. Third and finally, if I had killed her, where was the knife? I was there, present in the room with the body, but no murder weapon had been found. Not yet anyway. I began to breathe a little easier as I saw there wasn't enough evidence to connect me. Not yet. But the way these threatening letters had shown up with postmarks on my trail, I had to wonder what would show up next, and where.

The bartender brought a platter of food to our table. My medium hamburger, garnished with pickles, tomato and onion slices, and Jack's omelet.

I sipped from the mug of hot coffee. Strong, Colombian probably. I assembled my hamburger, unable to wait for Jack's return, and looked around for some ketchup and a dash of Tabasco, but found neither one. When I walked over to the bar to ask for them, I saw Jack at a pay phone under the stairs.

He seemed about to end his conversation. I returned to the table, and he joined me shortly after I sat down.

We made small talk about the food. I took a few bites of my hamburger, but I wasn't really hungry. Jack ignored his omelet and sipped at his drink. Anxious to return to our earlier discussion, I reopened the question of La Sardana.

"Has La Sardana ever been connected to art theft in this country before? Or in Europe."

"Howell tells me the theft of some Miros and a Picasso from a museum in Germany have been claimed by La Sardana. In this country nothing yet, although we suspect they might have been involved in our case. Actually, there were references to it in the first two letters but no direct claim. Phrases like 'Vermeer and Rembrandt belong to the Netherlands' and 'Plundered treasures in a faux palace.' There were others like that I can't recall just now. Not taking credit for the theft, but expressing support, solidarity, that sort of thing."

"Wait a minute, Jack. There's something wrong here," I said. "There was a man in Barcelona who I believe, and Interpol believes, was behind the museum theft. He's called the Dutchman, but his real name is Dieter Kockhorn. I had an encounter with this man, and he as much as admitted the theft."

"Are you sure of this?"

"Reasonably sure. The Dutchman is also very dangerous. Those two men recently found murdered in Barcelona were the Dutchman's men, and I believe he tortured and killed them for betraying him. I narrowly escaped being killed myself."

"How did you encounter this Dutchman?"

"His men kidnapped me from my hotel room and took me to a farm house in the country outside Barcelona."

"How did you escape?" he said.

"The Dutchman ordered one of his men to kill me and dump me in the woods. But on the way there I was able to turn the tables."

"Do you suppose he's involved with La Sardana?"

"Doubt it. The Dutchman's only in it for the money. He accepts contracts to steal art works for very rich and unscrupulous collectors. Interpol has been tracking him and his art theft business, working with the FBI in this country and other agencies internationally."

"This certainly turns a different light on the matter, Tommy. I think you should tell the police about this Dutchman." He paused. "Frankly, I'm overwhelmed by the entire business. Amy's death has really set me back." He paused again, and for a moment I thought he might break down.

"I'm going away for a few days to the Bahamas, clear my head and think about things. I'd like you to submit your report and your bill, including expenses through Monday, to Ted Wycliffe."

"What about the Dutchman?"

"Well, I believe that's now a matter for the police, the FBI, and Interpol."

"He could have used La Sardana to cover his tracks. That might explain the postmarks on those threatening letters. I know he's had his people in Boston. Maybe he's had me followed."

"Tommy, you've done all you could. A good job under the circumstances, but it's over now. I'm afraid I haven't any more heart for it."

I looked over at Jack's plate. His omelet was untouched.

Suddenly I felt caught between difficult emotions. I had sympathy for Jack and his loss. Naturally, he'd want to try to put all this out of his mind. But I was also afraid of what the police might make of those postmarks.

It was the most circumstantial of evidence, but it pointed right at me.

17
Friday, March 19
Boston, Massachusetts

Only minutes after I'd returned to my hotel room, the police came to the door with a search warrant. They must have been waiting downstairs for my return. Maybe Jack called them from his club. I didn't like thinking that.

The police went through my suitcase, the bathroom, all the drawers and closets, checked under mattresses and couch cushions. They were thorough. One of them found some condoms I had in a dresser drawer with my underwear. He looked over at me as if he was going to say something, but decided better of it. I sat watching television to take my mind off things. Nothing much was on, so I watched the evening news, local edition, for a few laughs, but there was nothing much to laugh about. Amy Louvenbragh's murder was in the headlines, and that was certainly no laughing matter. Neither was the notebook the cops turned up.

"This yours?" said the taller one with acne scars, pale eyebrows and no hair. He was holding the notebook by its corner in his plastic-gloved hand, as though it were dirty underwear.

"Yeah, I think so. May I see it?" It looked like the notebook had been in one of the drawers under some shirts. I hadn't put it there. It had been stolen from me a few days ago in this same hotel. I had a sinking feeling in the pit of my stomach. What was happening to me?

"You can look, but don't touch. I'll turn the pages." The detective set it down on the dresser top and opened the cover. I could see it was mine. Name, address and phone number on the inner flap. My preliminary notes about the Butler theft on the first several pages.

"It's mine," I said. "It was stolen from me last week. I have no idea how it got there in my drawer."

"Mr. Shakespear, we're going to take this in as evidence. I'll make you out a receipt." He placed the notebook and pen in a plastic evidence bag.

"Wait!" I said. "Am I under arrest?"

"Not at the present time. But if you'd like to come down to the station and make a statement, we'll be happy to take it."

His partner stood by silently during the entire conversation, neither speaking nor showing any reaction whatsoever. He was several years younger, dark, maybe Italian or Portuguese, and he seemed a lot tougher than the more talkative one. When I looked over at him, he looked away.

"I don't know. Is Sergeant Raymond on duty?"

"You can call when you're ready. Or maybe we'll call you." He and his partner moved toward the door, taking my notebook with them.

Turning back, he said, "Thank you for your cooperation, Mr. Shakespear."

I decided against going down to the station. Things seemed to be heading in the wrong direction. Instead of solving the art theft, I was becoming more and more involved. First the Dutchman, then art terrorists. Now I was being implicated in a murder.

Who could blame Jack for backing away? I would do the same if my fiancée were murdered, and the threatening letters just made it worse.

I sat down to make out a list of people to contact. That notebook would come in handy now, I thought. Instead, I picked up the telephone note pad provided by the hotel. It would do. Peavy. I wrote down Fred Peavy's name. Then Charley Howell. My mind wandered. I began to revisit the scene of Amy's murder. I could clearly see the body. The blood. Splattered everywhere as if her neck had been cut during the struggle. One arm free. The overturned chair. Her perfectly-manicured hand and the bloody finger that had stained my shirt. I doodled aimlessly thinking about the first time I had met with Amy Louvenbragh. Suddenly I looked down at the notepad and realized I had lost track of time. It was growing dark outside my hotel window. An hour had passed.

Still sitting in the dark, I called Shiva. I was feeling sorry for myself, and I needed to talk to a friend. As luck would have it, she was not answering. Maybe she was out or traveling on a job. Her machine took over and I listened to the latest trivia test. Who was the author of The Wizard of Oz? An easy one. Frank Baum. In what year was it written? Tougher, much tougher. I'd say 1939. Who was the original Tin Man? Hint: He withdrew from the production because the metal paint made him ill. No idea. Where does she get these questions?

"Shiva, it's Tommy. I'm calling from Boston. Back in the U.S. of A. Miss you. I'm coming back on Monday, just a few things to wrap up, but I'll be here through the weekend, so call me...." I tried to keep the fear and frustration I felt out of my voice. Until I told her, I didn't want her to know how much trouble I was in.

I placed a long distance call to the number Sam Bassett had given me and left a message. Elaine was out, too.

My dinner of poached salmon and peas arrived about seven o'clock on a rolling cart pushed by Manolo. I asked if he were Filipino, and when he smiled I could see he was missing a few teeth. I tipped him generously, probably a little too generously, but I was in a strange mood. I ate with the television off. I'd opened the drapes when the cops left, had sat by the open window writing down the names of people I would have to contact before I filed my report on Monday. As dusk settled in, I'd drifted off in a daydream, and now as I sat drinking Evian the snow began to fall. It was a pretty sight, the white flakes tumbling down through a glittering night sky. A spring snow to cloak the budding crocuses. I hoped it would be just a dusting, hoped it would not choke off the first bright blooms of spring, but knew that nature wouldn't give a shit what happened. Only people care about death and not all of them, I thought, and then the phone rang.

It was Elaine. Heard I was back. Horrible about Amy. Saw something on TV about me finding the body. How about going to that club on the south shore to meet Yards Malloy tonight? She said she had no plans, that Whit was tied up with some business all weekend. All weekend? Yeah, some leveraged buyout he was working on. She would drive the Volvo, pick me up out front in an hour and a half. No point in getting there much before ten. Missed me. Had to tell me something about Jack and Amy. Didn't know anything about threatening letters. La Sardana? Wasn't that a folk dance or something?

The Clamshell was an oblong brick building with a neon Miller sign in its grimy front window. The front door had been sealed off years before. There was a padlock on it and sidewalk dirt and debris had permanently settled into its corners and edges. Not much to look at from the road, but the Clamshell was right on the water across from the Boston skyline glittering in the distance. We walked around to the side. Snow had dusted the parking lot so it was easy to see footprints and tire tracks. There weren't many, two cars and a van with gangbanger graffiti on it in the parking lot. Five bucks each to the bouncer, a red hand stamp reading "Canceled", and we were in. The place was empty. Nearly empty, I should say. The band was setting up, the bartender was racking glasses, and a couple of under-aged girls in heavy makeup and pierced body parts were coming out of the ladies room.

We walked over toward the bandstand, picked out a table and deposited our stuff. I went over to the bar and ordered our drinks, a kir for Elaine and a fake beer for me. They had Sharps and Clausthaler. A choice, I thought to myself, what do you know? Things are looking up for us non-drinkers. When I returned to the table, Elaine was standing there with her arms around some guy in tight leather jeans with long hair, tattoos and a black Amnesty International t-shirt with the sleeves cut out. He had the looks of a model. Punk handsome and sensitive-looking, just the right mixture of danger and vulnerability for Elaine.

Elaine introduced me, and we shook hands. Yards Malloy. He began a handshake ritual that went through several distinct stages and ended up with slapping fives, both high and low. I'd been through it a few times before in the Seventies, so I was able to follow it mostly, though I stumbled a little in the middle. He was amazed, but showed it only with his eyes.

"You been inside, man?" he asked. I took it he was referring to prison.

"Not really," I said. "I got busted once for pot and spent a few days in jail, but that's it. At least, so far." He looked me over carefully as though deciding how much trust he could place in me. He motioned to me to sit, and the three of us took our chairs.

"Elaine says you're involved in an art theft."

Funny way to put it, I thought. I glanced at Elaine. "The Butler Museum had some paintings stolen. I was hired to do an investigation, to try to recover the art or get a lead that could help the agencies who are also investigating. There's FBI, Interpol and some others involved at this point."

"You're talking about the Vermeer and the Rembrandt?" said Yards.

"There were three Rembrandts, I believe." I corrected him.

"Not really," he said. "'The Concert' is a Vermeer and a great one. It's probably the most valuable of the paintings they ripped off. The Rembrandts were not of comparable quality. Way it is, two of them are probably not even Rembrandts. Whoever took them was no art lover and was in a real big hurry. Besides, if you're dealing for dollars, there were better targets in the museum, even in the same room. The Van Dyck or the Dürer for instance."

"Or the Titian upstairs." Was I competing with him?

"Yeah, it's marketable, but you know Titian was at least eighty-five when he painted it. In my opinion it's overrated. You could also mention the Giotto or the Botticellis, the

Raphaels or if you like American, there are half a dozen Whistlers there."

"Sounds like you know your art," I said. I was staring at a Mona Lisa tattoo on his left shoulder. It was three or four inches high and a fairly realistic rendering of the lady with the enigmatic smile. Yards noticed me staring at it.

"Yeah. I have had some experience with it, you might say." Yards was restraining an impulse to smile.

Elaine laughed and the two of them shared a familiar look.

She said, "It's also amazing to me why they left the Rembrandt self-portrait sitting there and took two Rembrandts which, as you say, were probably not authentic. I mean, that's assuming they had been sent for Rembrandt and Vermeer."

"Probable," said Yards. "From what I hear, it was a contract job."

"If it was a contract job, then how much would they stand to make?" I said.

"Depends on who you mean by 'they.' The handlers, the guys who take it out of the museum, they don't get much at all. I know that side pretty well. I used to set things up once upon a time. I'd usually hire the handlers, work with an insider I identified and be the contact to the head man. Of course, the head man pulls all the strings and owns the buyer. He makes whatever the buyer is willing to pay, less his expenses. There's usually a large amount to any insider who's involved."

"How does that work financially?" I glanced over at Elaine to show my amazement. She had her eyes on Yards.

The guy was fascinating, I had to admit. He talked with his hands, using them to punctuate his thoughts in a captivating and thoroughly convincing way. There were a lot of distractions around us, as the bar had begun to fill up with people, but I was focused on Yards' explanation. By the time he was done I had the feeling I understood how it might have worked. Even if I couldn't clearly recall all the details.

"The Vermeer alone is worth $75 million," he said. "The Rembrandt seascape $15 million, and the rest a total of maybe $10 million all together at most, and that's a hundred million, if you sold it at auction, but nobody is going to pay that much for stuff you can't show. So for that job, well, I figure a commission of 5% of the contract price, let's say $15 million total take, discounted, for the Butler job. So if it's all contracted, it would net the insider $750,000. Give or take."

"So let me get this straight," I said. "The guy at the top gets around fifteen million from the buyer and pays something to the handlers and to the insider, probably netting fourteen million."

"Maybe a little less. It varies. The goods have to be in acceptable condition. Sometimes the handlers screw that up. The insider doesn't have to worry about that one though. Usually he's paid up front just to grease the wheels."

"Who would the insider be?" I asked.

"Man, I figure that's your job," said Yards. "But there's usually several candidates—security, museum administration, curatorial staff. Could be almost anyone." He narrowed his gaze.

"I was thinking of the museum director." I said.

"The one who got her throat cut?" he said. "You found the body, right?"

"Yeah. She was in a position to profit from it and had opportunity."

"Tommy, I don't know," said Elaine. "Amy never seemed like the type to me."

One of the teenage girls with the band wandered over to Yards and began to massage his neck. She had a thin, pretty face. Neon-blue hair, white lipstick, silver rings in her nose and around her eyebrows. Young, though, with makeup covering her pimples.

"So what's the type?" I asked. I was conscious of the girl behind Yards.

Yards reached back as if annoyed and pushed her hands away, but she kept massaging his neck and rubbing her breasts against his head, suggestively. She smiled and stuck out her tongue at me revealing a silver stud embedded in it. I was distracted even if Yards was not. I wondered if she flossed that thing.

"There is no type," he said. "Although I usually looked for someone who liked to do drugs. You can get up close to someone like that pretty quickly. Otherwise, you've got your work cut out for you."

Yards stood up, and the girl backed off. She and Yards exchanged looks, but said nothing. He did not introduce her.

"I've got to go and get ready for the first set. Nice to meet you, Shakespear. Elaine, stay in touch." He put his arms around Elaine and kissed her. I looked over at the girl with the blue hair. She looked away and tried to act uninterested. Yards started to walk away from the table.

"Yards," I said.

He stopped and turned toward me.

"Yeah," he said. It was not a question.

"I'll be at the Four Seasons through Monday noon in case you think of anything else. And here's my number in California."

I didn't expect him to call, but it was worth trying to stay connected.

"California. You know, Shakespear, I hear the Dutch art ended up in California," he said. "Silicon Valley. A rich businessman, of course. And a jazz freak, the rumor is. Actually, it's more than a rumor. But, myself, I've never done business with him, so that's all I know. Supposed to be a big buyer, though."

I handed him the Clamshell napkin with my name and number in ballpoint. He stuffed it in the back pocket of his leather jeans. I made another mental note to get some business cards made up.

"Pleasure," he said. Yards returned to the bandstand, followed by little miss tongue stud, and strapped on his instrument.

I couldn't quite shake the idea that the Butler theft might lead back to the Silicon Valley. My own backyard. I remembered Sam Bassett had said something about a buyer in California. Coincidence?

But Elaine had something else on her mind.

"Tommy," she said. "I owe you an explanation."

18
Friday, March 19
Boston, Massachusetts

"He always did have a weakness for the young ones," she said.

"Exotic, too." We sipped at our drinks.

"I should think those ornaments would get in the way of a good time. Wouldn't you?"

"So what did you want to explain?" I said, changing the subject.

Elaine lifted her glass to eye level and peered at me through it. She pressed it against her forehead.

"Okay. It's just like you said. I was using you to get back at my husband. Whit had an affair, and I wanted to pay him back. I wanted to get his attention, hurt him, anything to make him notice me. Simple as that. So you were right. And I'm sorry. Happy now?"

"Happy," I said. But I wasn't, and I didn't fully understand. "So why me? Why not Yards? At least he's local."

"Because I wanted to make Whit feel insecure. I'd told him all about you and me on the Vineyard before we were married. So he sees you as a threat. Yards he wouldn't take seriously. Besides, I'm not Yards' type. He likes his women underdone."

"You admit you were using me?"

"Tommy, I was. Okay? But it's not like I don't care about you. I didn't scheme to get you out here or anything just to make Whit jealous. It was only when Jack said he needed someone else to pick up the investigation that I thought of you. And then I thought of how having you here might also…"

"Okay, okay, I get it. You know, Elaine, I really was in love with you. I mean, I can still feel how I felt back then."

Elaine reached across the table and took my hand. I took her hand, and held it, and brought it to my lips.

"We were good together, Tommy," she said, and she smiled. The ice in her eyes melted, and that smile went down into my gut. Elaine rubbed her hand against my cheek. I could feel the situation veering out of control again.

"Maybe we'd better get going," I said. "I'm still on Barcelona time, and it's been one long day." Elaine looked hurt for a moment. "Okay," I said, "How about one dance?" And she brightened.

"Just one dance?" she said. Give her an inch, she'd go for a mile.

"By the way," I said, remembering. "What were you going to tell me about Jack and Amy?"

The band was through with their sound check and ready to start the set. Yards stepped up to the mike and introduced the first tune.

"Jack doesn't know this, but I told you about how Whit had this affair?"

"Yeah?" I said.

"Well, it was Amy."

Elaine and I stayed on through the first set. We talked some more and danced some, too. She told me how she'd found out about Whit and Amy and that it had been a short-lived fling. Winslow was far too involved with his work to make very much of it. And Amy didn't want to lose Jack. Elaine had confronted them both one night when it was all but over, and she had agreed not to tell Jack. I wondered how Jack would feel now about Amy's murder if he knew.

The place had filled up with people and with smoke. At first, it was mainly college kids, and the locals stayed back toward the bar. We danced to "Can't Help Myself," an old Four Tops number that Yards' band had rearranged with a very funky set of rhythms. Yards laid down a nasty bass line. The sax player, who looked like the big guy with red hair in Sha-Na-Na, wailed on it something animal. He was raining sweat. His solo drew in some of the bar crowd. Pretty soon the bar area was vacant, the drinking crowd had moved up toward the band, and some of them had mixed in with the college crowd.

By the end of the song, everyone was dancing. It was a hot time, and the next tune was designed to cool things down. Elaine and I stayed on the floor and held each other for the slow dance. Elaine glowed with sexual energy, and I felt like I was back in high school. We pressed against each other and kept our bodies close. Halfway through the song, I looked into her eyes, and I knew I had lost it good. We stood in the middle of the dance floor, a few other couples gliding around us, locked tightly in embrace, kissing as deeply as we could wearing clothes, and gave ourselves over to whatever was coming next.

On the drive back from the Clamshell we were silent. I could feel the sexual tension and was afraid to speak. Elaine and I had no real business being together. We'd gone a lot further than I had wanted. And Elaine seemed to feel the same way. We just couldn't seem to stay away from each other.

Thoughts of Shiva kept intruding. I thought about our friendship and where it might be heading. I thought I might be falling in love with Shiva, though we'd never slept together, never crossed over to sexual intimacy. Yet, despite my feelings for Shiva I had this intense physical attraction to Elaine, and I didn't really want to shut it off. When we arrived at the hotel, Elaine parked at the curb and shut down her car.

"I'm coming up for a few minutes," she said.

I said nothing, and we walked into the hotel. We were alone in the elevator, and began kissing, touching each other, impatient, hungry for more. We floated down the corridor to my door, our arms around each other. The phone was ringing in my room, but I didn't answer it.

Alone in my room we stood looking at each other. Not touching. Not speaking. Elaine was like a dream I'd had every night for years. She was familiar but not the kind of familiar you take for granted. The kind of familiar you miss when it's away. I said it was good to be alone together. Elaine said not to go anywhere, that she'd like to take a shower. She'd be right back. While she was in the bathroom, I talked the room service clerk into sending up some refreshments and a dozen candles. I lit the candles and placed them around the room, turning out the lights to create a soft, romantic glow for Elaine when she came out of the bathroom. For the next few hours we basked in the candlelight's glow.

Elaine left a little before two, and I drifted off to sleep. The bad dreams began again that night. I was trapped in a room with no windows or doors. I felt the walls for a concealed opening but found nothing to hope for. I scoured the pages of a book for the answer to a question, and my hands grew larger, and pages of the book were too small for my fingers. I was chased by a little boy with a toy gun. I knew it had to be a toy but I ran all the same, afraid for my life. Wait, wait, he said. I stopped and turned. He shot. I looked down. There was blood on my shirt, my index finger was covered in blood.

It was an uneasy night. I awoke from time to time knowing why the bad dreams had come, knowing what I had to do to chase them away. In the morning, I told myself. I could take care of things in the morning. But I knew I had run out of ideas.

I knew I was coasting on fumes.

19
Saturday, March 20
Boston, Massachusetts

First thing Saturday morning I went back to the police station where I had been taken for interrogation. I asked for Sergeant Raymond and was told to wait. A few minutes later Raymond appeared and led me into a conference room, not the same one as before, but with the same look and feel. Pale green walls. Old wooden tables, black metal folding chairs. TV and VCR on a trolley in the corner. Same lingering odor of cigarette butts. I hadn't had breakfast yet but the smell put it out of my mind. Raymond sat across the table from me. In his hand he held a manila envelope.

"You didn't do it, did you, Shakespear?"

"No, of course not. But, I thought —" What accounted for this change, I wondered.

"I didn't think so. You're not the type for murder. I'll bet you don't even like violence much."

"I prefer to solve problems by other means."

"As far as I'm concerned, you're not a suspect. But unfortunately it's not that simple."

"Go on." What's next?

"There's been a lot of high-level attention on this one. Butler is a big name. Knows big people. And, of course, the woman was his fiancé. The DA could care less. He's on his way out. But the Assistant DA wants his job and he sees a political opportunity to score big on this one. He's pushing for an arrest. Not that I care much one way or the other what that putz wants, but if he can convince the DA..."

"I thought you said the DA was on his way out. What would convince him?"

"Well, he is on his way into private practice. That's another way of saying favors add up. It all depends on who lines up to lean on whom." Whoa! For a moment I was stuck wondering if Raymond had used who and whom correctly, but that distraction faded when I realized what he had said.

"You're saying the DA might go along because it would benefit him later on in private practice?"

"Yeah. That's about it." He opened the manila envelope. "Take a look at these pictures." Raymond handed me a stack of 8-by-10 glossies. They weren't pretty pictures. The shots of the body, especially the close-ups of her neck wound, were pretty gruesome. There were several pictures taken of the office set up, the blood spatters on the desk top and walls, one or two of the pool of blood on the floor. I glanced them over and returned them to Sergeant Raymond.

"See anything?" he said.

I hadn't, so I asked for them back and went through them again. Still nothing. "So what is it anyway? I can't see what you're referring to."

"Look at the ones of the blood on the floor." Raymond stabbed at the photos with his index finger.

I set the others aside and took a careful look at the two shots of the pool of blood. I told Raymond what I thought. It seemed like there might have been a footprint in the blood, but the resolution wasn't good enough, and you'd really need to see a close-up of that shot to tell if it was a footprint.

"Nope. Not a footprint. Here take a look at this." Raymond turned on the VCR in the corner of the conference room. "We made this tape at the same time as these photographs were taken. Look closely when it zooms in on the pool of blood."

The video tracked in on the body first, lingered on the neck wound, then pulled back to get the body and the pool of blood in one shot. Next a close-up of the pool of blood. Raymond froze the frame.

"See that?" he said. Raymond was pointing to what I had thought was a footprint. Just at the edge of the frame I could see Amy Louvenbragh's bloody index finger, the one that had stained my shirt. She had drawn something in the pool of blood. It looked a little like the number 12.

"Yeah. Is that a twelve?" I said.

"Or an R." he said. R for Raymond, I thought.

"Or maybe a K?" I said. There were two lines one either straight or curving slightly to the left. The one to the right had a wave in it but didn't quite touch the other line.

"All of the above," he said.

"If it was a K, I'd say it could point to this guy I was investigating in Barcelona. His name is Dieter Kockhorn. With a K. Alias 'the Dutchman'. Interpol is also tracking him for this art theft and others." I paused. "If it's a 12, I have no idea. The twelfth letter is L, but when you're dying I doubt you'd think like that." I paused again. "Of course if it's an R, there's you."

"Very funny."

"I guess it could be a D, too, or an unfinished B, or maybe an E or an M or a W, depending on if she was doing it right side up."

"But it looks to you like some sort of letter," he said.

"Yeah, it does. You know, the thought occurs to me, she was an authority on monograms, artist's signatures. I don't know what that means, but it might mean something."

"You think this Dutchman might tie in? How?"

"I don't really know. But let's assume there was an inside contact on the museum theft. Who would have been in a better position than Amy Louvenbragh? She even lived in the museum on the top floor. She had cozied up to Jack Butler, gotten hired on with fairly limited experience, except for her academic work on Vermeer. And even that points to possible complicity. She could have worked her way in deliberately to pull off the heist. She came to the museum only a short time before the theft. Let's say she and the Dutchman had a falling out over money after the theft. I know firsthand how vindictive he can be. Two of his men, the guys who probably did the job, turned up dead a short while ago in Barcelona. And they were tortured and mutilated before bleeding to death."

"Very nice, Shakespear," Raymond said. "But what was her motive in the beginning?"

"Greed, I assume. I don't really know what motivated her. I didn't know her that well."

"Well, it is plausible, but it's not going to make a case. And if the Assistant DA gets his train rolling, what we've got here won't stop it."

"There's still no murder weapon."

"That's right. On the other hand, you'd be surprised how often they turn up conveniently," he said.

"You don't mean what I think you mean," I said.

"Things do happen sometimes. If I were you, I'd get a lawyer ready just in case."

"I was planning to return to California on Monday or Tuesday."

"We know how to reach you," he said.

"Sergeant Raymond, do you mind if I ask what you plan to do with this evidence?"

"I really don't know what to do with it. I'll file a report on our interview and your speculations. Not sure whether anyone in the DA's office will want us to follow it up. It's pretty inconclusive, although at least it establishes one thing."

"What's that?" I said.

"She was probably still alive when the killer left."

MICHAEL G. WEST

20
Saturday, March 20
Boston, Massachusetts

The evidence Raymond had shown me seemed to indicate Amy Louvenbragh knew her killer. She had attempted to identify whoever that was by writing an initial in the pool of her own blood. If her death was connected to the art theft, as I supposed it was, then she probably had met with her killer earlier on the morning she died. My best working guess was that she had been an inside contact for the Dutchman. Something had gone wrong, or maybe the Dutchman had decided to tidy up after himself. If the two handlers were out of the way, then the inside contact could be the only remaining witness.

I hoped that Raymond would take good care of that evidence, especially the tape recording. If it disappeared or was erased, there would be no way to prove to anyone else that I wasn't the killer. Even so, the tape wasn't conclusive. I could have killed her and then used her finger to scribble a misleading letter or number in her blood.

I knew I'd have to find something else to prove my innocence, before I got swept up in some ambitious Assistant DA's power trip. The missing murder weapon was an important piece of evidence. I had a feeling that it might still be in the museum, but I didn't know where or how to begin

168

looking. Fred Peavy could be helpful in that. I'd give him a call and try to set something up. I knew I needed to know more about Amy Louvenbragh. Who were her friends? Elaine could point me in the right direction. Maybe Kara Penny-Worth or her boyfriend, Clark, could fill me in. Or Randall Stine, the gallery owner. There were several possible tracks to follow. I decided to check with Sam Bassett to see whether Amy had been at other museums that the Dutchman may have hit. Titus Moone, the previous museum director, might know something, too. And of course Charley Howell, Jack's other detective.

My mind was working overtime, and I was somewhere between high anxiety and panic. I really didn't have enough time to follow everything up in the two days I had left, but I had to try.

Back at my hotel I ordered breakfast. I was starving. While I waited, I began checking phone messages. There was one from the day before and one today. Shiva had just called, no message. Charley Howell had called yesterday and agreed to meet for breakfast on Sunday morning. I wondered who had called at midnight, but there was no message on that one.

After breakfast, I called Elaine but she was unavailable. I reached Clark at the newspaper, and, while he hadn't been especially close to Amy, he told me where to reach Kara. I caught her heading out to teach an aerobics class, and we agreed to meet afterward at Amy's apartment near Beacon Hill. Kara was taking care of Amy's cat. She had an extra key to the apartment and used it to look in on the cat when Amy went out of town. Since Amy's death, the cat had come to live with her.

I met Kara at Amy's apartment in the early afternoon. It was cool and sunny, warming up as the day went on. Last night's snow hadn't really amounted to much, and if the sunny skies continued through the afternoon the snow would all be gone by evening.

Amy's apartment was furnished simply, but elegantly. It looked like a magazine layout. Kara told me Jack had loaned Amy some things from his family's estate after the theft, when she moved out of her official quarters upstairs at the Butler. The afternoon light was soft and diffuse throughout the apartment, filtered through the linen drapes. I thought back to paintings by Vermeer and the way light came into Vermeer's rooms. Had Amy deliberately tried to create that appearance? But there wasn't anything of interest in Amy's apartment. It was clean and dust free. Every pillow had been plumped and set into place.

I had to wonder if the police had already combed through. As we stood outside on the sidewalk, I mentioned to Kara that I would have expected a little more disarray. Kara thought Jack might have hired a cleaning person to make the apartment more presentable for Amy's family when they came to claim her effects.

After leaving Amy's apartment I stopped by to see Randall Stine, the Newbury Street gallery owner. He was not especially sad about her death.

"She was an alley cat with a new shampoo," he said.

"Meaning what?" I said.

"Oh, come now, Tommy Shakespear. You can't play coy with me. You're the detective Jack hired to catch her."

"I'm what?" I was surprised to hear what I was hearing. Or thought I was hearing.

"Everybody said she was just a gold digger after Jack's money. But you and I know she had a different agenda."

Stine explained that Amy had wormed her way into Jack Butler's life in order to set up the theft.

"Why did she stick around then? I mean, the theft was two years ago. What's the point of remaining as museum director if you've accomplished your mission?"

"You know about the letters?" he asked.

"What letters?"

This was unsettling. How did he know about the letters?

"La Sardana, the born-again art terrorists, of course. You know, 'Return all art to the motherland, you imperialist swine!'"

"Oh, *those* letters. Okay. Let's suppose I do. I won't bother to ask how you know about them. But what do the letters have to do with Amy?"

"Extortion. She was such a greedy little bitch. Stealing the Rembrandt and Vermeer, the Manet and those Degas drawings weren't enough for her. So she made up La Sardana just to bleed Jack some more. Threatening herself was a clever trick to throw off suspicion, but she couldn't fool me."

"Interesting theory, Mr. Stine." I said. "Did she also cleverly make up her murder?"

"She got too greedy for her own good, Tommy Shakespear. Her partner probably did it because he had no choice."

When I left the RS Gallery, I felt almost dizzy. But the pieces were beginning to come together.

I was on my way to visit Dr. Moone in Allston near Commonwealth Avenue when I noticed someone was following me. I was riding on the Green Line trolley just beyond Kenmore Square. I'd stood up to offer my seat to a young woman who was very pregnant and carrying several heavy law books. After what Sergeant Raymond had told me earlier, I'd decided to be nice to all lawyers and potential lawyers at least until after this case was over. I might need one or two of them to defend me if that assistant DA pointed his ambition in my direction.

I caught a glimpse of another woman, not as young as the law student, and taller, wearing a navy-blue slicker and dark glasses. Her slicker was full-length with a hood and the kind of fold-over closures that I had on mine when I was a kid. Except mine had been yellow. I looked away. I had seen her before somewhere. She had been outside my hotel a few hours ago talking to the doorman, getting a cab, I'd assumed. Was there another time? Of course, I reasoned, it was a coincidence. But I decided to test that theory by getting off at the next stop. I was only about eight or nine blocks from Dr. Moone's apartment. It would be a pleasant walk, although the sky had begun to darken a little. The gathering clouds had cooled things off considerably. It might even snow again.

When the trolley came to a stop I eased my way to the exit door slowly. I didn't want to lose my tail, if that was what she was. I wanted to know why she was following me. I joined a small clot of passengers breaking free and stepping down into the street. We were in the divider between inbound and outbound lanes of Comm Ave, and there she was in her dark sunglasses, despite the darkening sky overhead.

She had short blond hair that wrapped her head like a helmet. Her hands and fingers were fine-boned. Her skin was fair, nearly translucent. I couldn't see her eyes, but I imagined they were gray, dull gray, behind those shades. Where had I seen her before today?

I approached her and spoke. "Excuse me, but do you know where I can find Boston University?"

"Which building?" she said. We were standing in the street surrounded by Boston University.

"Admin," I said. I was trying to sound like I had a purpose there.

"No idea. Sorry." She turned away from me and walked back toward downtown Boston. If she had been following me, she wasn't any longer. I crossed the street to the odd number side and walked the several blocks to my destination. I had the feeling I'd see her again.

Titus Moone lived in a two-bedroom flat on the ground floor of an older building on Comm Ave. The exterior was sandstone and brick veneer with false turret and battlement decorations. The lobby was limestone trimmed in marble, time-worn, but not run down. I found his name on the polished brass buzzer plate and pushed the button next to it. To my left a door opened.

"Come in, Mr. Shakespear," he said, "and make yourself at home. Titus Moone." We shook hands. "I'm on the phone right now, but should be off in a moment."

He slipped away into one of the rooms off a corridor to my right as I continued into the living room. It was fairly untidy. One tennis shoe sat smack in the middle of the floor. A colorful pile of clean, unfolded clothing brimmed over a blue plastic laundry basket next to the shoe. Newspapers, magazines, small stacks of unopened mail, mostly junk mail, and several coffee cups littered the low wooden coffee table at the center of a cluster of overstuffed couches and chairs. I sank into one of them and considered drifting off into a soft dreamy haze when he entered the room and hailed me.

"Care for some coffee?" he asked. I did. Actually I was getting hungry again. I'd had a late breakfast but no lunch. Coffee would have to do until I could get to some real food.

"Sure," I said. "Black, please."

"Care to join me in the kitchen? I brew it fresh." He didn't wait for an answer but led the way down the hall into his kitchen. I began to notice something. The apartment was not what you'd expect from a former museum director. There was no art anywhere. Not even an exhibition poster on the walls. There were posters and handbills, but they were all announcing political events. Walk for Hunger. Literacy Now! Jesse Jackson at Morse Auditorium. Act Up! Nuclear Freeze. In the kitchen there was more of the same. I had to comment.

"I'm surprised not to see more art on your walls."

"You'd expected Rembrandt, maybe."

"Yeah, something like that. You were the Butler Museum director. It seems strange that you'd have left it behind so completely."

"It's complicated," he said. He looked at me as if to say, you may not understand, and promptly changed the subject. "Any preference in beans?" Moone gestured toward a row of glass jars containing coffee beans. Some were roasted dark and oily, others shone with a light umber hue. I looked at the labels neatly printed in black ink. Costa Rican. Colombian. Brazilian. Blue Mountain. Yrgacheffe. Sumatra. Sulawesi.

"The Blue Mountain any good?" I wondered. Once it had been a great coffee. But recently a hurricane had hit Jamaica, encrusting the coffee crop with salt, destroying years of careful cultivation. Since then Blue Mountain had been hard to get and nowhere near as good.

"Not really. I buy it when I can, but it's nearly $40 a pound these days. Just not worth it."

"How about the Sulawesi? Celebes, whatever. That's my personal favorite."

"You got it. Great coffee. Low in acid, rich, full, caramel flavor." He scooped some beans into a grinder.

"Listen to me," he said. "I sound like a wine tasting." He laughed nervously. It was a high-pitched laugh.

Dr. Moone was a thin, intense man about my height. His dark hair was cut very short. Beard stubble. Either he hadn't shaved today or had molto testosterone. In one ear he wore a diamond stud. He looked like he didn't sleep much. There were dark caves under his eyes. I guessed he was around forty, forty-two.

"Titus. Can I call you Titus?"

"Sure. I'm Titus."

"Okay, I'm Tommy as far as that goes. Look. I'd like to cut to the chase. Dr. Louvenbragh was murdered. I found the body. I am an investigator working on the Butler theft. Let's see what else."

"Where's your card or license?" he said.

"Oh, you mean PI license?"

"Yeah, whatever," he said. He spooned the ground coffee into a gold filter basket.

"Uh. Well, I'm not formally licensed. You could call me a consultant."

"Meaning you work for Charley Howell?"

"No. Not exactly. I work for Jack Butler, or Fred Peavy, I guess, but I'm new to this line of work."

"Everybody has to start somewhere," he said. He poured spring water into his coffee maker, pushed the start button.

As the coffee brewed I gave Dr. Moone a quick synopsis. I left out Sam Bassett, the Dutchman, La Sardana. Basically, I told him what I thought he already knew. I wanted to see whether he had anything to add.

"You know, Tommy," he said, handing me a cup of fresh-brewed Sulawesi, "I got out when the getting was good. When I saw the news yesterday I thought, 'That could have been me instead of Amy Louvenbragh.' And what's more, it was a miserable way to live. I used to sit there in that monument to Beatrice Butler and just cringe. It's kind of a non-museum, you know. There's no life in it. You can't dispose of the art works or acquire new ones. They have to be displayed just as they are forever. It's really a mausoleum. Add to that the way those works were acquired, through bribery, smuggling, theft, and it's really a pretty sordid place. I'm glad to be quit of it."

"I understand you're doing social work now," I said.

"It's honest. Frustrating, heartbreaking at times, but at least you don't have to put up with a silly bunch of rich pukes."

"Like Jack Butler?"

"I didn't mean Jack especially. He's one of the nicer ones, a real human being, actually. And he's got problems like the rest of us. No, I meant the trustees and the benefactors. You have to constantly kiss ass to try to get the funds to keep the place running. Such egos you couldn't imagine. You've got to court them like young hustlers on the make. They know what you're up to, and they're determined to cut the best deal they can, including enormous amounts of fawning, flattery and ongoing social deference. Of course, from the foundation's point of view, it's necessary. Beatrice Butler had no idea how much running the museum would cost."

"Is that why the collection wasn't insured?" I asked.

"You know, that's a good question. I tried to convince the trustees that we needed to insure. Of course, to insure the entire collection would be impossible. Let's say it's worth five billion dollars. Probably less, but let's say five. One billion in coverage would cost $5 million. The full five billion for twenty-five. Where's that money going to come from? But, and this was my argument, it's not necessarily all or nothing. You could get lower coverage, say for $50 million, at around $250,000 a year. That's better than nothing, and we could probably have afforded that, but the trustees could never agree. To them, not insuring the entire collection, or insuring it for less than its total value, was somehow demeaning. So we went without."

"Would it have made a difference?" I asked.

"The stuff they hit was probably under $50 million. So, yeah, it would've."

I looked into my cup. I was running out of coffee and questions at about the same time, but I still had one or two more to ask.

"Any possibility someone at the museum was involved in the theft?"

"I've thought about that one, too. Hard to say. I really didn't know Amy Louvenbragh. She came in after I left. Not the typical background for running the Butler, but she did well despite that. Have you met Fred Peavy?"

"Yeah, why?"

"Probably nothing. I like him, don't get me wrong. He's always on the job, works long hours, really dedicated, you know. But I didn't hire him. He was there when I arrived in 1987, and I understand his background was a little iffy."

"Iffy?" Iffy was an odd word to describe a museum security chief. "How so?"

"He left the police force in Baltimore during a period when there were some corruption hearings. Nothing in his formal record, and I checked it, believe me. But this was a time when there was a lot of drug money floating around. It was rumored some of his colleagues in Baltimore had been connected with hashish and heroin smuggling."

I had finished my coffee.

"Well, thanks for the brew. I also appreciate your candor."

"No problem. Good luck with the investigation."

"One more thing," I said. I had a flash of myself in a dirty trench coat like Peter Falk as Columbo chewing on a cold Schimmelpennick cigar .

"What's that?" he asked.

"Ever hear of a group called La Sardana?"

"A rock group?"

21
Saturday, March 20
Boston, Massachusetts

Outside it had started to snow. Wet snow in big flakes. I was way underdressed and decided to try to hail a cab. While I waited at the curb I cursed the Boston weather. It had begun as a gorgeous spring day, but it had slid back into winter. The old man was dying. He lay on his death bed, white hair at his temples, gripping the sheets, holding onto his fading life, not yet ready to give up the ghost. I felt like calling in the euthanasia squad. Meanwhile, no cab, and now mixed in with the snow was a fine, hard rain.

I tried to put my mind on other things. I thought about touring Amy's apartment with Kara Penny-Worth. It had been far too clean and tidy. Who had been there? I thought about the blonde woman following me. Could she have been connected to the Dutchman or La Sardana? Why was she following me?

I thought about Titus Moone leaving his career behind. Did he have some motive for revenge? He might have harbored some vindictive feelings about the museum trustees. Clearly he had no love for them. Yet, when we talked, it didn't seem he cared enough to strike out against the Butler, and he did seem to like Jack. I thought about Sam Bassett and wondered whether he'd called. He may have news about the

Dutchman. Had he heard of La Sardana? I thought about Elaine. I thought about Shiva. After last night with Elaine, I wasn't eager to talk to Shiva because I wasn't sure what I would say. I knew I was afraid to lose what I didn't yet have with Shiva. Round and round, my head was teeming with unanswered questions, with maybe's and might-could-be's.

Finally, I spied an empty cab, and I waved it into the curb. Shelter at last. I was chilled from standing in the wet snow with only a pair of jeans and a flannel shirt. The shirt was damp, but this cab had some heat. I relaxed on my way back to the hotel.

When I got there I took a long hot shower to ease out the chill. Wearing the terry cloth robe the hotel provided, I ordered some tea and sandwiches from room service. I checked messages again and found Sam Bassett had called again. Shiva, too. And Elaine. Sam's message said to call whenever I got in. It was after midnight in Barcelona. I placed the call and he picked up right away.

"Bassett here."

"Sam, hi! It's Tommy Shakespear. Not too late, I hope."

"Not too late. I'm still up. I'm just having a nightcap to relax before bed."

"Any news of the Dutchman?" I asked.

"Nothing. Vanished into thin air. We expect he'll be out of sight until he has a new game going in a new city. I'll be returning to London in a few days."

"Too bad. I was hoping you might have had some leads." This was not good news as far as I was concerned. "I've got to wrap up my investigation by Monday, Sam."

"I hear you've had a bit of trouble at the museum," he said.

"Amy Louvenbragh was murdered in her office. I was on my way to see her when it happened. I found the body."

"The name was familiar, Tommy. So I checked into it." He was way ahead of me. "Amy Louvenbragh was working at the last museum the Dutchman hit. A couple of Miros and a Picasso."

"In Germany?" I said. I recalled my conversation with Jack Butler yesterday at his club. He mentioned La Sardana had been involved in a theft of Miro and Picasso works in Germany.

"That's right. Quite a coincidence, isn't it." Sam was slurring his words a little, but it was quite late.

"Listen, Sam. There's one more thing I wanted to ask. The museum got some threatening letters, supposedly from an art terrorist group. La Sardana. Ever hear of it?"

"Yes. What letters?"

"The letters demanded return of all art works to their countries of origin. There were three of them. The last one threatened Amy. It arrived the day before she died."

"Where were they posted?" he asked.

"This is the part I don't like much," I said. "They were postmarked from Boston, Herndon, Virginia, and Barcelona. I was in each of those places on the day they were mailed."

"Someone seems to be shadowing you." I could hear the clink of ice cubes at the bottom of his drinking glass.

"Yeah, that's right. Any idea who? I'm fresh out of ideas."

"None here, but I'll pursue it, Tommy. Be careful. I don't think you have to worry about La Sardana, but there might be others in Boston who would want you out of the way now."

"No problem, Sam. Like I said, I'm off the case after tomorrow. Heading back to Santa Cruz."

"One thing of interest," Sam said. "We've learned a little more about one of the Dutchman's big customers. The one from out your way, the Silicon Valley entrepreneur I mentioned. Apparently, he's quite a jazz fanatic. And a saxophonist. No name yet, but we should have it before long."

It confirmed what Yards had said.

"Any luck with the passenger lists?" I asked. I needed to know who the visitor from Boston was.

"I did get the request in, but not until yesterday. It may be a few days until we hear. I'll call you from London."

"Okay, Sam. I'm listed in Capitola, California. Shakespear, no E at the end."

"Roger."

After I hung up the phone I thought about calling Shiva back, but I still didn't have my feelings sorted out. Of course, I thought, they might never be sorted out. So I called.

"Shiva." She was in.

"Tommy, at long last. Are you okay? I saw in the paper about the museum director. What's going on?"

"I don't really know. I'm in the middle of something. And it's too complicated to explain on the phone. But I'll be leaving Boston on Monday."

"For where?" she said.

"Home. It's over. At least as far as I'm concerned. Jack wants me to wrap things up by Monday noon. Amy Louvenbragh was his fiancée or girlfriend, whatever. He's too upset to continue with the investigation. Anyway. It's over."

"The paper said you found the body. You okay?"

"Yeah," I said. "I'm okay. But it would be better if I left town, I think. There are a few strange coincidences in this case,

Shiva. Not enough to amount to anything yet, but it's almost like someone is setting me up to take a fall."

"For what?"

"For killing Amy, for instance."

"What? Are you kidding? Tommy, I think you should leave Boston right away."

"Yeah, I know. I've got a few more things to check into, though. I'll be leaving Monday, like I said."

"Anything I can do?"

"Nothing really, Shiva. Just talk to me. I need to hear your voice."

We made small talk about the weather. I said I was getting tired of Boston in springtime, and Shiva talked about how beautiful it had been in Santa Cruz. Warm and dry and sunny every day. I really had begun to miss the good California weather. When I looked out my hotel room window I could see the snow had turned entirely to a cold freezing rain. But I knew I was avoiding talking to Shiva about the thing that was most on my mind. I hadn't worked out my feelings yet about Shiva and Elaine. So I ended the conversation with Shiva feeling unresolved and guilty. As much as I hated to admit it to myself, Elaine was here and now. And Shiva seemed so far away.

I called Elaine, and we agreed to meet for dinner at an upscale pizza place around the corner from my hotel. She walked in wearing tight black stretch pants and sleeveless top with a loose-knit sweater hanging seductively off one shoulder. I went up to her, took her hand and kissed her bare shoulder. We shared a look that I hoped no one else caught. I was thinking about what we might do to each other when, with exquisitely bad timing, a friend of hers walked up to us.

He was, more accurately, a friend of Whit's. Elaine introduced us, then excused herself to the ladies' room. There I was, standing in this fancy pizza joint with someone I didn't know at all. He knew me, though. About me, that is. He was the assistant D.A. investigating the Louvenbragh murder. Just my luck, I thought.

He was about my age, maybe a few years older, but clearly he'd taken a different route through life. He was well-groomed, neatly-trimmed, wore gold-rim glasses and other conventional yuppie garb, although I had to admire his shoes. They were beat-up pebble-grain bluchers the color of varnished oak. I stood there in my hiking boots, my black t-shirt, leather jacket and jeans, looking something less than respectable to him, it would seem.

"You know who I am, don't you?" he said.

"You're the ambitious young assistant who wants to be D.A.," I realized he looked like a young George Will.

"Thin ice, Shakespear. Let me tell you something. We have enough evidence now. It's just a matter of the paperwork."

"You're bluffing."

"No bluff. If I were you I'd get a lawyer. And that's the last free advice you're likely to get for a while." He laughed, pleased at his joke.

"By the way, Shakespear, there's no point in involving Elaine or Whit Winslow any further in your affairs," he continued. "You'll soon be socializing with an entirely different class of people." He stood there smirking.

I said nothing. Why bother? He'd come up just to tell me he was the guy on the end of my chain. And he'd soon be doing some yanking.

Elaine returned. I let her know we were leaving, and she said good-bye to the up-and-coming Mr. Assistant D.A.

"What was that all about?" she said. "I could feel the chill."

"Nothing much," I said. "We're just not meant for each other." I didn't want to get into it with Elaine and ruin the rest of the evening.

The rain had stopped, and a faint mist hung in the air, lending halos to the street lamps in the dusk of early evening. We walked a few blocks to a sandwich shop with a pink neon sign in the window. Formica-top tables and wooden straight-backed chairs inside. The place seemed several degrees too hot for comfortable eating, and very dry. I took off my jacket and sat sweating in my t-shirt and jeans. Elaine took off her sweater. A Greek woman with jet black hair and powdered-white skin said she would turn the heat down but it remained stuffy and hot. We ate our sandwiches and drank our tonics quickly and left.

We said very little in my hotel room that night. We lighted the candles I'd spread around the room and revisited our lovemaking. The night passed slowly, and we did not look ahead. But for me something had been spoiled. It was like coming back to a familiar cool place by a river in the shade of the willow trees, finding litter left behind by others. We both knew I would be leaving Boston soon. We both knew it was a good thing, too.

I woke alone again. The telephone's insistent ring broke into the vault where I had laid my head and pried open my eyelids. I took the receiver in my hand as though someone had handed it to me. I was still on automatic pilot when I heard Whit Winslow say, "Shakespear, is my wife Elaine there?"

I assumed it was a dream and hung up the phone, but moments later it rang again. Again I answered it, but this time I had an answer ready.

"She's not here," I said.

Unfortunately, it was not Whit Winslow this time.

"Who's not there?" she said.

"You're not, for one," I said, thinking as quickly as I could. It was Shiva.

"Very funny, Tommy. You sure you're alone?"

Shiva had called me because of what I had told her last night, to make sure I was okay. Wouldn't normally call this early, but she had to drive north to Sacramento on business and was worried about me. She offered to pick me up at the airport. Maybe she could meet me on her way back down from Sacramento. I said I'd call back and leave her a voicemail message when I knew my flight time. She was in a hurry, had to go, bye.

The message light on my phone was blinking when I hung up the phone. I was afraid it would be from Winslow, and I didn't want to talk to him, didn't even want to know there was a message that could lead to a confrontation. I padded into the shower and turned on the water, full force, hot. I had to get ready for breakfast with Charley Howell.

We met at the entrance to the restaurant downstairs. There was a woman standing by the hostess desk. She was dressed in khaki with low-cut leather hiking boots, pleated trousers, tan cotton top and a tan sleeveless vest with about fifteen pockets visible. It looked like she was planning to go on safari. It was Charley Howell.

As I looked at her, I realized Charley Howell was the tall, thin, pale, blonde-helmeted woman who'd been tailing me the day before. Different clothes, but the same woman. The same woman I'd imagined would have flat gray eyes behind those shades. She didn't. They were lime green, flecked with yellow.

The hostess led us to a table near a window a good distance away from others eating breakfast.

"I spoke with Fred Peavy a few minutes ago," she said. "He wanted me to brief you on La Sardana. He also said you'd be terminating on Monday, tomorrow, that is."

"Look, we haven't really been introduced," I said. "Tommy Shakespear." I reached out my hand tentatively, but there didn't seem to be one coming from her side of the table so I pulled it back.

"Let's cut the crap," she said. "I'm Charley Howell. You know all about me." Actually I didn't. "And I know all about you. We're not going to be friends, and we're not going to be business associates, either. If you don't mind, I'd like to get on with this. I've got other things to do."

Cling-clunk, clunk. She was trying to light her thin brown cigarette with an old Zippo lighter, but it wouldn't fire up.

"Okay. I thought we could share a few insights on the case. But you're right. My job is done, really. So what's there to know about La Sardana?" I was relieved to see the waiter approaching us with a silver coffee pot.

"Not much. La Sardana is a splinter group that split off from the Provos in the late sixties. There were three founding members. They moved to Barcelona in 1969 and took the name La Sardana, some sort of emblem of the native culture. Two of them, a man and a woman, were killed in an accidental explosion about a year later. They were presumably preparing a bomb for some offending museum. There was one survivor, a German art professor named Dieter Kockhorn. He has been underground for the past twenty-odd years."

"The Dutchman." I said. It was beginning to seem a lot clearer to me how things fit together. But there were still quite a few missing pieces.

I drank the cup of lukewarm coffee in a single gulp and poured myself a second cup. Charley Howell sat ignoring hers. She lit her cigarette with a book of matches and coughed. She pocketed the matches, but I could see the familiar neon-blue logo clearly from where I sat. Boot Hill.

22
Sunday, March 21
Boston, Massachusetts

"What do you know about the Dutchman?" she asked. The waiter had taken our breakfast orders and was now just out of earshot.

"We've met," I said. "One brief encounter at a farmhouse outside Barcelona. It was last Tuesday or Wednesday. I was blindfolded, or rather, hooded at the time, however."

"You saw nothing?"

"I saw a lot of shoes, floor, dirt, gravel, that sort of thing. I also saw stars. Courtesy of the Dutchman's friendly conversation. Look, can we get back to La Sardana? I'd like to know the connection between the art theft, La Sardana and the Dutchman. It seems to me that's the key to solving this case."

"That's really not your worry any longer, is it?" she said. "According to Fred Peavy, you're off the case."

She was right. What could I say? But it angered me to have her rub my nose in it.

"But since you asked," she went on, "my guess is this Dutchman, Dieter Kockhorn, is behind the art thefts. Once he closes the deal, he uses La Sardana to tidy things up. He can get rid of business associates he no longer wants around and throw up a smoke screen to distract the police."

"So he killed Amy Louvenbragh?"

"Possibly." She played with her lighter. Cling, chunk chunk.

"La Sardana's a front for the Dutchman's dirty work." I had already figured this out.

"That's the way I see it," she said. It was obvious Charley Howell knew more than she was saying. I would learn nothing more from her.

"Well," I said, "I guess that does it for me. I'll be heading back to Santa Cruz on Monday."

"How did you like playing detective?"

If the waiter hadn't arrived with our food at exactly that moment, I think I might have tossed my cup of coffee in her face. Life sometimes rescues you from making the wrong move. Not often enough, but sometimes.

The waiter came up full of energy and breakfasty good cheer. Orange juice and eggs over hard for Charley. Sausage on the side. OJ, yogurt and granola for me. He left a fresh pot of coffee and the check.

"Ms. Howell," I said. "You don't mind if I call you Ms. Howell?" She just looked at me and stubbed out her cigarette. "I'll have to admit that I'm new to it. Being a detective, that is. I don't have a lot of gray hairs, yet. No scars or old bullet wounds. But I have learned one thing. Most detectives aren't all that smart. They overlook things that would lead them to the solution a lot quicker and with a lot less violence. They overlook important clues."

"Oh, spare me," she said. I probably should have, but I was frustrated and pissed off.

"For instance," I said, "What about the monogram?"

"What monogram?" she said.

"The one Amy Louvenbragh drew in the pool of blood next to her body."

"I don't know what you're talking about."

"That's what I mean about detectives," I said. "Breakfast is on me, Ms. Howell."

I picked up the check wallet, stood and left her sitting there. On the way out, I put it on my bill.

I went up to my room to get my leather jacket. Out the window I could see frost on the ground in the Boston Common. It was the very first day of spring, and it looked like a chilly one. Before I left for the Butler Museum I checked for messages. Sam Bassett had called. I tried him and found him in.

He admitted that Interpol knew of the connection between the Dutchman and La Sardana. In fact, although it had been kept confidential, La Sardana left a note pinned to the two bodies found at La Sagrada Familia. That the Dutchman had conceded the murders clinched the connection in my own mind. Barcelona police had hushed it up, Sam said, because the big tourist season was approaching. They didn't want to alarm tourists with thoughts of terrorists in Barcelona.

I asked Sam whether he was familiar with Charley Howell, and Sam said no, he'd add that to his list of things I'd given him to do. Anything else from your public servant, he asked? Still nothing available on the airlines' passenger manifests, but he thought by Tuesday at the latest he'd have that for me. Sam was leaving for London in the morning. He would fax me from there. I gave him Shiva's fax number and made a mental note to buy a fax machine right after I ordered business cards.

Sam said something else before he hung up that troubled me. He said maybe I should leave Boston, too, before things got uncomfortable for me. I asked him what he meant, and he said only that he'd been hearing my name mentioned as a suspect in the murder and that the police had some hard evidence. I agreed to leave on Monday. We agreed to stay in touch. It had to be the notebook and pen, I thought to myself as I set the receiver back in its cradle.

I arrived at the Museum by cab a little before it opened. I had been pre-cleared at the employee entrance, and I passed into the museum and went directly to Fred Peavy's office. I passed the museum director's office on the way. Yellow tape. The murder scene was still posted off limits by Boston Police. I really didn't want to re-enter that door. I kept my eyes straight ahead as I walked past. I found Fred waiting at his desk. He was wearing a black velvet suit. Okay, but it took almost a minute for my eyes to adjust to the tie he was wearing. It featured red and blue diamonds in a pattern apparently designed to induce a hypnotic trance.

"What's the occasion, Fred?"

"Don't ask, Tommy," he said. "Don't ask. Cause if you asked, I'd have to tell you about my wife and her hobby. No, no, hobby's not quite the right word. Obsession, that's more like it. I'd have to tell you about my wife and her obsession with china doll painting, and then, of course, the Crafts Fair at the Hines Auditorium, and the big soiree we are going to this afternoon over at the Marriott, and I really don't want to do that. It might put me in a bad mood."

It looked like it already had. "Okay, I won't ask. Besides, I have even more unpleasant things to talk about."

"Let's get to it. I'm in a hurry. By the way, you should know Jack's instructed me to work with you only until tomorrow. He says you're off the case."

"True. I'm probably wasting my time with this. Jack seems to have lost interest since Amy was killed. He wants to put it out of his mind. But I still have some unanswered questions banging around in my head. Like, where is the murder weapon? How did the killer get in and out unseen? Are we overlooking any evidence?"

"Another thing before we get started," he said. "The cops have been here poking around. I've been questioned here and down at the station. A lot of the questions were about you. Who you were, when you became involved, what your role was in the investigation of the theft. I got the feeling they were looking at you as a suspect."

Fred tried to smile, but it was like he was saying "It's fucked up, but that's the way the world works sometimes."

"I've been hearing that a lot lately myself. I think somebody has put them onto me, set me up to take a fall maybe. I hear there might be some politics involved. The DA retiring, another ambitious assistant in line to take his place."

"I ever tell you how I came to Boston?"

"No." I thought about what Titus Moone had said about Fred Peavy's sudden departure from the Baltimore police department.

"Maybe I will sometime." He thought better of it and changed the subject. "How about we take a look at the apartment?"

I had asked about the apartment yesterday when I set up the meeting. It seemed like a place that the police could have overlooked. Amy Louvenbragh had lived there until the theft. The museum was converting it into office space. Maybe the killer got in and out through the apartment. It seemed worth checking into.

"Cops check it out?" I asked.

"No," he said. "They didn't. Tell you the truth, it slipped my mind, too. But when you asked about it, I took a quick look around. Didn't find a thing."

He unlocked the door to the stairway leading up to the former home of Aunt Beatrice Butler and her successor occupants, the museum directors since her death.

"Watch out for stuff on the floor. You could trip or slip on something the workmen left behind."

"Then if I fell and hurt myself, I could sue the Butler Foundation for many millions."

"Right," he said.

"While I'm being prosecuted for the murder of its museum director."

"That would be ironic," he said.

"You mean mo-ronic, I think," I said. "Of course, the Butler Foundation doesn't have many millions."

I took a look around the large main living room. Traces of its former opulence remained. Antique wainscoting and wall paper, inlaid parquet flooring, a crystal chandelier hanging from the ceiling high above. All around were boxes and stacks of decorative art.

"Not quite ready to move into," I said.

"Another few weeks, probably. There's some more construction in one or two of the other rooms. Phone lines and lighting changes mostly."

"Is there an outside entrance?"

"Inside and outside, same key will open both locks. It's a master key of sorts." He handed it to me. It looked like any key. "Also fits the director's office."

"Anyone else been up here since the murder?"

"Not that I know of. We put a hold on construction until the police release the murder scene. It's still taped off, so..."

"Who has keys?" I asked.

"Several people, unfortunately. Dr. Louvenbragh had hers. Jack, of course. One or two others on the museum board."

"What's that?" I spotted something black and square on the window sill behind Fred. He reached out and picked it up. It was a matchbook.

"Just a matchbook," he said. "Probably a workman left it." He opened the cover. "Yeah," he said. "What I thought, empty. Somebody tossed it. Why?"

"Let me guess" I said. "Boot Hill." I recognized the cowboy boot logo.

"You win, but what's the prize?"

"I don't know. Can I have it?" I turned it over and looked at it, mentally comparing it to the matchbook I'd found at the Dutchman's farmhouse and the one Charley Howell had used to light her cigarette. It could be coincidence, of course. Boot Hill is a very popular place. But it could also be a link to the Dutchman and the murders. And with somebody who had been in Barcelona recently. Somebody other than me, that is.

"Take it with my compliments." I pocketed the matchbook.

"Sure that nobody else's been up here recently?"

"I doubt it," he said. "We've kept it locked and the renovation crew hasn't been here since Thursday afternoon."

"There is an outside door. Someone could get up here after hours if they had a key."

"Yeah. That's a possibility," he said. "I probably should have the locks changed." Then it dawned on him. "You know, it just occurred to me. We never changed the lock. I mean when Dr. Moone left. Of course, we should have, but when Dr. Louvenbragh arrived she just moved in. Moone may still have a key."

"Fred," I said, "I'll let you get on to your party. But there's one thing I need to ask. Earlier you said something about why you came to Boston, implying there was something going on in your life. Dr. Moone mentioned it to me yesterday. I'd like to ask you what that was."

He shrugged as if to say, "I might as well," and began. "There was some drug dealing going on in the department in Baltimore. Several people, fairly high up knew about it, may have been getting a cut. It went on for quite a while, and then somebody got greedy. A cop was found in his patrol car with a bullet between his eyes. His wife went public with what he had told her. Everything started to unravel. I wound up getting blamed. The dead cop was my partner. I had to retire on disability."

"Sorry," I said. "Dr. Moone suggested you might have been involved."

"He shouldn't go around spreading rumors."

"It stops with me."

"While we're at it," he said, "I have something you might find interesting. Titus Moone was forced out of the museum by the trustees. He was allowed to resign for personal reasons, and he made public statements about devoting his life to public service. But I'll never forget the day the trustees asked him to resign. I heard him walking through the admin wing ranting about the 'rich know-nothing assholes who rule the people's culture.' Those were his words, more or less, as I recall. When he finally left, he told Carole, his secretary, he'd get his revenge. Of course, no one took him seriously. He was emotional. A good museum director, but very emotional."

"He'd get his revenge, huh?"

"Yeah, but like I said. No one took him seriously."

"Maybe they should have," I said. "He had a key, opportunity, and revenge for his motive."

"Say, Shakespear," said Fred. "You're getting pretty good at this."

"You think so? I have my doubts."

"Yeah, I do," he said. "But watch out for the Boston cops. You really have no idea what motivates them. And sometimes it goes a funny way."

As we walked out my attention was caught by an open crate of red metal canisters. Fire extinguishers.

"Expecting a fire, Fred? Or, should I say, several fires?" Markings on the side indicated there were twenty fire extinguishers in the crate. I picked one up, turned it in my hands.

"It's the new fire code. Wall-mounted, one per room. Downstairs in the museum, too," he said.

"Making the world safe for great art," I said.

Fred took the canister from me and put it back in the crate. He turned toward me.

"Believe me, Shakespear, nothing is safe in this world."

23
Sunday, March 21
Boston, Massachusetts

The sky had darkened while I'd been inside the Butler. Thick clouds had congealed into a gray, colorless mass overhead. Another spring snow storm seemed a good possibility as I stood at the curb hoping a cab would happen by. It was cold and growing colder. I zipped my leather jacket all the way up and thrust my fists into the side pockets, doing a little dance to get the blood flowing. Maybe, I thought to myself, heading back to California isn't such a bad idea. The weather's warmer for one thing. I have friends and a new life building. What do I have here? No firm leads in this case, a matchbook from Boot Hill, an affair with a married woman that leaves me feeling sleazy. Worse yet, I am becoming a suspect in the very crime I am investigating.

As I shivered waiting for a cab, I kept thinking about Charley Howell. Something at the back of my mind kept trying to find its way into the light. Something about the prowler in my room when I first arrived in Boston. A woman, Sam Bassett had said. Charley Howell is a woman. Something about finding Boot Hill matchbooks at the Dutchman's farm house and in the Butler Museum. Charley Howell is a smoker. Maybe she mislaid her Zippo or it wasn't working. And the woman following me to Titus Moone's place turned out to be Charley

Howell. Working on another aspect of the case, Jack Butler had said. And what about Jack Butler? I really didn't want to speculate about Jack, but the facts kept pointing to him.

Finally a cab stopped and I crawled into a cocoon of warmer air. On the way back to the hotel, as my circulation resumed with a tingle at the skin and a warm melting through to my toes, snowflakes drifted down through the cold and gloom. I knew I was getting close to a breakthrough in this case, but I was afraid it would be too late. Job over as of tomorrow. Cops closing in on me. If Sam Bassett was right, I had to get out of Boston in the next twenty-four hours, or else. Besides, if I implicated Jack, I'd never get paid. And who would believe me, anyway?

I packed my things as soon as I got back to the hotel. I called Hank Greenberg at his apartment, hoping to find another place to stay, out of the eyes of the police and away from Charley Howell, but he was still out of town. Suddenly, I realized the phone was probably tapped, so I left him a message that I'd be staying in Boston for another week, or so. No need to alarm anyone. I told him to call me back when he got in.

Before I left Boston, before I went anywhere, I had to say good-bye to Elaine. I wasn't sure where we stood with each other. The past two days had been intense, to say the least. We'd started something up again, and I had to find a way to ease it back down. I called Elaine, and she was at home. Would she be free in an hour or so? The Four Seasons piano bar was a nice place for a drink. Okay, meet you in an hour, she said. Winslow was apparently still tied up with his business deal. I had to ask her if that was really him on the phone this morning. She'd seen him for breakfast and he'd said nothing.

No, it must have been a dream, she said. A nightmare, I said, the shortest nightmare on record.

I got there early. The piano player had just come on. He was tall, skinny and about thirty-six, with curly red hair thinning on top. Wore a tux and played bebop like he was trying to catch up to it. It was a stretch. All the notes were there, mostly, but he had to reach out for them. I listened to see if he'd get it, eventually, and after the first couple of tunes he made it all the way there. It was on a Thelonius Monk tune called "Between the Devil and the Deep Blue Sea" off the *Straight, No Chaser* album. Maybe I liked it because that's where I was.

I'd made up my mind to tell Elaine good-bye. Of course I was leaving town, but it was more than that. Something had flared up between us, and I knew it wasn't love. We had stumbled into something again that could only mess us up, if we let it. I had to talk it through with her, if only to get an understanding of what was happening that I could live with. That we could both live with.

Elaine walked in just as the piano player segued into another Monk tune, "I Didn't Know About You." I had to imagine the horn part, but the song couldn't have been any more apt. Elaine was wearing a black cocktail dress, no jewelry except for her wedding ring. She walked right up to me. I stood to greet her, and we kissed. Casual, familiar. Her lips were cool. We broke the kiss after letting it go on just long enough. Elaine smiled and shook her head. Not again, I thought. We settled back into our lounge chairs. I looked over at her and wondered if I could do what I knew I needed to.

We made small talk, snow in the weather forecast. The waitress brought us our drinks. White wine for Elaine and cranberry juice, a slice of lime for me.

"I had breakfast with Charley Howell this morning," I said. "In the first place, she was not what I expected, being a she, that is. I'd assumed Charley would be a man."

"She does have her mannish qualities."

"How well do you know her?"

"Not at all well, really. She's not in our circle, Tommy, but Jack's had her working on the case for over two years now. I think Fred Peavy recommended her. Or checked out her credentials or something. Anyway, she's supposed to be this great investigator, but she hasn't turned up anything. That's why Jack hired you."

"I think you had something to do with Jack hiring me, Elaine," I said. "Besides, with everything that's happened, Jack's laid me off. I'm being chased out of town, and she's still on the job."

"I still can't believe Amy's dead."

"Me either, and I don't buy that business about art terrorists either. La Sardana? Give me a break."

"Who'd want to kill her?" Elaine said.

"It had to be the Dutchman. Suppose Amy had been on the inside, and he decided to tidy up. My money would be on the Dutchman."

"If you had any money," she said.

"The only real question is, who's working this end of things. Someone has to be the local guy, someone close to the museum. Which reminds me," I said, "How can I get in touch with Yards?"

"Try information. He's living with someone named Kavanagh in Wollaston. That's without a U."

"C or K?"

"K."

I thought of the letter Amy had drawn in the blood on her office floor.

"Do you have a pen?" I asked. I drew the shape as I remembered it on a cocktail napkin and showed it to Elaine. "What does this look like to you?"

"Why?"

I told her what Raymond had shown me and why it mattered. "It means she was still alive when the killer left," I said. "So I couldn't have done it. See?"

"Unless you came back."

"Yeah, well."

I hadn't considered the possibility.

"You know," Elaine said, "It reminds me of the way Amy used to doodle when you talked to her."

I had seen that on my first meeting with her. She was drawing something that looked like a T.

"Is it a familiar doodle? Did she draw this one often?" I said, retracing the image I had drawn.

"No, but it looks something like the monogram she designed for Jack. JB sort of combined. One long nearly vertical line curving left for the J, and the B loops growing out of it. Like this," she said.

Elaine drew the monogram. It did looked a little like the thing Amy had traced in her blood. "Sort of like a 12. Jack had some shirts made with the design on his cuffs."

Suddenly the puzzle began to look like something. Enough pieces had come together to suggest an overall design.

"You don't seriously think," Elaine said, "That Jack could have had anything to do with Amy's death?"

"It occurred to me."

"It's really impossible, Tommy. He loved her."

"Maybe so. Suppose Amy had been involved from the beginning."

"And?" she said.

"Never mind...no, that wouldn't do it." I was having a hard time working up a plausible scenario. "Wait, I've got it. Suppose Jack was the inside man. Suppose Amy found out about the theft and confronted Jack. He would've had no choice. And maybe if he discovered Amy's affair with your charming husband, he could kill two birds, as they say."

"Awful. And I don't believe it, Tommy. Not for a minute."

"Well, I wish I had another suspect. I don't like it any better than you do."

"Have you checked into any other possibilities? Other suspects?" Elaine said.

"The short list is Jack Butler, number one. Behind door number two is Dr. Titus Moone, disgruntled former museum employee. Door number three, Fred Peavy, head of museum security, ex-cop with a cloudy background. And then, of course, there's you, Elaine. Let's see. What would your motive be?"

"Not funny, Tommy."

"Amy's affair with Whit?"

"Fuck you."

"Sorry, Elaine."

"Maybe you think it would be easier for us to be mad at each other. Not speaking. Just walk away, so you wouldn't have to face yourself and how confused you are about us."

The piano player took a break. He walked over to a table where some of his friends were sitting.

"I've thought about it a lot the past few days," she continued.

I sipped at my drink and took it in.

"Maybe I shouldn't have married Whit, but I shouldn't have married you either, Tommy. I'm probably not the wife type. Not your typical wife anyway. I know I haven't exactly been constant and chaste. Maybe I should have tried harder to be, you know, good, but it never felt that way to me. I've always gone by my feelings."

"Not always, Elaine."

I drained my glass and set it down on the table.

"Don't spoil it, Tommy. Being with you these past few days was as good as anything we had that summer on the Vineyard, but it's not a forever kind of thing."

"And now I'm leaving," I said.

"And that's just what I mean. Why should I have married you? No steady job. You're in trouble with the cops. I mean, really, Tommy, not a good bet."

She smiled when she said it, and I wasn't entirely sure she believed what she said.

"You really don't love Whit either," I said.

"Maybe I do, Tommy, but it's not like Family Circle or Leave It To Beaver. We have a life together, and it's a good life. Whit's not everything to me, I'll grant you that. But we enjoy what we have, and we're going to keep it going. We had a long talk about it today, and we agreed to work some things out."

Elaine surprised me. Committed to her marriage was not what I expected.

"Besides," she said, "What about your friend back home?"

"Shiva?"

"Shiva. The woman you're in love with, remember?"

"Elaine, in the past few days maybe I've lost track of myself. I don't really know what I feel right now. You always had that effect on me."

"That doesn't have to go away, Tommy. It means a lot to me to have that feeling with you."

"Jesus, Elaine," I said, "How do you sort it out? I mean, I can keep my mind only on one person at a time. "

"I just meant I won't forget you, Tommy," Elaine said. "And I don't think you'll forget me." She smiled as if she had something on me. I was getting dizzy sitting there listening to her. Either there was an echo in the room, or we were going around in circles. I had to break out of it.

"No, I won't forget," I said. And I knew I wouldn't.

In the lobby we hugged and kissed good-bye like old friends, even if a lot was still unresolved, and I went up to my room to get my luggage. The hotel operator had a message from Sergeant Raymond. I wrote down the number for later, waited a few minutes and walked out through a side exit. No point in attracting attention, if the cops were watching the lobby. Or if the front desk were to notify the cops on my checking out. I needed the next twenty-four hours for a few final errands before I left town.

The snow had begun to accumulate on the sidewalk, an inch or so, so far. In the cab I shook snow out of the grooves in my hiking boots. It sat on the floor of the cab in clumps like little white Monet wheat stacks blown down by the wind. Or tiny sand dunes. That was it, I thought, tiny sand dunes.

24
Monday, March 22
Boston, Massachusetts

Something was pricking the skin at my ankle. I lifted my head to see and, as I did, the dusty, faintly beer-tinged fabric of the TV-room couch peeled away from my face. I touched the indentations of the fabric pattern which had pressed into my cheek and kicked gently at the kitten clawing at my feet. Hank Greenberg's cat "Kaline," named for the Detroit Tigers baseball player, had taken my stocking feet for a clawing post. I meant the gentle kicks to dissuade him from further clawing, but they only stimulated his interest. Finally I rolled over, picked up the feline Kaline, and set him on my chest as I sat up more awake than I wanted to be at such an early hour.

Hank had returned from Florida on an evening flight to find me shivering on his doorstep with my suitcase for company. We greeted each other like long-lost brothers, which in a way we were. Hank was a few years older than I, but even when I was working for him, we were on a first-name basis and worked together like colleagues. His easy-going law practice always seemed more like a way of pulling in cash so that Hank could indulge in his sports passions, if truth be told, than the shark-infested, chum-strewn waters most urban law firms have become. Despite the fact that he was at the top of his class at Harvard Law School, serious money was never

Hank's motivation. Hank was a true eccentric and without affectation.

We ate kielbasa sandwiches and sampled a selection of non-alcoholic beers, while we watched a SportsChannel special on the coming baseball season. The Red Sox once again looked promising. If Roger Clemens had another Cy Young season, they said, then the Sox would be real contenders, if only there were a little better relief pitching, that is, and some more power hitting in the middle of the lineup. On it went into the early hours. I ducked out once to call Yards at the Kavanagh place in Wollaston, but he was out for the evening so I left Hank's number. It was well past midnight before I could tell Hank what had been going on. Needless to say, he was amazed at how much trouble I had gotten into during the week I'd been in Boston.

"Even if the police can link you to the La Sardana threat letters, I don't see how they can establish that you had a motive for murder. Better yet, there's no weapon, so where's the case? On the other hand," he said, "I think you jeopardize your position by leaving town. It can only worsen the appearance of guilt. If the police want to arrest you, you should probably turn yourself in."

Great, I thought. Maybe I do need one of those amoral, money-grubbing sharks, instead of Hank. I borrowed Hank's old Underwood typewriter and made up a two-page summary report and billing statement for Jack Butler's lawyer. I figured I should get the money sooner than later, in case the cops came knocking, so I decided to be on the doorstep with the bill when Ted Wycliffe, Esquire showed up for work. I debated calling Sergeant Raymond. That could wait until morning. Yards hadn't called back. I figured that could wait too. I was lying on Hank's dusty, smelly couch as I did all that deep thinking at around one-thirty a.m. The next thing I knew the kitten was clawing at my ankle, and it was early morning.

Hank was gone already. An early riser usually, I recall how he'd get into the office before everybody else and then sit there waiting for us, reading the sports pages, eating bagels he'd bought at Kupel's and drinking coffee by the pint. He'd left me the makings of breakfast and a fresh pot of coffee. I didn't know whether to feed the kitten, but I rummaged the cupboards anyway, found a small can of assorted animal parts in gravy and put the feedbag on for Kaline, while I drank coffee and thought about how I needed a plan.

It looked to me like I had to find an inconspicuous way out of town. If the cops had a warrant for my arrest, they'd probably already notified the airlines and car rental agencies at Logan airport. I considered taking a train or a bus, but the thought of five days traveling cross-country deflated that one. Midway through my second bagel, I realized that what I needed was a way out of Boston to, say, New Hampshire or Connecticut, where I could hop a plane to Chicago and then on to San Jose. That way I could avoid being nabbed at Logan while waiting for my row to be called for boarding. I had an open first class return which I could exchange. All I really needed was a way to the airport. Yards? He could probably turn up a car on fairly short notice. The only problem was I wasn't actually guilty of anything yet, so why get into stolen property? I decided I'd see if I could talk Hank into driving me out of the state.

The other thing I needed was cash. If I could get to Jack Butler's lawyer with my bill before the cops did, I could pick up my check. Hank would turn it to cash for me, and off I'd go. It seemed pretty simple. I was in the early stages of caffeine glow, midway between cups number two and three, when God is in his heaven and all's right with the world.

I took a long shower, but not a particularly satisfying one. Hank, it seemed, was using one of those water-miser showerhead inserts. Politically correct, yeah, but it made for a lousy shower, and because the water came out at a trickle, I had to run it forever to get the soap off my body and the shampoo out of my hair. Worse yet, his part of Boston had the kind of water that doesn't take the soap off easily. So, the net result was I used more water, not less, and came out feeling sticky.

While dressing I noticed I'd left some clothes behind at the hotel in my hasty exit. I had to make do with once- or twice-worn jeans and a cotton sweater. I looked outside. Not raining, but heavy, cold and damp. During the night, the snow had turned to rain, and the rain had washed away all traces of the fluffy white stuff. Up above, the sky was the color of a spare tire. I put on my hiking boots and leather jacket, grabbed the case report and bid a good-bye meow to Kaline.

It was twilight, brightening toward dawn as I slipped into the street. The phone was ringing, and it continued ringing while I stood outside listening to it, waiting for it to stop. Finally I had to move away from it. I walked with false resolution toward the subway and my encounter with Ted Wycliffe.

I was just inside the outer doors to the Harvard Square building that housed Wycliffe and Marks, when Jack Butler's lawyer came in from the street. He noticed me with a start, with the kind of reaction you have when someone who might be a mugger enters your peripheral vision. He was wearing one of those floppy Irish wool hats that make you look ridiculous no matter who you are.

"Oh, it's you, Shakespear." He smiled nervously, not quite sure I wasn't a mugger. Then, as if to assure I meant no harm to him, he invoked my first name. "Tommy, isn't it?"

"It is, Ted. How are you this morning?" I smiled back at him.

"Oh, fine, fine," he said, fumbling with his keys. "And you?"

"Been worse," I said.

At the moment I couldn't recall a time when it had been worse. Unless it was when I found Amy Louvenbragh's body. Wycliffe stood there with his arms wrapped around his briefcase, a newspaper stuffed into his trench coat pocket, while his fingers fumbled through his keys. I looked down at his feet to see whether he had those shiny oxbloods on.

Yep, and he hadn't forgotten to wear his rubbers, either. I wondered if he kept a shoe brush in his bottom drawer to give them a quick buffing when he took the rubbers off.

I followed Wycliffe into his outer office. He set a few things down on his secretary's desk and began turning on lights. No one was in yet, except us chickens.

"I brought the final report. Jack asked me to wind things up as of today. I've summarized my findings and tabulated the expenditures and billings. It's only a few thousand over the advance. I'd appreciate a check now if you don't mind." Actually, I was very close to desperate. I hoped Ted Wycliffe wouldn't give me any trouble.

"Well, of course, I'll have to review these figures and discuss it with Jack Butler. You realize we have to follow procedures," he said, adjusting his glasses.

"I've already been over this with Jack. He assured me there would be no delay with reimbursement." This would be my last attempt at civil reasoning. I could feel myself starting to boil.

"By the way, Shakespear," Wycliffe said, "Have you seen today's paper? Apparently, the police are close to making an arrest for the Louvenbragh murder. Take a look." He handed me the folded tabloid and turned to remove and hang up his trench coat and hat.

I peeled apart the wet pages to see the headline he'd referred to, then skipped down to paragraph three where I read aloud, "Speculation centered on an unemployed short-order cook from out of state who had been befriended by...." A moment later I looked up to see Wycliffe dialing a telephone in one of the offices off the anteroom.

I set the paper down on top of his briefcase and walked toward Wycliffe to confront him. When I got close enough to hear what he was saying it was clear he had dialed 911 to rat me out. I grabbed the phone in my left hand, and with my right open hand I shoved at Wycliffe under his chin, snapping his jaw shut mid-sentence, sending him staggering backward. I hung up the phone and slammed the weasel lawyer up against an enormous wall of books.

"Now let's get serious," I said, twisting his necktie. "I want you to write out a check for what Jack Butler owes me. And if you think I was the bastard who tore up Amy Louvenbragh, you don't want to find out what I can do to you."

"Okay," he said, choking, "The checkbook is—top drawer." I hadn't realized I was strangling him.

As I opened the drawer and removed the checkbook, Wycliffe's phone began to ring. I told him to answer it. It was 911 calling back. He made some noises into the phone about how it had been a mistake, no, no emergency, just a mistake, nothing serious, really, no really. Then he hung up, and I handed him a pen and he wrote out the check. Just as simple as that. I thanked Mr. Wycliffe for his cooperation, and I told him it had been a pleasure doing business with him. As I walked out of his office and through the anteroom toward the street, I was giddy with the realization that violence really can do wonders, if you're in a hurry. And I was in a hurry. I could hear police sirens less than a block away.

25
Monday, March 22
Boston, Massachusetts

Fortunately, there was a well-placed alleyway to one side of the Wycliffe and Marks office building, and I scooted through and then down the street parallel but in the opposite direction, away from the cops and their sirens. By the time I reached the subway I had worked up a heavy sweat. The sun was just getting up, and its rays cast a blue-gray light through the maze of low-rise buildings in Harvard Square. I began to feel dirty and somewhat uneasy.

As I slipped through the turnstile and stood on the platform waiting for the next train to Allston, I wondered why. It wasn't because of the shower, although my skin was probably swimming in soap and sweat. It wasn't because of the cops or their sirens, though I still could feel my heart pumping hard from the fear and exertion. It was because of the violence.

I'd had similar feelings in Barcelona after cracking into Onion Breath and escaping with him locked in the trunk, although at the time I hadn't realized why. Now as it came into focus, I realized that violence toward other people had made me a little queasy, and despite the initial exhilaration, the rush of power, it left me with feelings of disgust. No matter how much I despised that lawyer Wycliffe, smacking him around had cost me something.

I took the train across the Charles River to Hank's office in Allston where I found him behind the sports pages eating a bagel and drinking coffee. Needless to say, he was appalled at the story I told him of my encounter with Wycliffe. I tried to soften it by admitting how I felt about it, but that did no good.

"And what's more," he said, "You've probably now got assault and battery added to the other charges."

"You mean, they're going to hit me for murder and assault, too? Sorry, Hank, somehow the assault charge seems pale next to first degree murder."

"Yes, but consider how it complicates appearances. With the assault charge you look more guilty than without it." I thought about that one for a minute.

"How about the check? I need to cash it," I said. "Can you help me out there?"

"I've got some cash in the office safe I can let you have. I'll hold the check until later. I imagine that your friend Wycliffe will put a stop payment on it as soon as the bank opens."

"I don't suppose you'd drive me to the airport in New Hampshire."

"Nashua?" he said.

"I figure I can get a plane to Chicago from there and then on to San Jose by this evening. I don't want to chance Logan. The cops might have it staked out."

"Tommy, I want to advise you against it. You've already complicated things by assaulting the lawyer.

"We could probably argue that was self-defense. Say he attacked me with a wet newspaper, and I had to defend myself."

"Never mind that, Tommy, I want you to think about surrendering to the police. You've told me you may have an ally in Sergeant Raymond. We'll call him and arrange to go in to the station."

"I don't think so, Hank."

"I can't drive you to the airport. I'm not about to risk disbarment by transporting you across state lines, running from the police who have a warrant for your arrest. First degree murder. Forget it. You're a fugitive."

"Yeah, but I'm innocent," I said.

"So tell it to the judge."

That was that. He'd give me the money, but no way he'd take me to the airport in New Hampshire. He would, however, let me use the phone, and so I called Sergeant Raymond, just to see how things were.

"They made you for those threatening letters, Shakespear. The paper from your notebook, your pen. Not to mention the handwriting analysis. There's a warrant out for your arrest."

"Any fingerprints?" They'd forged my handwriting liked they'd forged the paintings.

"No prints," he said. "Where are you now?"

"No way. Look, what about the videotape you showed me? Doesn't that prove I didn't kill Amy? She had to be alive to draw in her blood."

"I thought about it some more," he said. "You could have come back to see if she was dead."

"You don't believe that."

"What I believe or don't believe don't make shit of a difference, Mr. Shakespear. We have courts for that. I'm just a cop."

"First degree murder?" I said

"Second degree murder, extortion, conspiracy, grand larceny," he said. It sounded as though he might keep going on indefinitely.

"What happened to loitering with intent?"

Hank gestured to me that I should hang up the phone. I didn't know how long it would take the police to trace the call so I said good-bye. No sense implicating Hank.

"I'll be in touch," I said.

"Don't call us. We'll call you," he said. Sergeant Raymond had a sense of humor after all.

Hank left the room to use the bathroom and get some more coffee. I took the opportunity to call Yards. He was asleep, according to the woman who answered the phone. She didn't sound any too awake, herself. But I insisted she get him, and she did, though it took a while. I didn't want Hank to hear any of it so I began to get antsy. I listened to the toilet flush in the other room, and then a little while later the door open and close. Then Yards came on the line.

"What."

"Sorry to bother you so early, but it's urgent," I said

"Who is this?" He did not sound pleased.

"Tommy Shakespear, Elaine's friend. We met the other night. The Butler art theft, you remember?"

"It's too fucking early for chatter. What do you want?"

"I need a car. I'll pay $500, but I've got to get out of town immediately, if not sooner. A little misunderstanding with the cops."

"You do it?"

"Do what?"

"Never mind," he said. "Meet me at the Buzzy's Roast Beef sign around noon. You know the bridge that looks like salt and pepper shakers? And have the cash. A thousand bucks, fifties or smaller. Understand?" Hank walked in sipping his coffee.

"Okay. See you then." I hung up and let out a lungful of breath.

"Who was that?" said Hank.

"Car rental company."

"Which one?" Hank sounded suspicious.

"Buzzy's." I pulled the first name I could think of out of the air. "Not one of the big ones," I said. "I figure the cops have them all wired."

I left Hank's around ten with eighteen hundred dollars in cash and headed back to his place to pick up my stuff. It only took ten minutes to pack, so I had a couple of hours to kill until I met Yards. Kaline wasn't doing anything so I spent the time with him. We watched a morning talk and variety show on TV, played with a yarn ball and discussed whether abstract art was humanistic or merely decorative. Baseball did not come up, except when Kaline mentioned a Leroy Neiman painting of Nolan Ryan. I might have imagined that. The time flew.

At twelve noon I was waiting for Yards at the Buzzy's Roast Beef sign near the Salt-n-Peppershaker Bridge. At twelve thirty I was still waiting. At a quarter past one, Yards pulled up at the curb in a red Subaru that was so grimy I hesitated before touching the door handle. It looked like it'd spent the past year in a mine shaft.

"Get in," he said, and I did.

"Whew!" There was nothing else to say. The car stank of Patchouli. I sat in it and looked around. A Grateful Dead sticker on the glove box, fast food bags and cartons littering the back seat, dirty clothes in a brown paper bag behind the driver's seat. After I set my suitcase down on top of the fast food cartons, I opened the ashtray and found a gathering of roaches. Not the kind that haunt your kitchen late at night, either.

"Got the money?" he said.

"Where were you? It's after one."

"Had to get some gas."

I handed Yards a thousand in fifties and twenties, and he counted it, smiling when he found it all there.

"That's it," he said. "It's yours, man. Be kind."

We got out of the car and walked around the car to check it out like you do at a real rental place. No major dents. I adjusted the driver's seat and got in. I started the car. Quarter tank. He sure didn't put much in.

Yards knocked at the passenger side window. I leaned over and rolled it down.

"Oh," he said, casually, "One more thing. I know things are hot enough for you as it is, but I heard something you might like to know."

"What's that?" I said.

"The murder victim. Amy Louvenbragh. She was working for the Feds."

"The Feds? Wait a minute. She was an art historian."

"FBI. Undercover," he said. "They recruited her as an informant at the museum."

"Amy was working for the FBI? So now I'm..."

"Explains why she was killed, maybe. At least that's the word I heard. The local cops and the FBI have been tripping all over each other to find a suspect. Way I hear it, the cops like you for it, but the FBI don't. That's why they haven't moved to tie you up yet."

"Wait a minute, Yards. How come you know this?"

"You'd be surprised if you knew who I talk to. Shakespear, you headed to the coast?"

"Maybe."

"Dutch art, right? Remember I told you the buyer was in Silicon Valley? I hear he's a jazz musician."

"I'm outta here, Yards," I said. "Thanks."

"No problem." Yards patted the pocket where he had the cash, then turned and got lost in the crowd on the sidewalk. I pulled into traffic and headed north to the Nashua airport.

As it turned out there was no Nashua airport. I found that out from the gas station attendant who refused to let me pull into the full service lane. He suggested a car wash down the street, and when I protested I had a plane to catch at the Nashua airport he gave me a strange look.

"You'll be waitin' a long time for that plane. Use the self-service lane. That car needs a sand blastin'. I aint touchin' it."

He gave me directions to the Manchester airport when I paid for the oil and gas. Eight-fifty. It took two full quarts and part of a third to bring the level up to the normal range. The car did smell like a rubber-tire bonfire. I wondered how much oil it burned and how much it leaked. I could already see a few drops on the pavement under the car. After throwing out the fast food cartons and the brown bag full of clothing, I drove off toward Manchester leaving a stinky cloud of black smoke behind.

I caught the first plane to Chicago from Manchester and changed planes there for San Jose. I had to change airlines, too, as I'd missed my connection on United. The ticket cost me seven hundred and twenty bucks and change. Not the best fare, but not the worst either. Anyway it left me with less than seventy five. Luckily, Shiva was home when I called from Chicago. She had a yoga class, but could pick me up afterwards. We didn't linger on the phone. We left a lot of things unsaid. I could tell she was dying to do the "I told you so, Tommy" routine, but mercifully she withheld it. We met by the luggage carousel at San Jose Airport. I was removing a greasy hamburger wrapper from the side of my suitcase where it must have hitched a ride clear across country. Shiva was all business.

"Tommy, let's get you out of here as quickly as possible. From what you've told me, there might already be a warrant for your arrest out here."

"Okay," I said, still not comprehending. "Take me home."

"Not home, you mail-order shamus. I've got to hide you out."

On the drive to Santa Cruz I kept falling asleep and then waking up as we ripped around another of the many hairpin curves on Highway 17 through the Santa Cruz Mountains. The car came to a stop at the end of a dirt road, and I woke up in the front seat of Shiva's car to see a man with long dreadlocks and chocolate brown skin standing under a porch light. Shiva embraced him and they spoke for a moment. I got out of the car, and the guy wearing dreadlocks said,

"Welcome, Shakespear. Naturally, I overstand the situation. Come inside, mon, and we will reason on it together."

Shiva had found me a hideout in the woods with a Rastafarian.

26
Tuesday, March 23
Santa Cruz, California

Fortunately, things were less exotic than they had first appeared.

Hedley Styles, my host, and, as it turned out, Shiva's tenant, was working on his Ph.D. in the History of Consciousness at the University of California, Santa Cruz. His dissertation was on jazz music and the evolution of attitudes toward it in different societal groups. Hedley's true love was reggae, not jazz, but there wasn't much of a market for Jamaican music in academia, so he opted for the more established subject until he could call his own tune. Besides, as he put it, "When you are in Babylon, to survive you must babble."

I liked that about Hedley. He was practical. He was also a snorer. As I lay awake on his couch wondering how long it would be before the cops came around, I could hear him chain-sawing redwoods in the next room.

In the morning Shiva appeared bearing still-warm bagels. Hedley put on some coffee and we chowed down on three-grain bagels that bore little resemblance to the East Coast variety, other than topological. That is, they were round, but then so were donuts. I liked them anyway, authentic or not, but

I didn't especially care for the news that Shiva brought with them.

"Last night when I got home I found this fax," she said. "From your friend, Sam Bassett. Here, you read it." She handed it to me and returned to her coffee.

I took the fax from Shiva and read it once quickly. I did not move my lips. Then I read it again and muttered to myself while doing it. Our man Bassett had done some more digging. He'd uncovered not only bones but also beaucoup bad news. Sam Bassett confirmed what Yards had told me. Amy Louvenbragh had been recruited by the FBI as an undercover liaison to Operation Bogart.

Señor Onion Breath had also turned up dead, dangling from a lamp pole near the Picasso Museum in Barcelona. Several fingers on each hand had been broken, one at a time it appeared. Ouch. I guess the Dutchman hadn't approved of my escape. The decomposing body parts—the head, feet and hands Sam found in the farmhouse tub—had belonged to the caretaker, but the torso was still missing.

Sam had also found a familiar name on the passenger list for Lufthansa on March 14. Charley Howell, Jack Butler's other investigator. Well, well, well. That could explain the Boot Hill matchbooks I found in the farm house and in the Butler Museum's upstairs apartment. That could also explain the postmarks on the La Sardana letters.

It now seemed likely that Jack Butler had concocted an elaborate frame in order to get rid of Amy Louvenbragh and pin it on someone else. No, not someone else, me. But why would Jack have become involved with the Dutchman? What could have motivated him to pillage his own museum? Sam also had that answer. The FBI had been investigating Jack because of large gambling debts he'd run up in the Bahamas. Amy was assigned to get close to Jack and find evidence linking him to the Dutchman and his art theft ring. Sam Bassett's fax warned me to steer clear of Jack Butler. A little late though. I'd already run my ship up on the rocks.

"Did you read this?" I said. "The Boston cops are after me for the murder of an undercover FBI informant."

Shiva shrugged. "Who knew?" she said.

"Enough with the levity. Pass the bagels."

"Your friend Jack has gotten you in pretty deep, Tommy."

"Yeah. At least I'm still alive and kicking. I wonder how long before they come after me.

Hedley had been silent until then. "You must not wait. You must take some positive action."

Like what, I thought?

Shiva stood up. "Tommy, I hate to leave you, but I have a business trip. An overnight to LA. I'll be back tomorrow." She looked at Hedley. "Keep an eye on him, okay?"

"I will do it," he said. Hedley turned toward me and smiled.

"Shiva, what's going on in LA?" I said.

"Nothing much. My usual video game circus. Games are big, bigger than movies these days. And, of course, everyone thinks that multimedia is some kind of second coming. But hey, those royalties do add up."

"I'd love to go with you," I said, "But I don't suppose that'd be too bright."

"No," she said. "Take a rain check. LA will still be there next week or next month."

"Unless the earth swallows it up."

"We should be so lucky."

We said good-bye on the front porch and embraced. After she left I could smell Shiva's characteristic scent, a mingling of bath soap, shampoo, and her own brand of musk. I wanted more. I wanted to undo everything I had done in Boston—Elaine, Jack, the Butler Museum—but now it seemed indelible, written in Amy's blood. I needed time with Shiva to see whether we could make something together that was fresh, but the Boston cops were sure to fax their fouled-up sense of what had happened to the Santa Cruz police, and I would have no time with Shiva, except on the run.

When I returned inside, Hedley had cranked up the stereo system and was enjoying a new Ziggy Marley CD.

"Tell me something, Tommy." He said, "Why, if the Interpol agent knows you are innocent of killing the woman in Boston, are the Boston police and the FBI wanting to arrest you?"

"I don't think the FBI does want to arrest me. I think they may still be holding back information from the Boston cops. But there are some funny politics going on, according to a police sergeant I met there. The district attorney is retiring, and his assistant is ambitious and has to make a name for himself so he can be the new DA. He needs a big arrest with lots of publicity. This case is his big break."

"Can the Boston police come here?" he asked.

"I doubt it. More likely they would arrange a local arrest and extradite me to Boston jurisdiction," I said.

"You need to check with the Santa Cruz sheriff, Tommy."

"Indirectly, maybe. Do you know anybody, Hedley? I sure don't."

"I will look into it," he said. "I have class in a little while. Maybe someone at the University can find something out."

"Just don't let anyone know I'm here or why you're asking."

"Help yourself to the music and any food you can find. Not much to eat here right now. I am going shopping later. We'll feast tonight. I-tal."

"Is that like spaghetti?" I figured that since Ethiopia had been under Italian rule, they must have absorbed the culture.

"No, mon. Ital means Vi-tal. Vegetarian food, no fertilizers, no preservatives. Nothing artificial, you see, Tommy Shakespear?"

"Righteous, dude." You can't help using dumb surfer expressions if you live in California. Naturally, I meant it somewhat ironically, but I didn't want Hedley to feel mocked, so I took a little something off the tone when I said it.

"Irie!" he said. Raising his hand in a wave, he went out the door.

"Irie," I said in reply.

I had no idea what that meant.

Part Three - A Dutch Reckoning

Behold, I send you forth as sheep in the midst of wolves:
Be you therefore wise as serpents and harmless as the
doves.

Matthew 10: 6

27
Tuesday, March 23
Santa Cruz, California

I spent the rest of the day in the house, afraid to go out, in case the Santa Cruz authorities had already been brought into the Boston agenda. There was a lot of reggae music to listen to, but, as Hedley said, not much food. I made a sandwich of sourdough bread and pesto sauce for lunch. It was that, or starve.

On the living room table I had piled up the CDs I was listening to. Sugar Minot, the Meditations, Culture, the Wailers, Peter Tosh solo, Freddie McGregor, Gregory Isaacs, the Abyssinians. Burning Spear. It was while listening to Burning Spear that I began to float away. It seemed to put me into a trance. His sound had a lot of dimension to it. More dimensions than I had remembered living in. Time and space multiplied.

I remember being struck by one thing which absorbed me for several hours. In the studio, Burning Spear seemed heavily produced. The instruments, a small orchestra of them, wove a loose and flowing robe of jazzy reggae. Their live concert CDs, in contrast, had a raw urgency about them that drew their listening audience in. It was a kind of revival meeting, and I felt I was physically there, listening to the messages of Marcus

Garvey and H.I.M. Haile Selassie through the mouthpiece of their ambassador Winston Rodney, aka Burning Spear.

I was not revived, though. I began to float away on the rhythms and soon found myself drowsy and then asleep.

When I awoke a light rain was falling on the roof and the sky had darkened enough to make me wonder what time it was. Not clearly evening yet, but late in the afternoon, was my guess. I glanced at my watch and saw the big hand on the two and the little hand on the five. I heard a chopping noise coming from the kitchen. Shrugging off sleep, stretching out of couch-distorted posture, I rose and padded through the kitchen door, where I saw Hedley surrounded by a harvest of vegetables. He turned and flashed his gleaming gold smile, nodding at me, and it seemed, inviting me in.

"Irie." I said to Hedley.

"Irie," he said. The sink and its vicinity was heaped with foodstuffs, many of which I'd never seen before. A vegetarian idea of heaven. I recognized sweet potato, plantains, scallions, avocados, lettuce, onions, red and green peppers, carrots, okra, radish, turnip and string beans, but that was just the beginning. There were herbs and fruits, too, I'd never seen. I soon gave up my vegetable inventory and wondered where Hedley had found it all.

"Tell me, Tommy, are you hungry?"

"Yeah. Very hungry. I couldn't find much to eat for lunch. I made a pesto sandwich I was so desperate."

"Pesto?" he said.

"You know, that green goop in the container in there." I pointed to the fridge.

"Ganja paste, Tommy. Irie."

"What?"

"You ate ganja paste on bread for lunch. I eat it on rice, but there are many ways to consume the herb."

I had blundered into his edible marijuana stash. No wonder I drifted off into a reverie listening to Burning Spear. I looked out the kitchen window into the forest. The rain was falling. I was standing in the kitchen with a genial Rastafarian who was chopping vegetables for a ritual feast, and I felt alone. I wished I were with Shiva somewhere, anywhere. Or, I wished I were alone. I wanted sunshine on a beach somewhere alone. But I was stone hungover in a mountain cabin with a Rasta, and it was raining.

"Don't get me wrong, Hedley. I appreciate all this. But I have been free of drugs for over two years, and I don't want to go down that path again."

"You consider ganja an evil drug?"

"Well, I didn't grow up in Kingston, Jamaica, like you, so naturally I do, yeah," I said.

"In the first place, Tommy, I was born in Atlanta, Georgia. My mother was Jamaican, but not my father, and I grew up in New York City. My point is it doesn't matter where you are from. It's what you choose to think and believe that matters."

"Like if ganja is dangerous, for instance?"

"Exactly," he said. "Just because the police call it evil, does not make it so. I believe they consider you a threat to society, too, at the moment."

"But that's a mistake they've made."

"I agree." he said. "The police make many mistakes."

He had me there.

"Well, okay. Let's just say that, the way I am, the ganja has too big an influence on my head. I get confused and afraid. I do things I later regret. Maybe the problem is with me, maybe with what I have chosen to think and believe, but it is not a good idea for me to do this herb again soon."

"Let not him that eateth
despise him that eateth not;
and let not him who eateth not
judge him that eateth," he said.

"Whoa! Who said that?" I wondered. Haile Selassie, maybe. Sounded pretty, but I couldn't follow those nots and Ediths all the way through.

"That is from the Bible," Hedley said. "Like 'Judge not, lest ye be judged.'"

We got through dinner without too much more philosophy. And it was delicious, all those flavors and textures. Not what I expected at all. We talked about cultures and how they impose their rules. In Hedley's mind, the rules you follow are up to you. I wondered how you'd get free of the rules when you can't see most of them. Hedley said you need the willingness to see. I asked him what this "Irie" thing was. He explained it was a state of essential "goodness," of being in tune with the Creation, free from the tensions of a corrupt world. I could relate to that. I also asked him why he said things like 'Yes, I' and 'I and I' and 'I-man' and he explained it was part of the Rastafarian philosophy to speak a certain way, accenting the positive vibration and especially the word 'I' which unites all people.

We moved into the living room and had coffee. Jamaican Blue Mountain. Now that was Irie. And at nearly forty bucks a pound I and I wondered how Hedley could afford it.

We spent the rest of the evening talking about reggae music and the local jazz music scene. Hedley smoked a little herb, and I got a little high just sitting there smelling that funky smoke. It turned out Hedley played bass and jammed around a lot. He knew all the local players. One in particular caught my interest, Andre Ziff, founder of Prometheum.

"I knew Andre fooled around with sax, but I never thought of him as a real player," I said.

"Ever hear him play?" said Hedley.

"No, not really. At Christmas Andre gave everybody at Prometheum a CD he produced, but I never listened to it. You ever hear it?"

"I played on it, man. I am shamed to admit it, but I needed the money."

"Where was it recorded?" I said.

"Up near the summit of the Santa Cruz mountains. He has a studio in his house there. Big house, state of the art studio equipment."

"The best money can buy, if I know Andre."

Andre Ziff was a self-made computer software millionaire and one of the first to crack the popular market for video games. Shiva had sold her last three titles through Prometheum and had told me quite a little about the legendary Andre that the popular press didn't report. Vain, very charismatic. Fascinating in the way that totally self-absorbed people can sometimes be. There were hints of a dark side to his behavior with his many women friends, but nothing specific had surfaced. Andre had lots of money and liked to let everyone know about it. One way was through excessive generosity, another was conspicuous consumption. Producing a CD of his own music was fairly typical of Andre's stunts. His parties were great, though.

"Tommy, you know about his art collection?"

What? He collects art? My pulse raced.

"What kind of art?" I said.

"Dutch art, I believe it is."

Was this the buyer Sam Bassett and Yards had heard about? Was Jack Butler somehow involved with Andre Ziff?

"Irie!" I said. "Hedley, did you see any of it?"

"Andre likes to show it off. He has a special gallery room he took I through when I went up to record with him last September. And a climate-controlled room with a big time lock on the door. Andre keeps some special tings in there. I don't know what."

I had some idea what might be in there. Climate-controlled, time lock. I thought back to the Dutchman in Barcelona. He had talked about men who rise to wealth and power and their passion for collecting art. Extraordinary men, he called them, with extraordinarily private collections. The missing Vermeer, "The Concert," seemed right up Andre's alley, and maybe the Rembrandts were, too. Who knows, Andre could have had a long term relationship with the Dutchman. I had to find out.

Before going to bed that night I called Hank Greenberg and Yards Malloy back in Boston. For Hank it was a sleep-disturbing call, but Yards was just getting revved up for a night of partying. Hank was still upset at me for leaving Boston. He warned me again to turn myself in before something else happened.

"Sorry, Hank," I said, "it's impossible. No one would ever go to the trouble to figure this out. I'd be put away as part of the new DA's election campaign. I can't take that risk."

"You're only going to dig yourself in deeper, Tommy. From what you say, the FBI is on your side. You have that contact at Interpol. Things should work out. I can make the arrangements here for you to surrender."

"No way."

"So why did you wake me out of the only sound sleep I've had in weeks?"

"Just to say hi," I said.

"Serious."

"Serious? Not really. Look, Hank, would you contact Sergeant Raymond and find out what they have and whether they've gone out of state with this? Do they even know I've left town? You can tell him I am considering surrendering, if you need to."

"Would that be the truth, or are you asking me to lie for you?"

"Just do it, Hank. I promise to consider it. That's all I can do. Okay?"

"Okay, Tommy," he said.

"By the way, there's no Nashua airport."

"Who said there was?"

"You did, Hank. Never mind. Go back to sleep."

Yards was considerably simpler, having less invested in conventional morality. Maybe, like Hedley, he saw the rules for what they were. Of course, he was a convicted felon. Yards agreed to ask around and see if anyone knew of a connection between Andre Ziff and Jack Butler. Or whether Andre had ever been part of the underground art market in the past. It was going to cost me to find out, though, no matter what he found out. Five hundred dollars. I didn't know where that money was coming from, but it was only money. Maybe Shiva could help.

Shiva. As I lay on the couch trying to find a position for sleeping, I let thoughts of Shiva clear out my mind. When I'd been in Boston, it'd been much too easy to become involved with Elaine. Much too easy, and while we always had a great time together, it was a transitory thing. Maybe that was why it was always exciting with Elaine. We had the hots for each other, but nothing more. No real relationship and no possibility of one.

Shiva was different. I cared about her and wanted her to care about me. Maybe there was a chance to have something that could last with her. She was independent. She had her own life and work, and yet there was a way in which we met on even ground. It had gotten bumpy recently and, I guessed, it was about to shake a little, but if we could make it through the next few days and weeks, I felt we could build something together.

Something with a guest room.

28
Wednesday, March 24
Santa Cruz, California

A second night on Hedley's couch put me in the mood for action. I couldn't face another day in the cabin or another night on that couch. First I had to get to my bike. I needed to get the kinks out of my body, to think things through and plan my next move, and I thought a long ride on my mountain bike would be a good way to do that. Riding always freed my mind. I knew Hedley would probably be reluctant to take me to Capitola against Shiva's wishes, so I rose early, dressed quickly and left the cabin as quiet as a snake.

A clear morning greeted me after a day cooped up inside, clear and cold as only a morning in the spring can be. There was a hint in the sun's rays of a warming to come, but only a hint. I shuffled along the dirt road. It was a short walk out to the Grade, and from there I hitched down into Santa Cruz, catching breakfast at Zachary's. I was running short on cash, down to fifty-five bucks, but it was worth it after yesterday's bagel breakfast, ganja pesto lunch and Ital stir fry. Don't get me wrong, I'm part vegetarian. It's just that there's another part of me that likes the tangy smell and greasy taste of bacon, sausage, fried eggs and home fries. I usually try to eat low-fat, but my body goes into withdrawal. This breakfast was a way of silencing that angry growl inside.

After breakfast I wandered out to Highway 1 and stood by the on ramp hitching. Hitching around Santa Cruz isn't all that safe anymore, but I didn't have any choice. It wasn't long before I caught a ride in the back of a flatbed truck bound for Watsonville. The truck stopped and I jumped in over a tire and a heavy chain. There were three men in back, Mexican workers. None of them spoke the language so we nodded, gestured, smiled greetings to each other. I pantomimed shivering. They shook their heads, smiled. It was cold, and the three men had already taken up the best spots, up against the cab where the wind wouldn't quite reach. That left me smack dab in the middle of the wind. I became an instant expert on airflow and turbulence, and by the time I jumped off at the Capitola exit, I was numb. My arms and legs seemed like somebody else's. I had a hard time convincing that person to move them the way I wanted.

Before long, I reached the hill heading down to the beach and the ice had thawed. Monterey Bay lay still in the distance, and only a few cars were moving down in the village, probably shopkeepers as it was too early for anyone else. I fingered the key in my pocket and walked down the hill toward my cottage. The cops might be watching my place, I knew, so I circled the block keeping my eyes peeled for squad cars or plainclothes guys eating doughnuts in unmarked sedans.

It had been almost two weeks since I'd been home. And there it was still waiting for me, just as I'd left it. I patted the wall just to the right of the door affectionately. It's been a long time, house, I thought. I slipped the key into the front door lock, and just then I felt something at my ankle and looked down to see Slinky, the neighborhood calico cat rubbing up against me. I could feel her purring and reached down to pat her when a whizzing sound and a loud crack! exploded just above my head. I looked up and saw a splintered hole in my front door. A bullet hole? I scooped up Slinky, pushed the door open and closed it behind us. My heart was beating fast. I took a deep breath to try to even things out, but my mind just raced. I paced. Who was it? Why were they shooting at me? Shit shit shit! What to do, what to do? Calm down, I thought, be cool.

I sat down in the green arm chair, and Slinky jumped into my lap. She flexed her paws and opened her claws, sinking them gently into my thighs. I scooted her off my lap, stood up and paced again, trying to think of what I could do. I picked up the phone, heard the dial tone and knew I had a line to 911. But I hesitated. Calling the police would just land me in jail and on trial for murder and all of the rest. Besides, somebody else would report the gun shot, and they'd be here in a minute. I peeked out the oceanside window first from one side, then the other, careful not to expose my body to the shooter. Nothing. It was Capitola in the morning.

I quickly changed into a pair of bike shorts and a cutoff sweatshirt, threw a few things into a nylon back pack, snapped on my helmet and gloves and wheeled my bike through the door off the kitchen. I leaned my bike against the outside wall in back and closed the door quietly, making sure it was locked. It seemed the right thing to do, but anyone who'd shoot at me in broad daylight probably wouldn't be stopped by a cheap door lock.

Mounting my bike, I pedaled swiftly through the network of alleyways connecting the cottages with the storefronts a few blocks away. I took every which way I knew, the most indirect route out of the village, weaving through the back streets, under the railroad trestle, behind the offices and stores and then through the residential areas. I took a winding route through Soquel, back across the freeway and then along the beach road toward the boat harbor, the Santa Cruz beach boardwalk, across the San Lorenzo River bridge and through the downtown area.

I arrived at Shiva's house about twenty minutes later. Traffic had been light until I hit Mission Drive and the thundering commuter herd. The west side of Santa Cruz was on its way to work. I had to weave through the congestion, avoiding drivers who couldn't be bothered to notice a bicycle, narrowly avoiding them, I should say. Shiva lived near the university in a neighborhood of large houses mostly inhabited by successful academics and other professionals.

As I turned into her semicircular driveway, I was reminded again that Shiva was into serious bucks. Winded from pumping up the steep ascent to her hillside perch, I dismounted and turned to look at the view across the bay that her videogames had bought. It was even more spectacular from the front bedroom, I knew.

Shiva's blue Lexus was parked in the drive, so I figured she'd returned from LA last night and was probably still asleep. I wheeled my bike around back through the arched wooden gate and parked it against the fountain in her formal gardens. Surrounded by dozens of floral varieties, I caught scent of some jasmine on a little breeze that rippled through. The fountain bubbled. I could feel the sun on my bare arms and face. Gunshots in Capitola seemed so far away.

I left my helmet and gloves in the garden and walked over pea gravel toward the back of Shiva's house, carrying the backpack in my left hand. I reached up over the laundry room door sill and found the key she kept there.

Once inside, I made my way upstairs to her bedroom at the front of the house. I moved quietly so I wouldn't wake her until I got to her door. I knocked and called her name, hoping she was alone.

"Tommy?" she said. I was still outside her bedroom door.

"Yeah, it's me," I said. "Okay to come in?"

"What time is it?"

I looked at my watch. It was a few minutes past nine.

"Shiva, can I come in? Are you alone?"

"What do you think, Tommy?" she said.

I guessed that meant yes. I opened the door and stepped inside. Shiva pulled the covers over her head and disappeared under a light blue blanket and matching comforter. For a moment I stood there looking at Shiva's lumpy outline under the covers, thinking how nice it would be to join her in bed. We had never slept together, never made love. When would we? Would we ever? I walked to the window, and I took a deep breath, gazing out into the sunny morning, the bay glittering in the distance as light glanced off the waves.

A small, dark bird swooped into view, cutting through the front yard on its way to some nearby perch. I've never been much at birds or plants, their names, I mean. And without a name the soaring bird became a projectile, a missile, a bullet.

"Well?" The voice, slightly muffled, came from beneath the covers.

"Well, what?" I said.

"Well, Tommy," said Shiva, "What are you doing here?" Shiva sat up, and I turned to face her.

"Someone took a shot at me."

"Somebody shot a gun at you? Where? When?" Shiva was now fully awake. She sat up in bed.

"Capitola. Outside my house, less than an hour ago," I said. "If I hadn't bent down to pet Slinky, it would have been over. Bang!" I made a gun with my right hand and shot it. I blew away the smoke.

"Did you see who it was?" Shiva reached to her bedside table, picked up a green hair tie and pulled her long blonde hair back into a ponytail.

"No. Nobody." I walked to the edge of the queen-sized bed and leaned my knees into it.

"You saw nobody?" she said.

"Nobody and nothing. Except the bullet hole in my door."

"Tommy, we have to call the police."

"Sure. The police. That makes a lot of sense, Shiva. We call the cops to report the shooting, and they come down to investigate. Let's see, Tommy Shakespear. Oh, by the way, we have a warrant for your arrest. Would you mind coming with us, Mr. Shakespear? You have the right to remain silent."

"Okay, okay," she said. "What, then?"

"I don't know." I sat on the edge of the bed and looked at her.

"You know, Tommy," Shiva said, "Slinky probably saved your life. I always liked that cat."

"You did?" I said.

"Yeah."

Shiva got out of bed. Wearing only a tank top, she walked calmly to the closet and took a pair of faded blue jeans from the shelf. As I looked at her, I wanted to freeze that view. Her blonde hair tied back in a ponytail reached nearly to the small of her lightly-tanned back. Her buttocks were firm, round and also lightly tanned. Not a tan line on her body. Slim and tan and blonde. She slipped into her blue jeans, zipped them up and turned around.

"Ready?" she said.

"Yeah, I'm ready. What do you have in mind?"

"Let's go back to the scene of the crime."

"I don't know, Shiva. Whoever it was could still be there, waiting for me."

"No way, Tommy."

"No way? Why?"

"If I was the killer, I'd try again, some other time, some other place. Maybe at night or early in the morning. But not at...what time is it now?"

"Nine-twenty," I said.

"Not at nine-thirty or ten in the morning."

"Oh, and what makes you such an expert? I'm the only detective around here, aren't I."

"Give me a break, Tommy. First, there's the bullet. Let's go find that. And then, while we're there, I think we should find some way to thank Slinky. Maybe a can of tuna."

"Oy!" I said.

"Yeah?"

"I just remembered I left Slinky inside my place."

"Another good reason. Let's go!"

On the way there, I told Shiva about Andre Ziff and his art collection. She didn't show much interest until I mentioned the climate-controlled room Hedley told me about. Shiva'd never seen it, nor the little gallery of Dutch paintings, but she'd heard Andre was an avid art collector. On the few occasions she'd been to Andre's house, he'd entertained out by the pool.

But if Hedley saw that stuff, she said, then it was there. Maybe the Vermeer or the Rembrandts were also there. Shiva recalled that Andre had a framed Vermeer print in his office at Prometheum. I'd never seen it, though. Of course, I wasn't on a first name basis with Andre Ziff, and I wasn't likely to be. On the other hand, I did want to get a closer look at Andre's office and his house.

We arrived in Capitola at ten past ten. No place to park. That was typical for Capitola, but not usually this early. It was shaping up to be a great beach day though. Shiva offered to drop me at my place so I could check on Slinky, but I thought we'd better stick together. I was a little gun shy, maybe. Besides, the cops were looking for me, and they might be investigating the gun shot. Anyhow we wandered around and finally found a place to leave the Lexus over by the trestle, a five-minute walk away. The village was bustling with Japanese tourists. There were four tour busses parked by the esplanade, the drivers standing around smoking, talking. A traffic cop was talking to them, probably trying to explain that no busses were allowed in the village. They'd have to move.

But that was it for cops. The coast was clear.

Shiva and I entered my cottage through the back door and found Slinky curled up on my bed. I went immediately to check for the bullet. Opening the front door I put my finger to the splintered perforation. No bullet. I looked again from another angle. Still no bullet. I could see clearly that the bullet had not passed through the door, but rather had embedded itself in the wooden frame. But it was not there now. Someone, maybe the cops, probably the shooter, had taken it out.

"Find the bullet?" Shiva came to the front door, holding Slinky in her arms like a nursing baby.

"No. It's not there." She looked.

"Here." Shiva handed me Slinky to hold, but to her credit the calico leaped to the ground and, landing softly, stretched out her back. Shiva squatted to look at the doorstep, and when she rose she held her palm out to me. "Splinters," she said. It looked like door scrapings from when somebody dug the bullet out with a knife.

"No point in sticking around here," I said. "Eventually, the shooter will come back here looking for me. He might not miss next time."

"Do you have any tuna?" She walked past me into the cottage.

"What?"

"For Slinky. You owe her, Tommy." Shiva was already in the kitchen, opening cabinets, browsing the shelves.

"The one to your right," I said. In a few moments Shiva had the can open and the banquet prepared. She returned to the doorstep with the tuna in a plastic bowl and looked for Slinky who had wandered around the side of the cottage. Shiva made a soft hissing sound and called out Slinky's name. The cat was back in an instant. In another moment she was eating from the bowl.

"Gotta pay your dues," Shiva said. It was a strangely intimate moment and not one you could predict. She touched me on the cheek, and then we kissed, briefly but deeply. I could smell the tuna on her fingers. Our eyes met, and a feeling passed between us, nothing words could fix or hold, an understanding.

As we left the cottage and walked back to Shiva's car, Slinky was still working on her tuna. I was chewing on a plan.

There were two places I needed to see. Andre Ziff's office at Prometheum and his house nearby in the Santa Cruz mountains. Night time would be the best time to visit them, and as I had no time to lose, tonight had to be the night. I wanted to try Andre's office first, to see the Vermeer print and look at his office files in case he kept anything there which could tie him to Jack Butler or the Dutchman. I really didn't know what to look for exactly, but I was not willing to wait for someone to shoot at me again. As Hedley had said, I must take positive action.

Positive.

29
Wednesday, March 24
Santa Cruz, California

Shiva was silent on the ride back to her house. I knew she had things of her own to think about. I wanted to ask about the trip to LA and if she'd worked a good deal on the distribution rights to Smash Attack II, but I waited. Maybe at dinner tonight, I thought, I could bring it up then.

We parked and went inside. Shiva led me into the kitchen, and I sat at the long harvest table. Coffee was brewing in a matter of minutes. Its aroma filled the kitchen. Shiva toasted some sourdough English muffins and joined me at the table, sliding a heavy mug of black coffee across its smooth wooden surface toward me. It smelled like liquid heaven.

"I've been thinking, Shiva," I said.

"Not again, Tommy. Last time you got a headache."

"Hey! This is good coffee."

"Live and learn," she said.

"Can't just sit and wait and hope all this trouble will go away."

"And?"

"You know Hedley?"

"Of course I know Hedley."

"I mean, I love Hedley and his heavy Rasta philosophy. You know, some of it came through to me. The part about positive action?"

I paused to see if Shiva'd nod in assent, but went on anyway when she didn't.

"So here's what I think, Shiva. Positive action. I think I've got to look into Andre, his office, maybe his house. When he's not there, of course."

"You mean *break in*, don't you, Tommy? Not *look in*. Are you crazy? You're already in trouble with the police in Boston. You want to add to that here?"

"Shiva, you sound like Hank Greenberg. The way I see it, I have three choices. One, turn myself in and possibly go down for something I didn't do. Two, sit around and wait until either the cops get me, or the shooter, which is a wonderful new alternative I've just learned about. Or three, do something. Considering them all, I like number three the best. Because it's my only real way out."

"Positive action," Shiva said. The way she said it I knew she didn't approve, but was becoming resigned to letting it happen.

"Positive," I said. "How about dinner tonight?"

"Dinner? Where?"

"The cabin. Hedley, you and me. We work out some kind of plan."

"Tell you one thing, Tommy. I'm not getting involved in a break in at my own company or at my boss's house."

"I thought you quit."

"Call it a leave of absence."

"Well, that's even better. I might need help getting in," I said.

"You're on your own, Tommy." A little more resistance to overcome.

"Well, how about dinner, then?"

"You cooking?" she said, "That I've gotta see."

And we did see.

That evening, the bony remains of the salmon we'd just eaten sat on a slab of redwood burl in the center of the dining table. Our plates were greasy. We'd turned to watch the sunset in progress. You could still smell the mesquite charcoal burning in the grill. I'd spent my last fifty on the dinner fixings, but it had been a feast to remember.

Under the table I was holding hands with Shiva, our fingers laced together like a couple of school kids. Tommy and Shiva sittin' in a tree. Hedley was toking on a fat joint of marijuana. Its aroma drifted across the room, a sweet, acrid scent that is unmistakable.

"I read this line today in a book of poems by the great John Ashbery," said Hedley.

"Who?" I said. Unfamiliar name. Shiva shook her head once, lightly, and shrugged.

"His book won a Pulitzer Prize. It was called *Self-Portrait in a Convex Mirror.* You must have heard of it."

"Sorry," I said. After Beatrice died I sort of lost track of poetry. I hadn't written a word in years, not even a letter. Until that two-page case report for Jack Butler.

"Well, what he says, 'Today is easy but tomorrow is uncharted...' has been with me all day, and," Hedley paused, smiling, "I think it's because it was the only line I could understand in his poem. In any of his poems." He laughed and expelled a huge cloud of smoke.

"I'd like to know what's so easy about today," said Shiva. She let go of my hand and scratched her head.

"Let me read it to you. Just a part of it," he said. "I would like to know your impressions of it."

"Okay," I said, "But we don't have to write your English paper for you, do we, Hedley?" He left the room to get his book, and as he did, Shiva put her hand on my knee."

"Tommy," she said. "You be nice to him."

We kissed, once, twice, a third time. When Shiva finally pushed me away, it sent a rush of desire tunneling into me. Hedley came back into the room, turning the pages of his book.

"Here it is," he said, standing by the table. "Tomorrow is easy, but today is uncharted..."

"Wait!" I said. They both looked at me. "That's the other way around."

An hour later Shiva and I were in her Lexus in the Prometheum parking lot.

"Go around back," Shiva said. "I have a key to the door."

We had driven to the Prometheum offices in Scotts Valley after putting John Ashbery to bed. I'd finally wore down Shiva's resistance, getting her to agree to a quick look-see to clear Andre Ziff of any further suspicion. Hedley wanted to come along, but I needed somebody at the cabin in case Yards should call back. Besides, he had that English paper to write.

Shiva had parked her car in the side lot, next to a pickup truck and a motorcycle. It was a cool night with a few high clouds dimming the stars. I'd worn my leather jacket. Shiva wore her all-blue Coogi sweater, a dozen shades of blue or more vibrating under the high-intensity lights in the parking lot.

We entered the building and passed through a corridor into the elevator bay. Just beyond I could see a large open space with sound-proof cubicles where the programmers worked. Where were the security guards?

"Hi, Shiva."

A nearly bald, wiry-limbed fellow with a wispy red beard walked through the elevator bay carrying a can of Jolt Cola. He didn't look up from the papers he was reading as he walked. He was wearing tie-dyed cotton drawstring sweat pants and a Grateful Dead t-shirt, barefoot. Around his neck was a string of rather large brown nuts. They looked like the same brown nuts as my seat companion on the airplane from Barcelona wore. He wore thick wire-rim glasses low on his nose.

"Ozzie, hi!" she said.

"That's normal?" I said.

"For Ozzie, it is. You used to work here, Tommy. Remember?"

"So did you," I said.

I guess it wasn't surprising to see someone so absorbed. Programming a computer was that kind of work. You lose track of time, lose track of where you are, and sometimes even who you are, especially late at night or very early in the morning. It wasn't that late though. Didn't feel that late, but my watch said ten thirty-five. As I glanced at it, the elevator chimed, its doors yawned open and into its mouth we went, pressing the black button for the third floor.

"I'm going to my office for a minute or two. It's down this way to the right. Want to come?" Shiva exited first from the elevator into the dim lighting of the corridor. At the end of the corridor to the left the cleaning crew had set up their supply post. As I looked down toward them I noticed many of the offices along the way were lighted, but uninhabited at this hour.

"Where's Andre's office?" I said.

"Down in that corner by the cleaning crew. They're probably doing his office right now."

"How about security?"

"They're usually in front of the building. Once an hour they walk around and look in all the offices. I think they have some sort of electronic device that reads bar codes at various checkpoints around the building. They're harmless."

"It's a living." I said.

"Yeah. Not much of one," Shiva said. "Are you coming?"

"I think I'll wander down to Andre's office and take a look."

"You don't want to wait until after the cleaning people leave?"

"I don't want to stick around that long," I said.

"Okay. I'll come with you."

As we turned to walk toward Andre's office, a man in a blue uniform emerged from the stair well. Security. He walked directly toward us. At times like that, when I'm about to be confronted, I usually feel a surge of exhilaration tinged with guilt.

This time, however, my nerves were really on edge, and for good reason, as we hadn't taken the time to work out a cover story. I was afraid he might ask us what we were doing in the executive wing at that hour, but he walked past us without any greeting or acknowledgment, intent upon his rounds.

"That was lucky," I said.

"Very," said Shiva. "He won't be back for an hour now. Once he leaves the floor, that is."

30
Wednesday, March 24
Santa Cruz, California

We arrived at Andre's office just as the cleaning woman was dumping a tall black wastebasket into a garbage bag. Its contents looked like ticker tape or confetti.

"Shredder," I said to no one in particular.

The woman looked up at me and then away. She was young and possibly pregnant, judging from her clothing. Her dark brown eyes and skin were radiant, but maybe it was the light.

"Necesito algo de esta oficina," said Shiva. I think. That much I could sort of understand. The rest was a blur. While they were talking, I slipped past them, past the secretary's desk into the inner office and took a quick look around.

Andre Ziff, for all his flamboyant extravagance, had a pretty ordinary office. Not what I expected at all from the consummate egotist. I had foreseen sweeping vistas of fountains and mountain-side redwoods. The office itself would be professionally decorated in opulent bad taste...vast mahogany desk with high-back leather reclining chair...polished chrome and black marble statuary...walls stacked high in red leather-bound volumes with uncut pages...Persian carpets... black leather guest chairs grouped around an onyx coffee table...wet bar fully stocked with expensive top-shelf liquors and crystal decanters....

But no. It was a very utilitarian space about twenty by thirty feet. There was a big wood-veneer desk with a blue fabric-covered desk chair behind it, a conference table and a couple of standard-issue gray office chairs grouped around it, piles of paper everywhere, empty soda cans, books without their jackets. In fact, no luxury apparent at all.

As I was taking this in, I heard another voice outside in the corridor. The security guard was asking Shiva what she was doing. Shiva said something to the cleaning woman in Spanish. Christ, I thought, we're cooked. I moved closer to the door to listen. She was speaking to the guard.

"I'm Mary Formanski, Mr. Ziff's administrative assistant. Andre, that is, Mr. Ziff, has asked me to pick up some papers from his office and bring them to his house tonight. He has an early flight back east in the morning."

"Where's the guy you were with?" he said.

"What guy?"

A few hours before we were holding hands, I thought, and now she can't even remember my name. How soon they forget!

"Guy about five ten, one seventy-five, one eighty. Looks a little like, oh what's his name, the movie star, always plays the wise guy...."

"I don't know. You've got me there," she said. "I was talking to someone earlier, a marketing executive whose name I can't recall. He's new here and we've not yet been introduced. He went down to get something from the soda machine, I think."

"You have some identification, miss?"

"Not with me."

"You're supposed to carry it with you at all times."

"Sorry. I've never had this problem before."

"We just have to be sure you are who you say you are."

Through the crack left by the open door I could see her pick up a framed photograph and gesture with it toward the security guard.

"Look," Shiva said. "Here's my family. Kevin, my husband, CeeCee and Eno, our children and our dog, J.C. Penny. We got him from the pound. Isn't he cute?"

It wasn't going to work, I could feel it. Shiva was acting up a storm, but the security guard wasn't buying. He was going by the book.

"I need to see the ID, miss," he said. "Or else, I'll have to escort you from the building."

I had to do something. But what? Burst from Andre's office and suddenly overpower the guard? Subdue him with my fists or a finger to the pressure point at the carotid artery on his neck? No way. Not my style. I crawled to Andre's desk. On it there was a telephone with several extensions, including one marked "Mary". I dialed Mary's extension. Next door I could hear the phone ring. Shiva picked up.

"Hello?" she said. "This is Mary." It almost sounded like a question.

"Shiva, hi, it's me. Tommy. Pretend I'm Andre. I'm calling to make sure you haven't forgotten to bring something or other. Will that help?" I could hear her expel a breath, count a beat, then reply.

"Yeah, Andre...I'm here now, but...Yeah, fine...well, one problem. I forgot my ID and the security guard...would you mind?...Okay."

Shiva held the phone out to the security guard. I could see him walk around the desk in the outer office and take the phone. I ducked down behind Andre's desk so the guard wouldn't see me.

"Hello," I said, "This is Andre Ziff." I tried to sound firm, important and a little weary at this hour of the night.

"Yes, sir, Mr. Ziff," he said. "Apparently your secretary left her ID at home. I was just asking her about it."

"And you are?"

"I'm Pete Cole with Valley Security. Night shift."

"Mr. Cole, do you know who I am?"

"I believe so, sir. You're Mr. Ziff, the big cheese around here, if I'm not mistaken." The guy had a way with words.

"That's right, I'm the big cheese. Now Ms. Formanski is getting some documents I need. You will assist her, I hope." I tried to imply his continued employment would depend upon it.

"Sir, thing is, she doesn't have any ID with her, and it's regulation."

"I will speak to her about it when she brings my papers. You will let her bring me the papers I need. Won't you?"

"Of course, Mr. Ziff."

"Thank you," I said. "Good night, Pete." As Andre, I was gracious, even grateful for his help.

After the security guard left to continue his rounds, Shiva and I took a good look around Andre's office. At first, I hadn't noticed the print, inconspicuous in its ordinary brown frame, hanging next to the office door. But when we closed Andre's door the better to rummage through his drawers, it all but leaped out at me. It was a high-quality photo reproduction of Vermeer's "The Concert," one of the missing paintings. I had a hunch it might be Andre's personal reminder of the treasure he kept in his vault.

I looked at the print. Vermeer had painted three musicians, or rather two musicians and a singer, in a room lit only by the light from an unseen window. Two tightly-coifed women, one the harpsichord or spinet player at left of center and the other, the singer, at right of center holding a piece of paper, flanked a man with shoulder-length hair seated nearly sideways on his chair, playing a lute. In the foreground on the black and white parquet floor lay a viola or bass fiddle of some kind. But here's what has always intrigued me about this painting. The lute player has his back to the viewer. Center stage, he has his back turned. Intriguing. Of course, the concert Vermeer painted was without an audience. Quite the opposite of Andre Ziff, who would record his jazz combo at company expense and give away his musical efforts in order to create one.

Meanwhile, Shiva was casing the room, trying all the drawers, doors and cabinets. The desk drawers and filing cabinets were locked. Nothing unusual about that. Not to be denied, however, Shiva went back to Mary Formanski's desk and found her spare key under the blotter, opened her top drawer and removed the set of keys to Andre's office. Within minutes we had opened every drawer, and our fingers had walked through every file. Nothing of interest had turned up, except perhaps for the loaded Pez dispenser we found in Andre's bottom desk drawer.

I wandered over to his window on Scotts Valley, or more accurately, onto the parking lot out front, and what did I see but a black-and-white police cruiser pulling up to the curb. It seemed the security guard didn't buy my act either.

"Uh, Shiva," I said.

"Yeah, what?" She was playing with the Pez dispenser, opening and closing the little Woody Woodpecker head. So far she hadn't eaten any though.

"I think we better leave quickly. Know any secret passageways?"

"Why?" She looked at me like I was crazed.

"Cops out front," I said. "They just got here, but I don't think we should wait for them. Do you?" I was already heading toward the door.

"What?" Then she got it and joined me in exiting Andre's utilitarian cave.

We ran down the hall toward the elevators, but Shiva urged me past them, around the corner by her office and toward the back stairs. As we closed the stairway door behind us, I thought I could hear the elevator chime its arrival on the third floor. Down in an instant, we ran through a short distance of corridor on the ground floor, past the elevator bay, through the side door and out the way we came in. We ran to the Lexus parked around to the side, out of view of Andre's office and the cruiser parked at the front of the building.

The Lexus fired up right away, and we glided out onto the access road paralleling Highway 17. No lights. We were rigged for silent running, and before my heart stopped pounding and my breathing settled down, we were safely out of shooting range. Not that anyone was shooting or likely to be shooting, but I'd feel a good deal safer once we'd put some more road between us and the cops at Prometheum.

Shiva did not breathe easy until we'd taken the most obscure possible path through the labyrinth of mountain roads between Scotts Valley and Soquel. We stopped briefly at Casalegno's store, a little mom-and-pop grocery and gas place outside of Soquel, just across the freeway from my cottage in Capitola. We called Hedley from the pay phone outside the store and woke him from a sound sleep to give him the latest bulletin.

"You found nothing?" he said.

"Well," I said, "Not exactly nothing. The Vermeer print was there just as Shiva remembered."

"And I found a Woody Woodpecker Pez dispenser. Tell him that," said Shiva over my shoulder.

31
Thursday, March 25
Santa Cruz, California

We spent the night in a motel near the freeway, unsure if it was safe to go home. I tried to reach both Hank and Yards unsuccessfully. No one was answering the phone at that hour, roughly four in the morning back east. Shiva and I lay on the bed fully clothed, holding each other. We laughed, recalling our scene with the security guard in Andre's office. We played with the Pez dispenser Shiva had found in his drawer. Like children whose parents were in the next room, we were whispering, tickling, giggling. I was determined to keep my hands off Shiva until this business was over. I didn't want any emotional complications in addition to everything else. Elaine had been a distraction, but Shiva would be a head-on collision. So I had it all figured out. Except for one thing. I knew I was already falling.

"Tommy," she said, "I know how you feel about me." Her eyes were moist, bright and green as clover. "So.."

"Hey, it's true, but...." I said. "Look, Shiva, we don't have to do anything. I mean it's late, and we're both tired."

She smiled. "Maybe not that tired."

Shiva stripped down to her underwear, and I followed suit, turning out the light, joining her in our cocoon of cotton bedding. As we lay in our motel bed, the cuddling led to kissing, and the kissing got almost too hot. We didn't try to stop it.

"Shiva," I said, "Are you ready for this?" I was having a hard time holding myself back.

"At this point, Tommy, I'm ready for almost anything."

"Me, too, almost. That's the word. I, uh, don't have a condom."

"No?"

"I think we should wait until this is over, Shiva. We can go away for the weekend. San Francisco, Monterey, Big Sur, maybe."

"All this excitement and romance, too. Come here, Tommy Shakespear."

We continued kissing, nibbling at each other lips, cheeks, ear lobes. And a few other places besides. Finally, when we had nothing left but sweet emotion, we lay together for a moment listening to our hearts beat. I could smell Shiva's warm, familiar smell. She felt safe and reassuring in my arms.

Turning sideways toward sleep, I wondered how the mess I was in could ever come out right. Then, deeply, almost instantly, like a vertical plunge into darkness I fell asleep with Shiva hugging my back. Snuggled like spoons, we slept in our nearly chaste bed.

I was the first to wake. It was a gray, foggy morning light that urged me to alertness, as a cool spirit entered the room through an opening in the thick blue curtains. A feeling of timelessness encircled me. I felt as though something were lifting me high above the room. I seemed to look down on the two of us sleeping there in our motel bed. The alarm clock on the bedside table glowed luminously, its red numbers unfamiliar hieroglyphs. Pulsing, they signaled danger. I felt myself drawn into them, as though a current were pulling me into the mouth of a cave. I knew the present and the future were one and the same. No matter what I would do, no matter what might happen, I could only be myself. What I would be tomorrow I already was. I looked at the faces of the people in my life, and they were like portraits in a gallery. Amy, Jack, Fred, Sam, Elaine. The Dutchman. Hank, Yards, Hedley. Shiva. Someone was missing. Was it me?

"Tommy, wake up."

I was awake, and yet Shiva was trying to wake me. Someone was missing. Where was I? I wanted to stay there a while, figure things out. Yet I began to feel myself reentering the room. The buoyancy that held me aloft began ebbing away. As this happened in a languorous slow motion, I became aware again of my own body, tingling with the bitter warmth you feel when your foot has gone asleep and then the blood revives it. Then Shiva's body next to mine.

"It's Thursday," she said. "I've got a yoga class at nine. We've got to get going."

"Wow," I said. "Shiva, I was someplace else."

"You're telling me? I've been trying to wake you for over a minute."

"Yeah, but the thing is, I was awake the whole time. Just someplace else."

"Oh, oh," Shiva said, "You're not losing it on me now, are you, Tommy?"

I told her what it had felt like. I told her about the clarity I experienced. How I drifted above the room and saw past and future. An out-of-body experience, Shiva called it. I was glad to know it had a name.

"It's probably a combination of things. The ganja paste you ate, for one thing. The stress of being on the run, shot at, chased by cops, whatever. Let's face it, Tommy, you've been through a lot in the past few weeks."

"But I had this clarity, this certainty." Besides, it was the first night since Amy's death that I didn't have any nightmares.

"Here," she said. Shiva threw me my shirt, and I put it on. We dressed, and as we dressed, I tried to explain to her what I'd puzzled over at the end. Someone was missing. But who?

"Aren't you afraid the cops will come looking for you now?" I said. "I mean, that Mary Formanski routine was pretty entertaining, but the guard didn't buy it, and the cops will have your description."

"Tommy, don't you think the cops have plenty to do without looking for someone who may or may not have broken any laws?" she said.

"What about this Mary Formanski? Won't they figure out you invented her?"

"There really is a Mary Formanski. She's Andre's admin, and we look a lot alike. About the same height, same hair color. Of course hers is dyed and..."

"Andre?" I said.

"And Andre is back east for a press tour. He'll be gone until Monday night or Tuesday. So it will take the cops a while to figure out if anything is really wrong."

"So we have a few days anyway."

"We only have a few minutes. My class starts at nine. Remember?"

"Okay. Can you drop me up at the cabin?" I said. "I've got to pick up the bike if I'm going to get around."

"You can use my car, Tommy. Just pick me up after yoga. I should be done at around ten-thirty."

We checked out of the motel using Shiva's credit card. Not a great idea, as it could be traced by either the cops or whoever was stalking me, but neither one of us had any cash. I was flat broke. We talked about that walking to her car through a wet morning fog that hung in the air like the mist in the vegetable section of an upscale supermarket. Shiva agreed to loan me a thousand dollars until I got straightened out. Really, it worked out to five hundred for me and five hundred for Yards, but I didn't want to share that with her at the moment. We'd go pick up the cash after her yoga class, then get some lunch, go to the cabin, pick up the bike, whatever. The whatever part had me a little worried. I felt peculiarly uneasy about what I should do next. Shiva was right. It had been a couple of pretty hairy weeks. Getting roughed up in Barcelona, the murder and getting blamed for it in Boston, having to run away and hide in Santa Cruz. And then last night. This was not like the detective books I had read. Those guys seemed to know what to do all the time. Even when they were chased into a corner, they seemed to have a sure sense for how to get out. Me? I was grasping at straws. And right now Andre Ziff looked like the only straw in town.

I drove Shiva to her class in downtown Santa Cruz, parked the Lexus and went into this coffee bar I know, the Jahva House. There are probably ten or eleven coffee houses in Santa Cruz, but this one has the best variety and choice of coffee beans. They've got my favorite, Celebes, in a dark roast, and they brew it strong. Besides, it's in an old engine repair shop, has a high-ceilinged, open feeling atmosphere with plants and books and music, and all kinds of people go there, Yuppies, students, street people, Rastas. It was one of Hedley's haunts, too, and I hoped I'd find him there. I walked up to the bar and ordered my usual Celebes and a three-seed bagel. Nearly cleaned me out. All I had was pocket change, until Shiva got out of Yoga class and loaned me the five hundred.

It was going to take a while for the coffee. I scanned the crowd, listened to the jazz that was turned a notch too high, looked out onto the back deck area, but I didn't see Hedley. Noticing there were few open tables, I picked out one that had a discarded newspaper on it and slipped my leather jacket over a chair to mark my dibs. It was a chilly morning so I hoped it wouldn't be too long before my coffee was ready. I sat and began to read the paper. The newspaper, our very own Santa Cruz Local, was a pleasingly thin amalgam of wire service reprints and local color. Nothing in the paper about our little misadventure last night at Prometheum. I checked the weekend doings. "Courage to Heal" incest survivor workshop, a local mystery author signing books, a long-board surfing contest, India Joze's Calamari Festival, the grand opening of a twenty-four hour gym....

"Celebes!" The coffee maker wore his hair long in a ponytail. His Pendleton shirt and jeans, again the fashion in Santa Cruz and beyond, had been the local uniform going back to the fifties, so they say. Surfers got it started, and now the grunge rockers from Seattle had revived it again. He handed me the hot mug and I retired to my corner table to think things over. As I was working my way through the Celebes, Hedley walked in. He was wearing a blousy white cotton shirt, black jeans and black Converse hightop sneakers, his dreadlocks up in a black knit cap and a red, yellow and green scarf around his neck. He approached the counter and waited to order. I walked over with my mug in hand.

"Hedley," I said. He turned toward me. "I've been hoping you'd show up here."

"Tommy. I have news." He was interrupted by the coffee maker's "Can I help you, please?" After placing his order for chai, an Indian tea, he rejoined me and we went to my table and sat down.

"Your friend in Boston called very early this morning."

"Who? Hank?" I said.

"I heard his name was Yards."

"Yards?" I said, "Did he have anything to tell me?"

"Yes, I. But Yards says you have to pay him first five hundred dollars. A deal, he said."

"Yeah. I guess I can work that. Thanks, Hedley." His chai was ready, and when he returned to the table I filled him in on last night. We agreed that the next move had to be checking out Andre's house. Shiva had said Andre would be out of town through the weekend. That would give us a few days to get a good look at Andre's collection, if we could somehow get inside his house, one, and two, his gallery vault. Hedley drew out a sketch of the floor plan as he remembered it. We discussed ways of gaining entrance, and I decided on posing as a pizza delivery. It was clear from his expression that Hedley wasn't entirely sold on my plan.

"I think we should talk this over with Shiva, Tommy," he said.

"Why, Hedley?" I said, "Everybody likes pizza. And, if he has anyone living there with him, or any hired staff, they'll want to see what kind it is. Mushroom, extra cheese,

269

pepperoni, No anchovies, of course. Then we throw a bag over their heads, tie them up and we're inside."

In the end I agreed to talk it over with Shiva. I had had a second cup of Celebes by then and was completely wired. I had seen the clear light and knew my plan was perfect. That's when Hedley said he would make me a present of his Burning Spear concert poster, the one I'd been admiring last night during our salmon feast. It would be a guiding spirit, an emblem for my quest.

"It will settle I up," he said. Hedley meant that I needed something to steady my mind, which was, I had to admit, jumping around like a jackrabbit. We finished our drinks and, as it was nearing ten-thirty, we went together to pick up Shiva at her yoga class. Hedley would leave his car until later. It wasn't parked on a meter, he told me. There was an alley behind India Joze a block away where he always stashed it.

As we walked to the Lexus, I felt as if there was a cloud moving above and just behind me, cooling the air at my back, sending a chill up my spine. But the sky was blue, clear blue, and the sun stood still just above the line of buildings to my left. I was unlocking the driver-side door when Hedley cried out. The windshield shattered, and I heard the first cracking sound and then a second and a third. My face scraped against the outside mirror as I fell to the pavement. I heard Hedley go down on the other side of the car. I lay there on the street for almost a minute afraid to move, but there were no more shots. Turning on the ground toward Hedley, I could see him lying by the car, motionless. His green, yellow and red scarf caught my eye, and then I saw more red. It was a splotch of red at the back of his bone-white pirate shirt, and it was spreading.

He'd caught a bullet meant for me.

32

Thursday, March 25
Santa Cruz, California

I jumped up and ran around the car to Hedley. He was pushing against the ground as if he wanted to get up, but he had no strength. He fell back down and grunted in pain.

"Hedley, don't move. You've been hit. Stay put. I'll get an ambulance." My mind was churning like a gerbil in a wheel. I was totally panicked.

"Tommy, wait!" he said. "Come here." I was halfway down the block by then, but I returned to his side and knelt down close to him.

"What do you need, man?"

"Look, Tommy. I do need an ambulance, yes. But you do not want the police to know who you are." Hedley was obviously in a great deal of pain. I wondered how he could focus his mind on anyone else in such a moment. "Take the keys from my pocket here, mon. The right one." He grimaced in pain , trying to move his arms and point to the pocket with his hand.

"I'll get them, Hedley. Don't try to move." I reached into his pocket and found the keys. I held them for Hedley to see. He closed his eyes and rested his hand on my arm.

"I rest my eyes now. Tommy, be cool. Irie." He was seriously wounded, alive, but for how long?

"Irie," I said.

Christ! I thought to myself. Not again. I thought back to when I was seventeen in Boston kneeling on the sidewalk next to Kid Ory. I took a quick look around. I don't know why I expected crowds of people and sirens and police running to the scene. Maybe I've seen too many movies or read too many books. The street was pretty quiet. Maybe nobody heard the shots. Maybe people were afraid. I know I was scared, but I was more afraid for Hedley than for myself.

Across the street and down half a block, a meter maid was slipping a parking ticket under the windshield of a blue Volvo. Setting his hand down gently on the ground, I got up and began running toward her, shouting to get her attention. When I reached the meter maid, I pointed out Hedley's body lying beside the Lexus.

"Look," I said, "That man has been shot. Call an ambulance, please."

"Just a minute," the meter maid said. She was filing a ticket receipt. It angered me that she didn't immediately look up when I told her someone had been shot. Christ! What were her priorities?

"Didn't you hear me?" I said.

Up the street a small crowd had begun to gather around Hedley, mostly people from the Jahva House. Others spilled out the doorway and stood back on the sidewalk. The meter maid, having taken care of her administrivia, now swung into action. Brandishing her walkie-talkie, she called for an ambulance as we ran together toward Hedley.

"Everybody back off," she said. "Give the man some room to breathe."

One of the people I'd seen in the coffee bar was looking at me strangely. She was wearing Birkenstock sandals, jeans and an Antioch College sweatshirt. Her hair was red and curly, cut too short for the roundness of her face.

"Officer," she said. "That's the man who shot him. He shot Hedley. Arrest him!" She was pointing at me.

I began laughing, nervously. The small crowd turned to look at me accusingly. The meter maid was busy calling for police. It wouldn't take long, though, for the cops to get there. Headquarters was only two blocks away.

"Come on, get serious," I said. "No way it was me. They were shooting at me, too." I pointed at the windshield. "Think I'm that bad a shot?" I said. It was a dumb thing to say, but for some reason, maybe I was nervous, it slipped out.

"He admitted it." "He's got a gun!" "Get him." Others in the crowd began to chime in.

"I've got to see some ID." The meter maid had holstered the walkie-talkie and had her hand out for paper.

"Don't let him get away!" My red-haired vigilante stepped up to grab me by the arm. I felt cornered. I looked at Hedley lying on the ground. He was unconscious. In the distance I could hear sirens I assumed belonged to the ambulance or the police, maybe both. It was time to leave. I looked up at the sky, and it was blue, all the way to heaven. I took a deep breath. Abandoning caution, I decided to bluff my way out.

"That's right," I said. I thrust a fist into my leather jacket. "I've got a gun. So nobody better try to follow me. Or you'll catch a bullet."

I turned and ran toward where I knew Hedley had stashed his car. It was only a short distance away, and I reached it in less than a minute. The old brown Buick was open and started up right away. No one had followed. I could hear more sirens now and knew I had only a few minutes to get lost. I eased the car through the alley, onto Mission street, left at the town clock and cruised by San Lorenzo Lumber where the Mexican workers congregated, waiting for day labor jobs. The cops would be along soon, I reasoned, but they'd be looking for one guy on foot or in a car, not a car full of men. So I rolled down the window and waved four guys over to the car. Cien dólares, I offered, lacking the Spanish for anything less. No questions asked, they piled in and we drove off toward Highway 9 and the Santa Cruz Mountains.

Now what? I was being chased by cops in Boston and Santa Cruz. My roster of crimes was growing—art theft, murder, assault, and now, attempted murder. I was transporting a carload of illegal aliens, probably, who thought I had a day's work for them. And, to add insult to injury, Shiva had been waiting for me at the health club for almost an hour. Meanwhile, her windshield had been shattered, and her friend had been shot. A little black storm cloud seemed to be following me around, and I had to do something about it. Getting to a phone was first.

In Boulder Creek, I stopped at a gas station, filled up the tank and used the pay phone. I called the health club, and they located Shiva in the parking lot still waiting for me. It didn't take long to explain what had happened.

"Forget the car, Tommy. I'll get it later. Pick me up and take me to the hospital. Someone has to be there for Hedley."

"It might be a little crowded, Shiva," I said.

"What do you mean, crowded?"

I hadn't yet explained to Shiva about the carload of Mexicans.

Luckily, the Buick was a wide-bodied gas guzzler with ample room for three in the front and three in the back. Shiva squeezed in between Che and me, and Xavier got in back. The other two guys, whose names I never got, didn't seem to mind, but they'd had the back seat all to themselves on the way to Boulder Creek and then to the health club.

We had a problem though. It was the kind of problem where you have three sheep on one side of the river and three wolves on the other shore. The boat will only hold two animals at a time, and if you leave two wolves with one sheep, it's lamb chops.

I had a Buick full of Mexicans and no place to put them. I had to get my bike up at the cabin and give Shiva Hedley's car to drive. Her Lexus would be impounded, and besides that I didn't want to be stopped by the cops in Hedley's car. But, meanwhile, Shiva needed to be at the hospital to watch out for Hedley. So Che, Xavier, and the other two guys and I dropped Shiva at the hospital to check on Hedley, and I drove off toward the cabin with my four new friends. Of course, once I got to the cabin and picked up my bike, unless it fit in the trunk, I'd have the problem of where to put Che, Xavier and company when I returned to the hospital to leave the car for Shiva.

So far I hadn't thought of anything for them to do for their hundred dollars. I kept on postponing that hoping something would arise. I had other things on my mind.

"Make yourselves at home, guys. There's food in the fridge," I said. Che said something to Xavier and the others, and they nodded and went into the kitchen.

I picked up the phone and called the hospital. Shiva answered the page and brought me up to date on Hedley's condition. He was critical. The bullet had shattered a rib and punctured a lung, coming to rest near his spine. At the moment Hedley was in emergency surgery, and the outcome was uncertain. We'd know more in a few hours. Shiva was crying. Her friend was maybe dying. And it was all because of me and the Butler art theft case which had swerved way out of control.

I called Boston. I had no reason to expect Yards would be in. He rarely was when I called, but I tried him anyway. He answered on the first ring.

"Yeah," he said.

"Yards?"

"This Oscar?"

"No, Tommy."

"Tommy who?"

"Tommy Shakespear," I said.

"Sorry, I was expecting this other call. You got the five hundred?"

"Yeah, I got it."

"No tickee, no washee," he said. A real businessman.

"Yards, look. I'm in a bit of a bind. Yeah, I've got the dough. Or, I can get it, and I can get it to you in just a few hours by Western Union."

"So? Why don't you send it?"

"I've got this problem with the cops here."

"Let me guess. You need a little time right? But you can't wait for the information."

"That's it."

"Sorry. I tell you what I know, and you disappear. I never see my five bills. Forget it."

"Yards, we've done business before. What did I pay you for that car? A thousand bucks? I only used it for a couple of hours. And you probably sold it to someone else after me."

"And?"

"Yards, I got a friend who took a bullet in the back less than an hour ago. He's in the hospital now, and he might not make it. If you've got some information for me, maybe it'll keep someone else from getting shot and killed."

"Okay, Shakespear, but you better not be bullshitting me. And I'm going to expect you to keep your part of the bargain once you get clear of this. Five hundred in cash, remember."

"Yeah, it's a deal. I'm good for it, Yards. Now what've you got?"

"First, there's no personal connection between Jack Butler and Andre Ziff that I know of, and, believe me, I've looked in lots of places you wouldn't think of looking. Ziff was a big benefactor of the museum though, corporate donations, and then two years ago his large annual gifts stopped. Before that, he used to fly to Boston on business and go to these parties at the museum for suckers like himself. Medieval music concert, schmooze with the board. That kind of thing."

"No connection to Jack Butler?" I said.

"Not really, no. Not that I could find. They knew each other, but that's it. Tell you one thing about your friend, Butler, though. He has a gambling problem. Big time."

"I've heard. Anything else?"

"Yeah, one other thing. There's a contract out on you, but you already know that from what you said."

"Know who took it out?"

278

"No, I got it from the other end. The supply side, you might say. But you would be interested in this."

"What's that?" I said.

"The shooter is supposed to be a woman."

33
Thursday, March 25
Santa Cruz, California

As I hung up the phone, I knew Yards had to be wrong, at least in part. Andre Ziff had been courted by Jack as a buyer for the Dutch paintings even before they were stolen. Jack had used the Butler Museum as a catalog, and Andre Ziff's donations were a kind of earnest money, giving him the right to browse. Andre had picked the Vermeer, maybe the Rembrandt and one or two others, unless there were other buyers, which there maybe were, and the Dutchman's crew removed the paintings from the museum with Jack's knowing cooperation. Dutch Masters to go. And, after the theft, no more Andre Ziff donations. He had his paintings and moved on. More likely, he had forgeries and the Dutchman kept the originals, but the thing that bothered me was Jack's role in it.

Maybe Jack had run into a blind alley with his gambling debts, and there was no way out except to work with the Dutchman. Maybe, and I could understand his desperation and his hypocrisy. He had been plundering a family treasure just as his Aunt Beatrice had done to stock it in the first place. But then it had gone beyond plunder. Way beyond. Amy Louvenbragh's murder had changed all that. If it was Jack, and I didn't see how it could be anyone else, he had crossed the line from merely reprehensible to inhuman. And now he had hired someone to murder me. Someone who had shot an innocent bystander. Someone who had put Hedley Styles's life in jeopardy. Yards was probably right about the hit. It made sense that it was a woman. Charley Howell was a woman, and Charley Howell worked for Jack.

I got the yellow pages out and started calling every motel in Santa Cruz asking for Charley Howell by name. I figured she'd be brazen enough to continue using her own name, as she had done when she flew to Barcelona. She had to be thinking I wouldn't suspect her, and she was right. Until now.

The clerk at the Gaslight gave me some guff about not disclosing the names of their guests, so I came up with a line about having missed my sister at the bus station, and, yeah, Charley was an unusual name for a girl, but that was Mom, and, well, Mom had passed away after a long illness, and we were supposed to be at the funeral home in less than an hour for Mom's wake. The clerk, whose name was Angela, had lost her Dad a few months ago, and she could relate, she said, to our loss. She was still processing her grief, she said. Unfortunately, Charley Howell was not registered there.

I must have called twenty motels. I hadn't known there were that many in Santa Cruz, but with the Boardwalk and surfing as two major local tourist attractions, I probably should have. Finally, a bingo at the Motel 6. The clerk had just come on duty, and yes, they had a Charley Howell. Did I want to be put through to the room? Not just now, thanks. I'll call back later. Just making sure Charley's arrived.

Shiva did not respond to the page when I called the hospital to tell her the news, and I heard some strange noises from the kitchen, so I set the phone down and went in to see what was going on. My hired hands, it seems, had gotten into the ganja paste. They were passing the bowl back and forth, eating the stuff like two-finger poi, licking and slurping and giggling. I took the bowl from Che and put it back in the refrigerator. He had become my liaison to the group, so I explained to him using my best Spanglish that we were going back to the hospital to find Shiva, and we were taking the mountain bike. He helped me to load the bike into the trunk. Xavier and the others piled into the Hedleymobile and were talking and gesturing excitedly. I went back into the house and grabbed my backpack, making sure I had what I needed in case I didn't get back to the cabin that night.

On the way to the hospital I had an idea. At the time it seemed like a half-baked idea, and in retrospect it probably was, but I really didn't have any others, so I went with it. I pulled off the road near the entrance to Roaring Camp, set the parking brake, and turned to Che, who had grown more and more silent.

"Che," I said, "¿Puedes drive the automobile? Can you drive?"

"Si?" he said. I was not convinced.

"Okay, Che, let's try this. Quiero... I want you to drive to the hospital. Quiero que..." I made steering wheel motions with my hands.

"You want me, ah, drive car?"

"Si," I said. "Drive car. Okay?"

"Okay," he said. But he sat there.

"I mean now, Che. Let's change places. Cambiar, entiendo?"

Che shrugged his shoulders and stepped out of the car, nearly falling down in the process. He regained his equilibrium quickly and came around to the driver's side door. Meanwhile,

Xavier and company were laughing and punching each other, obviously enjoying Che's pratfall. I slid across the seat, wondering how much ganja paste Che had eaten before I took the bowl from him. As I changed positions, I glanced into the back seat and the laughing stopped. I smiled, and they smiled. Smiles all around. Che sat behind the wheel and slipped the car into gear. He released the parking brake, and we were off. So far so good.

When we reached the hospital, I sent Che inside to locate Shiva, while I sat in the car with Xavier and the other two. He was gone quite a while, and when he returned, there was no Shiva. Where was she? Something seemed wrong, but then Shiva was unpredictable. Maybe she went to get something for Hedley's room. I was beginning to get hungry, and the Mexicans responded with enthusiastic nods and smiles when I suggested a pizza, so we went to a place near the Boardwalk that made real New York-style pizza. Che drove. I was trying to decide whether he could be trusted with the car.

I called the hospital from the pizza place, but still no Shiva. Hedley was out of surgery, but he was still in intensive care and his condition was listed as serious, whatever that means. The pizza cleaned me out. I was literally down to my last dime, and the pay phone took twenty cents. So no more calls, it was time to take on Charley Howell, mano a mano. Well, actually, I had four extra guys, if I could manage them.

We got to the Motel 6 in one piece, although two of the guys had fallen asleep in the back seat. Che parked, and I got out of the car. We were across the street from the motel office which faced toward the street. Two two-story wings ran back parallel at right angles to the office. It was a cheesy-looking motel, but, of course, it was cheap. I asked Che to stay in the car with the others. I was taking a chance with Hedley's car, but I needed to trust Che in case anything went wrong. The motel clerk was a long-haired guy with very few teeth. His face was bright red, his gray hair tied back in a ponytail, and the skin on his nose had that granularity you see with long-time street drunks. I caught a whiff of something sharp, I wasn't sure what, on his breath.

"My sister's staying here, from out of town. We're goin' to our mother's funeral. What room is she in?"

"What's the name?"

"Howell. Charley Howell."

"She expecting you?"

"Yeah. I'm late, in fact."

"209. On the left, stairs just around the corner."

"Thanks."

"You want me to call her?"

"Nah. I'll just go up and knock." I hoped he wasn't going to insist.

"I didn't think so," he said.

I was on my way out when he thought of something else to say.

"Tall one, isn't she?"

"Yeah. She's a tall one." Getting closure with this guy was difficult. I opened the door.

"What happened to you?" he said, indicating the bruises that had faded to a mustard hue. No time for that. I kept going out the door and crossed the street to the car.

Che was the only guy still awake in the car. I could see the other three guys in the back seat leaning against each other in the various stages of sleep. Xavier's mouth was open. One of the other two guys was snoring. A thin trickle of drool had worked its way over his chin and down to the hollow in his neck. I explained to Che that I needed him to come with me and asked him for the keys. He followed me across to the stairs and up and around to the motel room the desk clerk had indicated.

Room 209. The shades were drawn. I needed to get a look inside, but since Charley Howell would recognize me, I decided Che could be my eyes and ears. I asked him to knock on the door and give an excuse for going into the bathroom. I told him to say, "Plumber. I need to check the pipes. Problem in the room below." We rehearsed it twice just down the hall from 209. In whispered tones I heard Che say it all perfectly. What a find! He'd be worth his hundred bucks if he could pull this off.

I positioned myself just out of sight, where I would be shielded by the open door. Che knocked at 209. There was no answer. Che knocked again. When the door opened, he took a step back, obviously surprised by Charley Howell's appearance.

"Perdóname," he said. "Plumber. I need to check the pipes. Problem in the room." His accent cut through his lines like a chainsaw.

"What did you say? I didn't call a plumber. I don't have a problem. Go away."

Che was persistent, however, despite his nervousness. He began again, but this time a few of the words got mixed up.

"Problem. I need to check the plumber. Pipes. The room below."

"Yeah?" Charley Howell was hesitating. Che's sincere manner seemed to have found an opening. He tried again.

"Yes. Claro. Problem in the room below. Check the plumber. You want to bring the manager?"

Charley Howell finally gave up. I could hear her grunt in disgust.

"Wait a minute."

She closed the door and we listened to some bumping sounds coming from the motel room. A minute or two later she opened the door.

"Okay, amigo, make it quick," she said.

Che entered, and the door closed behind him. Che was gone for a while. I could hear some more banging around, and then I could hear Charley Howell's voice raised in a scream.

"Get out, you idiot! Look at this mess!"

Che exited, shrugging his shoulders. He was a splendid actor, continuing to play his part even as the door slammed behind him.

"I come back to fix the toilet. I come back," he said. He was talking to the closed door.

I motioned to him to come to where I was hiding and Che came toward me with a very worried look on his face.

"The lady, your friend. She is in there, I think. In the closet." he said.

"Who? Charley Howell? The tall woman?" I was puzzled by what he could mean. "Of course she is."

"No, señor. Is the friend of yours. From the hospital. You call her Shiva."

It took a moment for me to realize what Che had just told me. Shiva was in the room. Charley Howell was holding her hostage, probably planning to use Shiva to set me up.

"Look, Che. We've got to get her out. Her life is in danger. Muerte, you know."

"No problem, señor. I fix the toilet." Che explained that he had stuffed a roll of toilet paper in the bowl and flushed, flooding the bathroom and thoroughly clogging the toilet. I was ecstatic. I hugged him.

"Okay, Che. Go and get the rest of the guys. Wake them up and bring them here. Right away."

It seemed like a long time, but it was probably just a few minutes until my four new friends came up the stairs toward 209. I was waiting for them two doors down. I explained to Che what I wanted him to tell the others. We were ready. He knocked.

"Fix the problem. Need to fix the toilet."

Charley Howell opened the door just enough to peek out.

"Not you again," she said. "Look, I'll fix it myself. Get lost."

Che stuck the toe of his boot in the open crack.

Charley Howell tried to close the door but there were suddenly five of us pushing our way in. I could see no sign of Shiva, but there was a packed suitcase on the unmade bed. Charley Howell was getting ready to leave. She pulled out a gun and waved it at me, but Xavier hit her from the side, and Che and the other two piled on. There was a lot of screaming and yelling. During the hubbub I took out the can of Mace Shiva had given me and sprayed Charley Howell in the face. She was still holding the gun but, luckily, it was pointing toward the TV set when she began firing. The TV exploded in a shower of glass. But the Mace had done its work. Charley Howell was writhing on the floor, retching, vomiting, nearly blinded by the direct hit. She wasn't alone. When I sprayed her I accidentally hit one of the Mexicans. He was not a happy camper. I took the gun from Charley Howell and asked Che to keep an eye on her, while I went into the bathroom to wet a towel for the Mexican man I'd sprayed. I found Shiva tied up in the closet where Che said she'd be. I untied her and helped her out. We embraced standing in an inch of water from Che's flooded toilet.

"Tommy, thank God!" she said. "Is everyone all right?"

I explained about the Mexican I'd accidentally sprayed and Charley Howell and the gun. Shiva got a towel and went to take care of the guy I had sprayed. I went over to Charley Howell, who was sitting up now with flakes of broken glass in her hair. Still sick from the Mace, she had vomit on her clothes, her face was teary and flushed, but it hadn't dimmed her nastiness any that I could see. Che kept the gun pointed at her. He was clearly relishing his day labor.

"So you were the shooter," I said. "You're going to go down for kidnapping, attempted murder, maybe even murder one, if Hedley doesn't make it. We've got the gun. Ballistics will do the rest."

"Shakespear," she said, "You're dumber than I thought. First place, that's not the gun. Second, you can't prove kidnapping. And third, say it's destruction of property and disturbing the peace. I can trade you for a lesser charge, maybe get off completely."

"How do you figure?"

"You're wanted in Boston for murder, theft and a few other charges. I'm a private detective hired by the Butler. Fred Peavy will back me up."

"Fred Peavy?" I said. How did he fit in?

"I'm working for him."

"I thought you were working for Jack Butler," I said.

"Maybe he thinks so, but I work for Fred. Museum security, special detail. You're in deep shit, my friend."

Out of the corner of my eye, I spotted something square and black on the bedside table. It was a Boot Hill matchbook. Fred Peavy, not Jack Butler. Something was wrong here. Meanwhile, I could hear police sirens only a block or two away. I had to get out. I got the keys from Che and told him I'd leave them on the front seat once I got my bike. Either he or Shiva could drive Hedley's car. I knelt down to talk to Shiva who was helping the guy I sprayed. I whispered to her.

"Meet you on the pier at eight tonight. Gotta go." I kissed her cheek.

"Careful, Tommy. Don't go back to your place or Hedley's. They'll be watched," she said.

Before I left I took out the Mace and gave Charley Howell another shot in the face for good measure. She screamed a string of obscenities and choked on her tears. I wanted Shiva and Che to talk to the cops before Charley Howell had her say.

Fred Peavy, though, and not Jack Butler. Now that was something to think about.

34
Thursday, March 25
Santa Cruz, California

As I waited for Shiva on the Santa Cruz pier in the fading light of early nightfall, I thought back to the last time we'd been there together. Two weeks ago I was about to begin my new career as a detective. I had ten thousand dollars in the bank, a first class ticket to Boston and reservations at the Four Seasons Hotel. Shiva and I were on our way to dinner at the Sea Breeze.

Now I had cops on my trail. Now I had no place to stay. Now I had a friend lying in critical condition in the hospital because of a bullet meant for me. I had not solved the art theft nor the murder, though it looked pretty clear to me now that Fred Peavy and the Dutchman had been working together.

I'd lay odds it was the museum's own director of security, Fred Peavy, who cut Amy Louvenbragh's throat. So FP, not JB, was the monogram Amy Louvenbragh tried to draw in her blood. I'd bet it was Fred Peavy who sent Charley Howell to take the pen and notebook from my hotel room. It was Fred Peavy who wrote the La Sardana letters, then had them posted to incriminate me, who sent Charley Howell to visit the Dutchman in Barcelona, warning him to scare me off. I'd bet Fred Peavy had Charley Howell plant the pen and notebook in my room for the cops to find and then sent her after me to make sure I didn't come back to testify in Boston. I was pretty sure the Boot Hill matchbooks had not been planted, and they further proved the link between Fred Peavy and Charley Howell. Had Fred Peavy been setting up Jack Butler to take the fall? When I appeared it must have seemed to him like a gift. Tied in a pretty blue bow. I was going to have to take that gift back. Blue ribbon and all.

I heard the Hedleymobile even before I saw it. Shiva was behind the wheel. She parked it across from the Sea Breeze and stayed in the car. I looked at my watch. 7:35. I reeled in my line and handed the pole to the man I'd borrowed it from. I thanked him for the loan and told him I was sorry I hadn't caught anything for his dinner. I'd figured it would make a good disguise. At least I got in some practice baiting hooks and casting lines. I left my bike where it was, locked against a pier railing. Just to be safe I walked the long way around the Sea Breeze restaurant. Anybody following Shiva? Didn't seem so. I approached the car from the passenger side, opened the door and got in.

"Do I smell fishy?" I held out my hands.

"Just keep your hands to yourself, Tommy. I'm in no mood."

"Okay, sorry," I said. "You're thirty minutes early. How's Hedley?"

"Still in intensive care and listed critical. The doctors were able to get the bullet out. There was some damage to the spine. They've repaired the rib and the lung puncture. He'll be in bed for quite a long while, the doctors say. But I don't think he's going to make it. They say it's less than fifty-fifty." She looked very upset.

"What about Charley Howell?" I asked just to change the subject.

"I was able to convince the officers that she'd taken and held me in her motel room so they'd consider kidnapping charges. She's also liable for the damage to the motel room, the TV and the flooded bathroom, although that's small stuff really."

"What about shooting Hedley in the back? And attempting to murder me." I was getting pretty excited and concerned that Charley Howell might get away.

"Tommy, I don't know about that. She claimed the gun was for self-defense. The police were interested in whether she had a license for it. She was insisting that they should be chasing after you. Che was great, though. He kept saying 'I never seen that gentleman, and I been here the whole time.'"

"Speaking of Che," I said, "I owe him, and his friends, some money."

"No you don't, Tommy. You owe me. Four hundred and fifty dollars."

"Four hundred and fifty? What's the fifty for?"

"A tip. What are you, Shakespear, a cheapskate?"

She had me there. I decided to move on. The way I saw it, there were two things I still had to do in order to clear my name and set things straight. One was investigate Andre Ziff's art collection. If he had Vermeer's "The Concert," that would tie him into Fred Peavy and the Dutchman. I needed to get the Vermeer back or at least try. Maybe it wasn't the whole magilla. There were several other pieces missing from the theft, but it was at least one tangible link and the most valuable of the stolen works. I knew I'd stand little chance of finding the Dutchman. He had been too much for Sam Bassett and

Interpol, Operation Bogart and the FBI. But if I could corral Fred Peavy, that would be one important link in the chain. Maybe FBI could sweat some information out of him that would lead eventually to the Dutchman. So, that would be task number two. Get Fred Peavy. Although first I had to tackle Mr. Andre Ziff.

"Shiva," I said, "Want to come with me tonight? I'm going to take a look around Andre's place. He might have the missing Vermeer in that vault of his. And who knows what else is in there."

I explained the plan I had worked out with Hedley. We would pose as a pizza delivery, and if someone answered the front door we'd throw a bag over his head and tie him up. Andre would be back east for another few days and so, I reasoned, in the worst case we'd find his woman friend at home. Maybe a servant, a cook or a maid.

"No kids, right?"

"He has two kids, a boy and a girl, but they live with his ex-wife in L.A.," Shiva said.

"So maybe nobody's home."

"Probably Andre's friend Suki will be there. She's not one of my favorite people. Remember when you were laid off?"

"How could I forget?"

"Suki was sitting in Andre's office the day before. I went over to see Andre about something he'd forgotten to say to the press. Smash Attack PR stuff. Anyway, there she was, sitting in his office with the list of people who were going to be laid off. She asked me if I wanted to see the list, but I wasn't interested. I knew I was okay, and you and I both knew you weren't going to make it. So Miss Suki SleepAround sat there cracking jokes about the people she didn't like who were going out the door.

Guys mostly. Guys I knew she'd slept with. She was playing the Red Queen. 'Off with his head. Off with his head.' I really didn't think it was funny."

"A real sweetheart. Well, if she's home, she might recognize you, Shiva."

"You, too, Tommy. Don't forget, your picture's been in the paper. An artist's rendition, that is."

"Not much of a likeness," I said.

"Hardly does you justice."

"Justice? Don't talk to me about justice...now where were we?"

"Disguises," she said. "We're going to need disguises."

Before we left the pier I put my mountain bike in the trunk of the Hedleymobile. It was dark now, and across the water the lights of Beach Flats glowed like fallen stars behind the Boardwalk as we drove down the pier and into town. We stopped at an all-night supermarket and bought a few things for the assault on Andre's, including plumbers tape, two cotton bags, a package of pantyhose and a few lipsticks. Shiva insisted we eat before going to Andre's, so we had some sashimi, some hand rolls and some maki at Mobo Sushi. I tried one of their exotic specialty rolls called The Sidewinder. It's getting hard to find just plain raw fish anymore.

The drive to Andre's place was over Highway 17, through Scotts Valley and off onto an intersecting road into the hills toward the east. Once we got off 17, the roadway was transformed into a mountainside trail, barely wide enough for two lanes of cars. Luckily, there was almost no traffic. We wandered among towering redwood groves older than the Rembrandts, older than the Vermeer, older than the ancient

Chinese urn I had no hope of recovering. Shiva was silent. I had a torrent of thoughts coursing through my mind. Thoughts about time and tradition, about art and ancient trees. Probably I was psyching myself for invading Andre's home and stealing back the treasures he'd illegally purchased. Probably I was justifying yet another wrong that could never right the endless chain of crimes stretching back through human time as far back as memory itself. Probably. But I knew I was going to do it. And I knew I was risking something more than my life and Shiva's. Trouble was, I didn't know what.

We parked the car about one hundred yards from the gates to Andre Ziff's estate, facing out toward the road in case we had to make a quick escape. By the light of the interior lamp, Shiva applied my makeup, and I applied hers. First we pulled a sleeve of pantyhose down over our heads so that we looked nearly unrecognizable. Then we applied the lipstick in war-like markings faintly suggestive of aboriginal tribal tattoos. Pink and purple lipstick.

"Now, Tommy," Shiva said, "Which pizza place is it that has delivery people who look like psychopathic killers?"

"Yeah, well. So we changed the plan a little. We can say we have a pizza for Ziff—that might get whoever is home to open the door—as long as they don't look through one of those peep holes."

"What if nobody's home?"

"Would be much easier," I said, "But then we'd have to figure out how to kill the alarm system first."

"So maybe it's better if Suki is sitting around doing a lot of nothing as usual."

"You don't like her."

"Chances are, though, with Andre out of town, she'll have some young stud she's picked up playing house with her."

"You really don't like her," I said.

"How did you guess?"

I glanced up toward the house. There were lights on out front and in several of the many windows facing front toward the drive.

"Well, somebody's home," I said. "Let's go see who."

35
Thursday, March 25
Santa Cruz, California

"Remember, Shiva, no names," I said. "Except Andre Ziff. Him we should know. After all, it's his house we're robbing. But we don't know Suki, if she's there, or anyone else. Okay?"

"Whatever you say, chief." Shiva saluted. I took it as a mild rebuke, but it was my gig. She was just along for the ride.

Shiva was looking mighty strange in her panty hose and lipstick mask. I'd drawn thick purple lips and wavy pink eyebrows, alternating pink and purple parallel stripes diagonally on both cheeks and a thick pink line running down her nose. I hated to think what she'd done to me.

As we approached the front door I could hear a dog barking somewhere in back of Andre's house. Soon another joined in, and the two of them began a rousing chorus of the Carmina Burana. Or maybe it was "Mack the Knife." Who knew. Anyway, we looked at each other and wondered silently how we'd handle the dogs if they got loose.

The house was a two-story California ranch house faced entirely in thick redwood planking. It might've had the look of a barn converted to living space, if it hadn't been striving so hard for that image. Clearly, it was designed for dramatic effect, but to me it was merely offensive. To use redwood in such an extravagant fashion was ostentatious and outrageous. Redwoods are ancient, sacred trees. Shiva had convinced me of that during a long, late-night conversation last fall when we were camping under the redwoods in Pfeiffer State Forest down in Big Sur. When we reached the porch, Shiva gave me a look that went something like, "Do you believe these assholes?"

I grabbed a large rock and smashed the front porch light. It made me feel better, and the dogs started barking again. Shiva rang the front door bell, and we stood there in the dark waiting for someone to answer. Inside the lights were all on. There had to be someone home, but it was after nine. Shiva rang the bell again.

Finally, after a minute or two we could hear someone saying, "I'm coming, I'm coming, just a minute," and shouting to the dogs to be quiet.

We moved to either side of the little peep door as it opened, and a very beautiful Asian American face peered out. I guessed it was Suki. I signaled to Shiva who began speaking from her position just off the front porch and to the right.

"Pizza delivery!"

"Pizza?" Suki said, "I didn't order a pizza. Where are you anyway? I can't see." It was very dark. Suki seemed to be trying to peer out into the darkness.

"I have a pizza for Ziff here."

"Oh, ok, Andre must have ordered one," she said. "What kind is it?"

Suki opened the front door, and we leaped onto the front porch in tandem, slamming against the door and sending Suki sprawling backwards onto the black and white parquet floor. I pulled a white cotton laundry bag from my back pocket and placed it over her head, wrapping it tightly around her neck with plumbers tape. Suki would be able to breathe through the cotton, but she'd be hot and uncomfortable in there. I knew because I had tried it on myself during the ride up to Andre's house. Shiva got an arm chair and sat Suki down in it, taping her arms to the arm rests and her feet to the front legs. For good measure, she wound the shiny silver tape around Suki's slender chest, fixing her to the back of the chair. I had the feeling that Shiva was enjoying this part. During the entire time, about five minutes in all, Suki was silent and fairly docile. I wasn't sure why. I would have been kicking and screaming for help if I knew somebody was home. When we had Suki all wrapped up, I spoke to her.

"Listen to me. I have a gun here and it's loaded. I'm pointing it right at your head. Can you see it?"

"No, I can't see anything. But please don't hurt me. I'll tell you anything you want to know. Please." She was near tears.

"Where's Andre?"

"He's in his studio recording something. In the back of the house."

"Where exactly?"

"You go through the wing on the right, next to the last door on the left. His music room. There's a glass wall so you can see if it's okay to go in."

"Why isn't he still back east?"

"He came back tonight. Some kind of problem at Prometheum. An important meeting in the morning. I don't really know any more."

"Okay," I said. "We're not going to hurt you as long as you sit here quietly. We're going to put a gag in your mouth to make sure."

I stuffed a ball of panty hose remnants into her mouth. The cotton bag was in the way but some of that went in, too. A few twists of tape around it would hold the gag firmly in place. I could hear the dogs barking again so I went into the kitchen. Andre's kitchen was done in stainless steel and black, very industrial looking, but also very spacious. There were two ovens, a microwave, and a huge glass and steel refrigerator like you see in restaurants. At the center was an enormous cooking island with a JennAire grill. All around the periphery were cabinets with glass doors so you could tell at a glance what was inside. I went to the refrigerator and found a piece of steak about the size of my shoe, set it down on a butcher block and sliced the steak in half with a cleaver.

Looking around, I noticed that the kitchen door facing the backyard had a pet entrance cut into it, and that concerned me. If those animals got in the house, there could be a problem. I opened the door and quickly tossed the steak into the back yard. That, I reasoned, would occupy the dogs for a while. The microwave looked heavy enough—in fact, it was too heavy for me to lift alone, so I recruited Shiva to help me secure the pet door from those dining Dobermans or whatever they were. Together we set the nuke down in front of the pet door to prevent the dogs from getting in the house. Then we set off to find Andre.

"How's Suki?" I said. We were out of earshot and heading down the wing where Andre kept his recording studio. Shiva could not contain herself. What began as a smile soon turned into a giggle and it would've gotten worse if I hadn't cautioned her to wait until later to count up our chickens.

"Fine," she said.

"You seemed to enjoy taping her to the chair. Real pro."

"A pure pleasure, and I'd do it again any time. As for 'real pro,' believe me, it was strictly personal."

We arrived at Andre's studio and could see him sucking hard on a saxophone. Sweat was pouring off his brow. I wondered what it sounded like but the studio was so thoroughly soundproofed we had to content ourselves with the visuals. But that was enough. Barefoot, Andre had all three hundred pounds of himself in motion, shaking like a whole lot of jelly poured into a red-and-white Hawaiian print shirt and faded blue jeans. His hair, cut short and even shorter on the sides, glistened with his perspiration. He was wearing earphones.

We burst into Andre's music room waving our hands, screaming loudly and looking like psychotic killers in demented warpaint. I ripped the earphones off his head and shrieked at him something I'd heard in a movie once.

"We're going to kill you, motherfucker! Get down!"

Instantly, Andre dove for shelter behind an amplifier. He covered his head with his hands and arms and lay on the floor whimpering. For just a moment I felt sorry for him, and I walked over to him and kicked him in the ribs with my running shoe. I ordered him to shut up and listen to me. Brandishing a water pistol, I commanded Andre to get up from where he lay cowering on the floor, and with Shiva walking behind me I ordered him to take us to the picture gallery. I summoned up more dialog from the baddest movie I'd seen.

"You know what we're after, Andre. The Dutch Masters. Okay? Now let's do it or we'll do you."

Like Suki, Andre was cautious and quiet, compliant. They both must have seen the same sick movie I saw. He nodded, said something like "Okay, okay don't hurt me," and got up on his somewhat unsteady legs. After dusting himself off and checking out our weird faces for a moment, Andre lead the way through another studio door into a picture gallery set up for reading, listening or meditation. The floor was covered in thick carpeting, a soft white fluffy pile suitable for just about any prone pleasure. In each corner were futons flat on the rug with several colorful pillows and a knit shawl or blanket. Earphones, books and CDs sat on low tables by each futon, as though to accommodate several different readers, listeners or meditators at the same time. On the walls hung watercolors by Matisse, Dufy, Chagall and somebody else I didn't recognize, selected for their graceful figures and relaxing color tones. A decorator's touch, no doubt.

The climate-controlled room lay beyond it through a door that had a combination lock, something like a bank vault but less obvious in appearance. Andre stopped and began to turn around. I stuck the water pistol in the back of his neck and ordered him to continue.

"Andre," I said, "Don't even think of turning around, or I'll blow a hole in your neck you could stick a guitar through." I was overcompensating again, but then I only had a water pistol.

Before I knew it, Andre had the lock open and was entering his inner sanctum. Shiva followed close behind. I brought up the rear. Inside the vault it was a bit cool and dry, not to mention dark. I told Andre to stay put, and Shiva went looking for a light switch. When she switched the lights on, we all stood there blinking in silence for a moment. Andre, of course, had seen it all before, but even he seemed to be in awe of the paintings he had stashed in his gallery vault. The Vermeer occupied a place of special honor, it seemed, but then it was his latest acquisition. It was framed in a heavy gold leaf over wooden molding that was more ornate than it needed to be. Andre had made his point a few times more, as the painting had four baby spots trained on it, and, just below it, he'd fixed a thin brass plaque identifying his trophy, "The Concert."

Having seen what I came to see, I motioned Shiva out of the room and ordered Andre to follow her out. In the meditation room I looked at Shiva and winked.

"Go check on the girl," I said. I was enjoying this tough guy talk, I'm afraid, a little too much. Under her pantyhose and lipstick mask, Shiva rolled her eyes at me. She wasn't going to put up with it. Andre caught the gesture.

"Hey, don't I know you?" Andre was staring at her. He seemed to be on the verge of recognizing Shiva. Not good. I repeated my suggestion.

"Go and check on the girl," I said. "Okay?"

Shiva left the room. Andre was still puzzling over her identity, and I was getting ready to tape him up like Suki, when I heard barking just down the corridor. Yelping followed soon after, and I could hear Shiva running toward us, shouting things like "Oh shit," "Shit shit shit," and "We've got to get the hell outta here, now!" Andre whistled, calling out to his dogs in a singing, chanting holler.

"Baby, Baby, Baby. Come here, Baby. Come here, Sucker, Sucker." Baby? Sucker? Where in God's paradise did he get those names?

And in a moment of pure idiocy I still don't understand, I said, "Andre, you're dead!" and I shot him in the chest. That did it! Andre looked down at his wet t-shirt, his face showing puzzlement, and after it dawned on him all I had was a water gun, he charged me full on. All three hundred pounds of him hurtled toward me, collided with me, and sent me flying over a table and sprawling flat onto a futon, ass over teakettle, as they say.

Now I was in deep water with sharks circling. The dogs were just outside the room. I could hear them yelping and barking in a confusion of anger and pain. Andre lay on top of me, his sweaty body stank like stiff socks and old jockstraps. He'd knocked all the wind out of me, and I thought for minute I had a broken rib or two. This time it was over, finally over. I had nothing left. I was about to beg Andre for forgiveness and pray he'd let me surrender to the cops, when I felt Shiva kick Andre in the butt.

"Get up off my partner, you fat slob," Shiva said. She kicked him again, and he began to get up.

"You can't tell me what to do," Andre said. He was feeling pretty confident now. I lay there beginning to breathe again.

"Ya wanna bet?" she said. At that I rolled over to take a look. Just in time to see Shiva unleash a blast of spray, pepper spray it turned out to be, into Andre's fleshy face. He howled, and all at once I knew why the dogs had not bothered us and why they had been barking and yelping in pain. Shiva had used her pepper spray on them.

It took a while, but eventually we got Andre taped to a chair in his studio. While Shiva removed Suki's gag, and, reluctantly, made her more comfortable, I inventoried the paintings in Andre's vault. I found the stolen Rembrandts as well as several other notables, including a Holbein and a Van Dyck, that had not come from the Butler. Apparently, Andre Ziff had been a client of the Dutchman's for some time. I wrote out a note to the police, explaining the situation and why they should consider Andre an art thief or, at the very least, an accessory before and after the fact. Also, I suggested they call Jack Butler in Boston. On the way out, I pocketed a high-quality miniature tape recorder from his studio. Something to remember Andre by. Shiva led the way.

Meanwhile, Baby and Sucker, Andre's pair of matched black Dobermans, were nowhere to be seen.

36
Thursday, March 25
Santa Cruz, California

The last thing I did before Shiva phoned the Scotts Valley police and we exited Andre Ziff's splendid estate, was to call Jack Butler. I had a feeling he would be asleep. After all, it was on toward midnight in Boston. Needless to say, Jack was surprised to hear from me, though at first he was more than a little irritated at being dragged from his dreams. However, when I told him what I'd found in Andre Ziff's private gallery, he seemed to wake right up and become almost cheerful.

"So, Jack," I said, "Am I back on the case, or what?"

"As far as I'm concerned now, you were never off the case, Tommy. How soon can you be in Boston?"

"In that case, I'll need a ticket to Boston on United, a room at the Four Seasons and a little walking around money. I've had a few expenses in the meantime. We can update our accounting later."

"That should present no problem," Jack said.

"Oh, and you'd better book those reservations under another name. How about Winston Rodney?"

"Who?"

"Never mind, Jack. I'd need ID. So I'll have to use cash."

Shiva drove like a maniac to SFO. Under normal conditions you'd allow, say, ninety minutes from Santa Cruz to the San Francisco airport, but we didn't have that kind of time. We didn't have much time at all, and if I had stopped to calculate it, we'd never have tried. The United flight to Boston, the red eye, was the last plane out, and it would leave at ten. We exited Andre's place in the Hedleymobile, spinning dirt, gravel and pine sticks at around nine five or nine ten. No way you can make a ten o'clock plane, I told her. Shiva just smiled. Her face was smeared with lipstick where it had come through the pantyhose.

"You'd better clean up some, or they won't let you on the plane," she said.

I took a look at myself in the vanity mirror and for the first time saw what Suki and Andre had seen. Yecchh! I looked like a pink and purple nightmare. It wasn't easy cleaning the lipstick off my face, but eventually I found a rag Hedley had been using to wipe the inside of the windshield.

"Thanks for saving my ass back there," I said. "I was done for, you know."

"You have no idea how funny it looked, Tommy. You were lying there with old Andre on top of you like a couple of sea lions mating. I had to fight off the impulse to stand there and laugh."

"Anyway, thanks, partner."

We cut through the night in the Hedleymobile blasting reggae music, the windows rolled down, whipsawed by cool winds streaming in and the pulsing sounds of Burning Spear pushing out from six pairs of speakers Hedley had installed. You'd think we were a couple of high school kids the way we sped down the highway and onto the freeways, passing cars, weaving in and out of night traffic. Shiva has what it takes to be a stock car racer, everything, that is, except a southern accent and an auto parts company to sponsor her. When we got to the airport it was a little before ten. We ran inside to get my ticket, which Shiva paid for with a credit card. Luckily, the plane was delayed until ten-thirty. We could breathe a little easier. I found the bathrooms, and we washed our faces. At the security checkpoint Shiva handed me a wad of fifty-dollar bills. It reminded me I owed her beaucoups bucks.

"Take care of yourself, Tommy," I said in a mock-feminine voice. "I'm out over two thousand dollars if you don't come back." I said it, not Shiva.

"Stop," she said. "Tommy...?"

Maybe I was scared she was thinking it. She wasn't though. Tears welled up in her sea-green eyes.

"Tommy, I don't know what I'll do, if I lose you. Or Hedley, of course."

We embraced, and I could feel her heart beating. I felt very small.

"Thanks, I'll take a pillow and a blanket."

A thirty-something flight attendant with short black hair and too-bright eyes, was walking through the cabin offering sleep accessories. I was going to need some sleep. We'd land in Boston around six a.m. The cabin was quiet, fewer than half the seats occupied. I put the earphones back on and tuned in some classical music. The seat reclined at a touch, and up came the foot rest. I pulled the gray-striped blanket over me and settled back into my pillow. I knocked once at the door in the Land of Nod, but no one was home to let me in. Taking off the earphones, I shifted my position and knocked again but still I could not get past the front door.

Charley Howell, Andre Ziff and now Fred Peavy. Two down and one to go. One heavy ex-cop, to be precise, with two probable murders under his belt. I'd have to be very careful with him, if I didn't want to end up as victim number three. It had taken the help of four stoned Mexicans to subdue Charley Howell, and if Shiva hadn't been packing her pepper spray, Andre would have pulverized me under his three-hundred-pound meat hammer. By going after Fred Peavy alone, I was taking a pretty big chance, but maybe he wasn't expecting me. At least I'd have that in my favor, unless Charley Howell had gotten through to him. On second thought, I probably didn't have surprise on my side, but I did have Jack Butler. I wondered how to reconcile Jack's "No problem" response to my request for money with what Yards had told me about his gambling debts. Maybe Yards had gotten it wrong. Maybe Jack wasn't behind the eight ball after all.

Finally the door swung open, and I dozed off and slept like the virtual dead, until the captain announced our descent into Logan Airport. It was an aircraft carrier landing, a rough touchdown and heavy on the brakes. Nobody applauded. When we docked at the terminal I made for the taxi stand, and as I had no luggage to delay me, I was into a cab within five minutes of landing. The driver was a career cabby, he informed me, not one of your college kids or immigrants. He'd been born and raised in the shadow of Bunker Hill, well, not literally, but in that vicinity. Garrulous to a fault, he had worn me down to numb indifference before we'd emerged from the Sumner Tunnel into Boston. It was a cool spring morning, sunny and clear with only a few puffy white clouds in the sky above the girders and concrete of the expressway.

Suddenly, on a whim, I decided not to go to the Four Seasons. It had nothing to do with the cabby, it had nothing to do with anything I could point to. But I was guided by this feeling that I should stay clear of the Four Seasons, where I was expected.

I directed the cab driver to take me to another hotel I knew. Not the Ritz or Le Méridien. Too similar in class. Someone tracking me would think of them right away. Not the Westin or the Marriott. Too obvious. I wanted a hotel you might overlook, like the Copley Plaza.

The Copley Plaza had been taken over by a national hotel chain but still had an old-fashioned elegance with architectural furbelows in every direction. Elegance in the old Boston style. And it was in a convenient location. I checked into the Copley Plaza under the name Winston Rodney, using a two hundred dollar cash deposit. It took a lot of talking to convince the desk clerk. A thick middle-European accent informed me I'd have to settle my account in cash daily, unless I had a credit card to present to her. Fine with me. I went upstairs in the old elevator to the right of the front desk and wandered through the maze of hallways until I found my room. Dark. I opened the windows. Still dark. My room was tucked away under a sculpted overhang in the shade of the John Hancock Building, and I could see no sign of sunshine.

Exhausted, I fell upon the bed and tried to think of how I'd handle what I had to do. Nothing, but nothing, came to me.

I awoke groggily around nine and made a few phone calls. Robotic, I was going through the motions, as the stress of the past two weeks had at last short-circuited my brain. Shiva was out, so I left a message I'd call back. I called Yards and arranged to meet him at the top of the John Hancock at two. I called Jack Butler and set up a meet for noon, the same place. I reminded Jack of my need for cash, and he agreed to bring along some folding green. After I hung up from talking to Jack I dropped off to sleep again.

When I awoke again it was just past eleven. I called Shiva back, and we had the most whacked-out conversation in which I learned that Hedley's condition had improved slightly. Just enough to get her hopes up. The Santa Cruz cops now had both Charley Howell and Andre Ziff in custody and, oh by the way, that guy Tommy Shakespear, a fugitive from Boston, a murder suspect and co-conspirator in an international art theft ring, was now at large in the Monterey Bay area. He was still considered armed and dangerous.

I confess it gave me pleasure to know the cops thought I was three thousand miles away.

37
Friday, March 26
Boston, Massachusetts

I took the elevator to the top of the John Hancock Building just before noon. I wanted to be there before Jack arrived in case he was followed. Through the glass walls of the Hancock observatory, despite an increasingly gloomy sky, I could see Cambridge, the blue, gold and red domes of Harvard, the boathouse on the Charles. In another direction, out to the southwest, I could just make out Fenway Park, and imagined Hank would be looking out that way if he were here. Directly below the tower were Copley Plaza, the Trinity Church and lots of people standing around, sitting on benches, or coming and going through the little concrete park between them.

Jack was late, and I wandered around the exhibits, reacquainting myself with the colonial history of Boston, listening to the battle reenactments, browsing the historical documents hanging on the inner walls. The Hancock Observatory was popular with tourists, and it was easy to see why, but that Saturday it was not crowded. The weather man had forecast thunder storms, and it looked like his prediction was on target. The sky was now inky black and thunderheads, forming for the past hour, roiled up in the sky like squid tentacles. So when Jack arrived I had to conceal myself behind a pillar as I watched to see whether he had come alone. In the elevator with him was half a troop of girl scouts dressed in full uniform with two guiding women in attendance to shepherd them. I waited for a second elevator and when the remaining scouts arrived with another leader, but no one looking like a cop, I walked over to where Jack stood. He was looking to the east and the Boston Common, and he was alone.

"Jack, it's me," I said, "Your old friend Winston Rodney. How have you been?" He turned and held out his hand.

"Winston. It's been too long."

We shook hands and moved back from the glass observation wall, standing near a formal replica of the Declaration of Independence with the bold, outsized signature of John Hancock. Now in the company of our founding fathers I was ready to receive a few of our dead presidents—in particular, Jefferson and Grant. Jack took out an envelope which held the historical figures, and I stuffed the envelope in one of the flap pockets of my leather jacket. The other held the miniature recorder I'd taken from Andre's. I showed it to Jack and explained.

"I think we're going to need some evidence of Fred Peavy's role in this. I don't suppose you've found anything in the museum which would help here?" I said.

"Nothing, I'm afraid, Tommy."

"Winston."

"Sorry. Winston." he said. "I've been through Fred's files personally and found nothing at all."

"He must keep the records at home, then. Can't imagine not keeping any records."

"I've had to place Fred on suspension. I phoned him this morning and requested he stay away from the museum for two weeks while we sort things out."

"You did what?"

"After what you told me last night, I felt I had to inform the board. We canvassed by phone this morning. All agreed Fred Peavy should be suspended, pending the results of your investigation." I was aghast. So much for the element of surprise.

"I appreciate the vote of confidence, Jack. I really do. But did you consider that might put Fred on alert?" I was being uncharacteristically diplomatic. I wanted to say, "Jesus H. Christ! What the fuck did you do that for? You could get me killed!" But for some reason my better instincts prevailed.

"Winston, as you know, the Butler is an institution governed by the bequest of my aunt Beatrice as well as the many informal traditions that have evolved over the years. I am not free to act independently of the board. Suspension is warranted in this situation. Some years ago we took similar action with a museum director, as you may know." That would be Titus Moone, if memory served.

"Okay, but let's not involve the board further in this," I said.

"Agreed. By the way, I did call to let you know I was polling the board. But you were not yet checked in at the Four Seasons." Whoops. Well, it was a trade-off. I couldn't risk the cops, so I missed the board meeting. Que sera, sera.

"Jack, I'd like you to call Fred Peavy and invite him to the Butler to meet with you. You can say that, given the many years you've worked together, you wanted to hear him out, man to man. Despite the board's official position, you consider him to be innocent of any wrongdoing, and you want to see if there is some way you can help prove his innocence."

"His innocence? Isn't that laying it on a bit thick?" he said.

"Of course. No way he'll fall for it, but it doesn't matter. Fred will probably want to play his part, too. I bet he will agree to meet you. Let's make the meeting for about four o'clock this afternoon. Your office at the museum. Okay?"

"All right. You're the detective."

"You said it. By the way," I said. "You can leave a message for me at the Four Seasons. They'll hold it at the desk until I check in."

"I will let you know when I've confirmed the meeting."

"Oh, Jack?" I said.

"Yes."

"I heard from someone that you were into some gamblers pretty heavy in the Bahamas. You work that out yet?"

"How did you...?" Jack was caught off guard.

"A connection. Nobody you know. So, what's going on there? Anything to worry about?"

"Fortunately not. It was a temporary cash flow problem. I was able to dispose of some securities and take care of it. Not to worry."

"Sure about that?" I said.

"Certain."

"Sorry. I know it's personal, but I had to ask."

Yards showed up on time. He was wearing a shiny black Members Only jacket left over from 1985, black jeans and motorcycle boots. He was carrying a package with a yellow ribbon tied in a bow. I knew what was in the package.

"Over here," I said. "Let's hear about the redcoats." We went into the room with the big model of Colonial Boston in the center of it and listened for a while to the tape of gunshot and galloping hooves, as the patriots won another skirmish.

"You owe me five bills from last time," he said. Yards was always to the point. He played with one end of his mustachio and smiled. Snidely Whiplash.

I handed him five hundred dollars in fifties in an envelope from the Copley Plaza which I'd prepared after my meeting with Jack. I had a second envelope in my pocket ready with another five.

"I'm having second thoughts," I said.

"Your choice, Shakespear."

"I know."

"But you wouldn't want to go in there naked."

Yards had a point. I knew Fred Peavy would be armed. I just hadn't made up my mind whether I would be.

"That guy back in Santa Cruz who got shot?" I said. "Hedley?"

"The Rasta."

"He's in pretty bad shape in the hospital. Might not make it."

"Happens," Yards said.

"Yeah," I said. "It happens."

And then I knew I wouldn't take the gun.

I called the Four Seasons when I got back to my hotel and told them I was checking in this evening. Were there any messages? There were two. Jack Butler confirmed the meeting at four. Sam Bassett left a number for me to call in London. Sam Bassett? How would he know I was in Boston? I called the number.

316

"Sam? Good to hear from you."

"Shakespear. How's the weather?"

"Fine, Sam, but how did you know I was in Boston?"

"We have a tap on Jack Butler's line. With his permission, of course."

"Anyone else listening in?" It concerned me that the Boston cops might know I was in Boston.

"I am sorry you've had such a rough time of it, Tommy."

"You and me both. But I'm still alive. And so is Hedley Styles."

"Fortunately." Sam Bassett, like Yards, took killing as normal, but I didn't. I hoped I never would.

"You didn't answer my question," I said.

"Yes, they're listening."

"Who exactly?"

"The FBI. The Boston police surveillance team," Sam said.

"They know where I am?"

"Not at the moment."

"They know about the meeting between Fred Peavy and Jack this afternoon?"

"They do. I called to tell you about it."

"Sam," I said, "I'm going to be there to confront Fred Peavy, get something to implicate him. And clear my name."

"Not a good idea. I'd suggest flying to the Caribbean and sitting in the sun until this blows over, Tommy. You'll only get yourself in deeper, and maybe you'll get somebody else killed."

"Too late, Sam. Much too late."

"Cheerio," he said. "I'll light a candle."

38
Friday, March 26
Boston, Massachusetts

I was late getting to the Butler Museum. Jack and I had planned to rendezvous at three-thirty in order to prepare for Fred Peavy's arrival, but I had miscalculated badly. While I was on the telephone talking to Sam Bassett, the sky had let loose with rain and thunder, and by the time I came down in the elevator the rains had become a torrent. Trying to find a taxi in such heavy rains in Boston was a frustrating experience, and I had reason to be anxious about getting to the Butler on time. I waited outside under the hotel awning for about an hour unable to find a free taxi. I considered taking the subway, but kept thinking a cab would come along in another minute, and of course, eventually one did, and I sprinted to it through sheets of rain, stepping over and around the little rivers flowing on the sidewalk and in the gutters.

When I arrived at the Butler, drenched from my mad dash to curbside, and to the shelter of an alcove, I found the administrative wing closed. Jack Butler's office was unlocked, and no one was inside. I headed for the stairway to the upstairs apartment. The door was unlocked. Before I went upstairs I turned on the tape recorder in my jacket pocket. My only weapon.

"Close the door behind you, Shakespear."

No mistaking Fred Peavy's voice. He still sounded like a cop, even if he had gone bad along the way. I did as he ordered, came up the stairs and into the renovated space. In the past week it had become a warren of offices. Not fully furnished yet, floors and walls still bare, there were cubicles, desks and chairs, tables, filing cabinets, and computers in boxes stacked here and there. Jack Butler slouched unconscious in an ergonomic desk chair, trussed up with phone cord, his face bruised from a savage beating as Amy Louvenbragh's had been. On the desk in front of him were a knife and a necktie. I guessed the necktie was to gag Jack Butler, and I knew what the knife was for. Fred Peavy stepped out from behind a filing cabinet. He was wearing leather gloves and holding a gun. I knew he'd have a gun. He waved it at me.

"Make yourself at home, Shakespear. I'm so glad you could come. Jack Butler tells me you've been over to Andre Ziff's."

"Yeah, Fred. We found those paintings you stole for him."

"Andre should be more careful with his art collection. Sit down," he said.

I took off my leather jacket and slipped it over the back of a black leather desk chair, the tape recorder whirring away in its left flap pocket. I sat down and looked at Jack. His lips were cut and swollen, and his right eye was nearly closed from the swelling around his cheekbones and eye sockets. He remained unconscious though his injuries looked back at me pleadingly. I turned my attention to his captor.

"Nice gun, Fred," I said. "Looks like a pretty serious weapon."

"Standard police issue. In Boston, that is."

"What kind is it?" I really didn't care what kind it was, but I couldn't think of any other way to stall him. I had to think of a way to turn the tables.

"Nine millimeter Glock semiauto. Holds eighteen rounds fully loaded. Enough to fill you full of holes, Shakespear, if you get any ideas."

"Fred, I've got some money here."

"It's not for sale," he said. I think he was pretty pleased with his joke, because he smiled in a sneering sort of way, baring his yellowed front teeth. Then he had another thought. "How much money?"

I reached into the flap where I'd stashed it and pulled out the envelope to show him. It was the envelope with the second five hundred I'd made up for Yards. I waved it at him.

"You can have the money. Let us go. The cops know we're here. It's already too late to get away with this."

"Don't be an asshole. If I want the money I take it. Who's to stop me? You? Or maybe Jack Butler here." His smirk widened.

It didn't look like I was convincing Fred. He grunted as he gestured toward Jack with the Glock. The gun seemed to get bigger every time I looked at it. I stood up and pointed to the knife on the table.

"Is that the knife you used on Amy?"

"Pick it up, Shakespear."

"Why?"

"Pick it up. It's going to have your prints on it this time."

Then I saw it. There was a bright red fire extinguisher hanging on the wall next to me. Within arm's reach.

"Take the money," I said.

I tossed the envelope with five hundred onto the desk. It hit and slid across the desk past Fred and fell on the floor. Fred turned to follow it with his eyes, and as he did I made my move. I grabbed the fire extinguisher from the wall and slammed it into the side of Fred Peavy's head. The blow was a glancing shot that ricocheted off his shoulder and caught him just below the ear with enough force to send him across the maple desk.

Fred must have seen galaxies of stars, but somehow he shook it off and remained conscious. Tough ex-cop. But he'd lost the gun. Reaching up to feel the place where I'd hit him, his hand found the raw abrasion the metal band on the red fire extinguisher had cut into his neck. I scanned the room for the gun that went flying from his other hand when I hit him. Fred still seemed unaware he'd lost it, though a bit dazed, and that gave me a couple of beats to make my move.

I stepped into the desk chair and springing up, I launched myself into the air, reaching down with my hand to fend off the far edge of the desk. Landing on the floor just beyond it, I found myself alongside the nine millimeter Glock semiautomatic. In an instant Fred was there, too, and we wrestled. Matching arms, elbows, legs and body weight for a purchase on the gun which now lay just out of reach. Though Fred was larger and probably stronger, I was quicker, more agile, younger. I squirmed my way out of his grasp and took the gun in my hands.

When I turned toward him, holding the gun level at his heart in my two hands, I expected him to reach for the sky, grab air, but no such luck. He bulled into me from his wrestler's crouch, just as I would have said, "Freeze!" and the gun went off twice in rapid succession before I knew what had happened. There was a frozen instant as though time, and not Fred, had obeyed my unspoken command, and he was all of a sudden gone, dropping hard on the ground like a stone. Stone dead. His weight draped around my legs like a shroud.

Quickly, I stepped back in something like horror. Revulsion mixed with terror. A sudden, turbulent wave of nausea broke, and I was in the whitewater soup. I looked down at the gun I held, then to Fred's lifeless body lying on the floor. The gun in my hand felt like power I had never wished for. Never wished for, and now had to live with. I set the gun down on the desk alongside the necktie and knife, and I knew I'd crossed a line somewhere. I'd done a thing I'd never be able to undo.

I reached into the flap pocket of my leather jacket and took out the miniature tape recorder I'd borrowed from Andre. I snapped it off and rewound the tape. I showed it to Fred Peavy where he lay dead on the floor and to Jack Butler sitting unconscious in the chair. And then I played them both the concert I had taped. It was music to my ears.

But neither Fred nor Jack could hear a word.

39
Three weeks later
Capitola, California

So I won't bother to tell you all the nitty gritty little details about how the FBI and the Boston cops came in and tidied up the mess I'd made at the Butler Museum. Or how they behaved like rival street gangs in church. They were surprisingly friendly to me. Not that it mattered. I was numb from everything that had happened.

Sergeant Raymond acted like we were old drinking buddies. He had been doing some sleuthing on his own and had found that the scrawl Amy Louvenbragh made in her dying moments resembled a monogram she'd designed for Fred Peavy, as a birthday present, no less. Some gratitude.

Of course, Fred Peavy was dead. I was responsible for that, and I would have to live with it forever. A heavy weight to carry with me. It would take time to deal with, but I had time.

Fred's taped confession corroborated the physical evidence at the scene—the way he'd tied up and beaten Jack Butler, the knife that he'd used to cut Amy's throat he'd intended for Jack, too. Charley Howell and Andre Ziff were only too happy to trade testimony for reduced sentences, and they had plenty to say about Fred Peavy. According to Charley Howell, Fred had concocted the La Sardana letters, and

Charley had posted them when she followed me to Barcelona. Andre Ziff admitted doing business with the Dutchman through Fred as his intermediary. Andre's statement gave a pretty clear picture of how it had worked from the buyer's end, including dates and dollar amounts. There had been other thefts, too. Meanwhile, the FBI had seized his art collection, refrigerator, house and all.

I guess that made the case for Boston's new D.A., although he probably wasn't eager to renew our brief acquaintance. Don't think I'll be calling Elaine Winslow for a while, either. She and her husband Whit have a few things to work out between them. Jack was right, I shouldn't have been involved. I just hope I can find a way to explain it to Shiva.

Never did call my mother. I keep intending to write, but she's already gotten the news from CeeCee and Johanna by now. Better that way. I figure a call or a letter from me would just start up a lot of the old stuff with Dad that we've both no interest in revisiting.

Since I had to remain in Boston for a few weeks while the Boston police and the FBI sorted things out, I called Hank Greenberg. He was not particularly impressed with the way I'd handled my first case as a detective, but then Hank's given to scoffing generally. When I told him about the luxury box seats I'd gotten from Jack for Opening Day at Fenway Park, he changed his tune. Suddenly I was his prodigal son, and it was time for a barbecue.

The Red Sox won their opener, too. It was a close one, good pitching on both sides, but the Sox batters got the best of the Green Monster. Two home runs in the middle innings to even the score. And a home run in the bottom of the ninth decided it. Hank was elated, of course, but I knew it was only a matter of time before our Fenway fan extraordinaire would again plunge deep into melancholy, heartache, and grief.

Jack Butler was in pretty bad shape for a week or so, but he showed his gratitude when we got together at his club. Jack finally got around to telling me what had been on his mind that night at Elaine's party. There had been rumors about Andre Ziff. Unsubstantiated rumors about a secret art collection some said was pornographic. Jack had suspected that Andre might be involved in the Butler theft, but had nothing much to go on. Sam Bassett and Yards had caught wind of it, too. Neither the FBI, nor the Boston police had followed that trail. It had seemed too unlikely that a successful businessman, a museum trustee moreover, could possibly be involved. My return from Barcelona had coincided with Amy's murder. Jack's mind turned elsewhere, and then all the evidence began to point to me.

We talked about the likelihood of the recovered paintings being authentic. Jack said the board of trustees would insist on having them validated by experts before returning them to their places at the Butler. Personally, I believed the Vermeer and the Rembrandts to be the Dutchman's fakes, and I doubted the originals would ever be returned. They were most likely long gone with the Dutchman, hiding with the other priceless treasures in his vault. Somewhere who knows where. So there would be little chance of Sotheby's paying the reward, though with Jack I expressed every hope. It seemed a pyrrhic victory, and I wasn't happy to acknowledge that. Especially since I'd nearly lost a friend in its pursuit, and Jack had lost Amy.

Hedley's on the mend now. When I got back from Boston and dumped my stuff off in Capitola, the first thing I did—after airing the place out—was visit Hedley in the hospital. He was in a semi-private room with one roommate recovering from hepatitis and two empty hospital beds. The IV tubes are out now and he goes to physical therapy twice a day. In a wheelchair. Still, he's alive and given every chance of recovering fully, though it'll be a while before he's back in action. We talked for a while, a very short while because he was tired out from his therapy session. When I left the hospital I drove up into the Santa Cruz mountains. I took the Burning Spear poster from Hedley's cabin and brought it down to Hedley's room and put it up on the wall next to his bed. Winston Rodney, reggae ambassador worldwide to His Imperial Majesty Haile Selassie I. Hedley flashed me a smile that shone like a sun. Irie!

So now the Santa Cruz cops no longer seek out the infamous fugitive Tommy Shakespear, but for some reason the newspapers carried *that* story on page fourteen, next to recipes for ceviche and pesto and the salmon fishing forecasts. It would be quite a while before people stopped giving me funny looks, before they stopped staring and pointing. No matter. Since I got back, I've made friends with a few of the local PIs, and they say it goes with the territory, like the nightmares I've been having. At least I've got my health.

Besides, I already have another client. Ichibano, a 453-pound Hawaiian Sumo wrestler, who has been touring the U.S. arenas with a traveling Sumo exhibition, has been charged with smothering a male prostitute in his hotel bed in San Jose, although he swears it was an accident, and I believe him.

One strange thing, though. Sam Bassett, if that *is* his real name, probably doesn't work for Interpol. Interpol, Hank informed me at the Red Sox opener, doesn't have any agents. They're an information clearing house, computers and databases, that kind of thing. No operatives. So who's Sam Bassett, and why was he involved with this case? I tried calling him in London at least a dozen times on that phone number he gave me. No answer. I tried calling the Interpol main number, but they say no one named Sam Bassett works there. Hank thinks he's British intelligence or CIA. I don't know. It may be a while before I can figure out that one.

Meanwhile, I'm going on vacation with Shiva in Big Sur for a while. We've got stuff to work out, sure, but I've got a feeling there's something between us we can build a relationship on. We're going to camp out in the redwoods, swim in that cold, rocky stream she used to play in as a kid, go for long walks on the beach and sit together in the dark by a campfire—maybe find a way to bring some quiet to our lives. I sure hope so.

Minimum, I'd like get a lot closer to nature and as far away as I can from art.

ACKNOWLEDGEMENTS

I would like to thank my former agent, the late Jane Jordan Browne, for her help back in the day. I would also like to thank Thaw Malin III, a fine Island landscape painter, and Judith Partelow, a wonderful Cape Cod actor and director, for their assistance in getting this book to print.

ABOUT THE AUTHOR

Michael G. West, a graduate of Williams College and the Johns Hopkins Writing Seminars, is the author of several novels, including the Tommy Shakespear Mystery Thriller series. He has worked as a dishwasher, short-order cook, housepainter, shingler, sheetrock taper, private tutor, taxi driver, college professor, freelance book editor, computer programmer, industry analyst and strategy consultant in several countries and on both coasts, north and south, in the U.S. He currently lives year round on Martha's Vineyard, an island off Cape Cod, Massachusetts.